JAZZ HANDS

Eleanor Gwyn-Jones

OMNIFIC PUBLISHING
LOS ANGELES

Omnific Publishing
1901 Avenue of the Stars, 2nd floor
Los Angeles, CA 90067
www.omnificpublishing.com

First Omnific eBook edition, December 2014
First Omnific trade paperback edition, December 2014

The characters and events in this book are fictitious.
Any similarity to real persons, living or dead,
is coincidental and not intended by the author.

Library of Congress Cataloguing-in-Publication Data

Gwyn-Jones, Eleanor.
    Jazz Hands / Eleanor Gwyn-Jones – 1st ed.
    ISBN: 978-1-623420-90-1
    1. Contemporary Romance — Fiction. 2. Breakup — Fiction.
    3. Cruise Ship — Fiction. 4. Theater — Fiction. I. Title

                10 9 8 7 6 5 4 3 2 1

Cover Design by Micha Stone and Amy Brokaw
Interior Book Design by Coreen Montagna

Printed in the United States of America

It started like a ripple,
as if his breath near her had blown like the wind
against her still seas, puckering the surface of her.
When he caught her eyes, it stirred her current, her core,
pulling her like the tide. And when he put his arms around her,
waves crashed and it was devastating.

Chapter 1

The cab bounces in and out of another pothole, knocking my head against the window. It's like a slap from the universe. What had I been thinking? Why had I lied about having a hotel? *Of course I haven't booked a hotel! I just flew three thousand miles across the Atlantic to race to you, stand on your doorstep and tell you I loved you, Cole! Of course, I don't bloody have somewhere to stay, because I was supposed to be with you! But no, there you are watching TV cozied up with some blonde.* Some blonde he called "Sweetie!" Ugh. Why do I always have to be so…bloody British? Suck it up, suck it in, and walk away, head held high. My upper lip is so stiff, it might be in rigor. Or maybe that's the cold. God, it's like Siberia here.

The cab sweeps around the corner and there, standing alone, an illuminated building almost like a fort on the edge of the city. Its brightness casts spotlights on the tarmac and uplighters on the old stone, like theatrical beacons signaling safe haven.

"There! Can you drop me there, please?"

"At the Radisson? Sure thing." *The Radisson? The Radisson! I remember the Radisson.*

I fumble for change, the feeling in my fingers almost entirely gone, and he lifts my two suitcases to the curb.

"Thanks, honey, take care."

He speeds away, and I lumber up the front steps, no doorman or bellboy to help me at this time of night. In all of my in-flight scenarios, we were supposed to be deliciously wrapped around each other's naked limbs by now, promising—between an unstaunchable flow of kisses—that neither would ever let go, ever again. Instead the only thing I'm wrestling with is baggage. I stop for a breath on the top step—oh dear, there are only three—and survey the Electric City. Well, here I am Scranton, Pennsylvania! Stranded. Without my unfiancé, hotel-less, in a city lacking a functioning passenger railway service and midnight buses! Couldn't have gone better!

I heave the heavy glass door open wide enough to slide in one case, then myself, then the other, like some clunky transformer.

I vacillate between feeling hopeful and empowered, to frightened and lost. Right now, the latter is winning. *But you are here, Enna! Buck up! You made it here!* And, there are certainly worse places than this beautiful old railway station, now a hotel.

The deserted lobby echoes with the sound of my four wheels. I meet no one, not a soul, as I wheel my way across the marble, turning in to a little bar. I remember this! We had downed late-night drinks there and called it "The Affair Bar," the perfect spot for an illicit rendezvous. Unpeopled it feels like a deserted set, a sepia-tinted still, just a row of empty leather-topped stools, the wisp of old cigar smoke, hanging like a sleeping spirit. *It's the people who make a place.*

I wheel through to the larger bar, the one with the enormous chandelier. We had danced in this room. Cole had slid his palm to the small of my back and whispered hot breaths in my ear. I try to recall what or why or when we had been here, but the conversation vanishes down the rabbit hole of memory. We had fun here. We were a team here.

Will everywhere I go in this town be preceded with echoes of us, ghosts of happy memories I can't seem to catch or hold on to?

A woman looks up and stops wiping down the granite counter top.

"I'll have a cup of tea. Hot tea, please."

The bartender lifts a questioning eyebrow.

"If you're still serving."

She looks at the empty stools to the left and the right of me and seems to consider her reply. Maybe the thought of staying open merely to serve some strange foreigner with two huge wheely cases and clearly a head full of baggage, is not appealing. "Sure. But I gotta close at two."

"I also need a room. Is it too late to check in? I didn't see anyone at reception."

"It's never too late. I'll buzz the front desk and let them know. Just pick up the key and sign your paperwork when you leave here. You Australian?" she asks without looking, tossing the rag into the sink and reaching for the pyramid of mugs stacked on the end of the counter.

"British."

"Ah."

"Close."

"Huh?"

"We sent our convicts there, transported to Australia, or Tasmania, so it's a similar root of the language," I spiel with surprising alacrity.

It's twelve twenty-five in the morning. I have no plan, no reunited fiancé. Unfiancé apparently has a new girlfriend, and I am now resigned to getting a hotel room that will probably cost me half a kidney. I am, in fact, for all intents and purposes, to use the proper Anglo Saxon, fucked. Yet, here I sit, the cases that contain the remainder of my transatlantically-uprooted life sitting up at attention around my ankles like loyal Springer Spaniels. I'm drinking tea, pride wrapped around me like a flimsy pashmina, exchanging niceties with the sole employee—her name badge says "Larissa"—at an old railway station bar, faded and jaded but stoically ignoring and carrying on. It's all very British. I should get a bloody T-shirt. Someday I will find this ironic. Someday.

"My family was from Ireland. Way back. Don't see too many Brits here in Scranton. What brings you here?"

Ah! The million dollar question. The man who was my fiancé. The man who I left. The man who flew to England to find me lifeless on the bathroom floor. The man who got me to the hospital just in time. The man who saved me. The man who, just a short hour ago was blissfully—what?—snuggled up on his black leather sofa with the leggy blonde in his arms. The man who let me spill my heart at his door, a messy fountain of feeling, and still closed it firmly in my face and let me wheely myself away.

"Work," I reply, burning the roof of my palate with the scalding water. "I'm here looking for work." It just seems easier.

"Pickle."

It was the nickname that melted my marrow, the syllables that he could utter from the other side of a crowded room, and I would feel them on my neck as if he had whispered directly to that silky spot beneath my earlobe. He could, in fact, deliver any kind of poison, but served with that particular condiment, it would always taste sweet to me.

Pickle.

I place the mug back down on the granite countertop. Cups, theaters, hearts all plummet to ruin when held in my hands. My vertebrae fuse together, unbendable, as if the mere sound of his voice — the single word he has uttered — has dissolved my bones, some oral alchemy which changes calcium to chromium and marrow to oil. Paralyzed, I'm unable to turn around. I want so desperately to believe it is him yet don't trust my eyes to prove my ears.

Larissa starts to say something about being closed but stops before a grammatical sentence is complete.

"That was very romantic." His voice sounds different, lubricated. "You should have called first."

I finally locate my tongue stuck firm to the roof of my throbbing palate, like a fleshy mussel obstinate in its hardened black shell, but say nothing.

"She's gone. She really means nothing, you know."

I look up from my tea, the bagged leaves still infusing their ruddy stain through the water, and I raise my eyes to the mirror behind the counter. It is him. He's lost weight. He's grayer around the temples. He's wearing the Ralph Lauren hunter green sweater I bought him on that shopping trip to New York when he spent oodles on me, when he wrapped the most scintillating sapphire around my neck, and all I could afford to buy him was an inadequate jumper. He's Cole, with those hazel eyes and that strong, square jaw that I just want to hold in my hands. I take the inventory of him that my tongue and my ego and my verbal bulldozing did not make time for an hour before.

There is so much I want to tell him still. So many directions this could play out right now. I roll clips from different scenarios in my brain. This is a real-life improvisation.

You're an actress. You're a director, Enna! Think! Being witty, being sharp, being accusatory—all knee-jerk reactions that will make him defensive. Tell him what you really want. Be open! Be honest! You've thrown your heart over the line once today; why stop short now?

The muscles in my tongue lunge into action. "How did you find me?"

Enna! I inwardly scold myself the second the words are through my lips. *What does it matter? Who cares if he's the fifth member of the A-Team trained to track you down. Focus!*

"It wasn't hard. There are only a few cab companies, and a British accent is kind of distinctive. Besides, I know you have a thing for beautiful old buildings. I didn't think you would resist staying here."

"Well, seeing as I have no career left and will almost certainly be in debt soon, I thought, why not do it in style?" I mean it to sound fun and flippant. It trails in the air between us, sad and inappropriate. I look at him and pull a small, uncertain smile tightly across my teeth.

He looks at me and turns away to the bar. "I'll have a Jim Beam. Double. Light on the ice."

Larissa takes a tumbler, swirls ice cubes around it, throws the ice away, places three cubes in, cracks the metal tags as she unleashes a fresh bottle, and pours a hefty glug of amber. The liquid fractures the ice, and the rich, syrupy color highlights the little cracks on the surface. We watch this seamless production. I'm aware of every little detail, suddenly hypersensitive to this intermission, both keen and reluctant to get to the conclusion.

Cole swirls the tumbler—it looks tiny in his hand—and then pours practically the entire measure down his gullet.

Wow.

He shakes his head and sucks the air through his teeth.

That's a new…what? Thing? Habit?

Enna, stop thinking! Start doing!

"I don't care about her. The other woman." *Other woman? Shit, I'm a walking, talking cliché.* "If you say she's nothing—she's no one—I'm relieved." And I really don't care about her. Truly. It wasn't as if I was the Virgin Mary during this…hiatus, but Will? He can rot for all I care now. It is all about Cole. It's amazing how one can switch off or on like a tap when betrayed or loved unconditionally. And Cole does love me. He flew to England and found me when

I needed him most. "I just want you to give us another chance. I want to find a way to brush this whole thing under the carpet and start again."

"Ha!" He chuckles. *Chuckles?* "You know that one of the strange laws in Pennsylvania is that it's illegal to sweep things under the rug?"

"What?"

"It's true. It's a law."

Oh. "I mean, figuratively. I mean, let's just start over again. Can't we?"

"You make it all seem so easy." He sits on the stool next to me.

Larissa looks sheepishly through her fringe. She seems unsure of what to do or where to put herself, whether to get him another drink or skulk back into the kitchen. After a sway of hesitation, she tops up his glass and silently vanishes through the swing door.

"You can make it complicated if you choose. But it *is* easy when you know what you want."

He says nothing.

Despite the exhaustion, the starvation, and the sheer delirium of the past few weeks, or maybe because of that, I continue, blinkers on, a body of jolted nerves and adrenaline firing the same ineffective message through my body: *I must—I have to—make him see.* It all seems so obvious to me now.

"I know what I want, Cole. Take a moment. Please, just take a moment. Think of how special it was. When we would sit, as we are now, but interlaced, knees locked together, talking, listening, eating, drinking, doing everything together, not being aware of anything or anyone else but the other."

He looks away from me again toward the large, distressed mirror on the other side of the bar.

"Listen to me! Don't you remember? Remember that time we went up to your friend's cabin out by Montrose? The group was all hunting, but you stayed with me. You wanted to take me on the quad and show me the trails. It felt like you wanted to show me the world. You cut the engine, swiveled around in your seat, and we kissed, and we touched, and as you breathed on my neck, I looked up to the trees standing sentinel around us, I thought I could never love anyone as much as I love you. Cole, it doesn't have to be complicated. I know I hurt you, but if you love me—if you ever loved me—give me a second chance."

His eyes remain fixed away from me. *Did he hear? Did he get it? Did he remember that magnetism?* It was chemical, biological. It certainly got very animal.

"Please?" Oh God. *Do* I sound like I'm begging? I sound like I am begging. Mum would walk away. She'd hold her head high.

I sit waiting for his response for what must be over a minute. He is resolutely silent.

I pull out a five dollar bill and leave it on the bar. I stand.

Oh, stop me!

Stop me!

Stop me!

I turn the bags around. *He's not going to stop me. Again.* I start to wheel. *Motherfucker.*

"Enna."

I stop walking immediately, of course. Mum wouldn't like it, but I want to leave no shadow of a doubt that I am committed.

"Enna, I can't forget. You left *me*. After everything, after looking me in the eyes and telling me what you told me, you left. I'm loyal. I'm committed. I spent over fifteen thousand dollars in applications and legal advice to get you here — that should tell you something — then you waste that money, waste that visa, leave for your theater and some actor. That...that *killed* me, Enna. It makes me sick, physically sick, to think how quickly that all happened. Exactly how long was it before you jumped from my bed to his, Enna? And then — what an ass — I still come when you call and find you practically dead on your bathroom floor. So don't tell me that I'm a bad guy and that I don't care. I just have a hard time believing you right now. And I don't honestly know if I can ever forgive you. The trust is gone."

It's a verbal bullet and it strikes me in the stomach.

"I'd take a bullet for you." Didn't he say that once? A million tears ago.

He raises his glance and catches my desperate, disbelieving stare. *He doesn't trust me?* But he's the person I would trust with my life. How could things have become so skewed? So screwed. I look around, taking in once again the cold marble and granite, this empty, unused chamber, and I realize that there is nothing left to say. I have served my heart on a plate, and he has sent it back, untouched. I can't *make* him trust me. The more I say that he can believe me, the less he will — isn't that how it goes?

What if I were to just fling my arms around him and squeeze out all of his doubts? What if I suggested he come up to my hotel room? Could I wrap my legs around him and slowly, tantrically remind him of all that was good and true and full of wonder?

I nod, mentally balling up these inadequate suggestions and tossing them away, and instead I take a step toward his stool, kiss his cheek, take one last deep inhale of the scent of him—oh God, how can I not be with this man whose mere smell triggers something unholy in me—and I whisper in his ear. I kiss him a second time because, well, his cheek is there—and fuck it, I want to—and I awkwardly wheel myself and my large cases through the bar.

It's not a graceful exit. I am trying for dignity, and pride, and getting out of the room before my face trembles and gushes a flash flood of tears, but one of the unwieldy cases catches on a chair leg. As I tug it to heel, it knocks the chair to the ground with an almighty clout.

I should stride on, leaving a trail of downed chairs in my wake, and I do try; I roll the cases one table further before I have to turn around and, ridiculously, bob and excuse the clumsy scene, like some chastened maid from *Downton Abbey* or something. Oh God, rejection and humiliation, complete! I pick up the fallen furniture. Both cases then clatter to the floor from their upright position, and as I swoop to grab their handles and leave the room, I look back at the man who I thought would be watching, to see that he's not. He is facing the bar, his head in his hands, his stained glass beside him, drained empty.

Chapter 2

How do you win back someone's trust? This sounds like an eminently "self-helpy" topic. Surely there must be a guide, a *Dr. Phil* episode, something I can research online. I will get to work tomorrow. As soon as I get my bearings, I'll head to that coffee shop on the square, if it's still there, and I'll caffeine and Wi-Fi up.

My mind whirls as I remove what little eye makeup I haven't cried off. What a fucking day. I have been up approximately twenty-six hours. I think I'd be forgiven for plummeting headfirst into the pile of cushions that decorate this palatial room, but the routine of cleansing, exfoliating, washing, rinsing, moisturizing, and balming gives some kind of comfort.

As I lie between the starched, cool white sheets, my pink and puffy lids so heavy, it occurs to me that maybe, maybe he'll tap at my door. He'll come to me. He'll knock one back at the bar—Dutch courage and all that—and he'll be there. Maybe he already tapped at my door, but I didn't hear. Maybe with the faucet running and my thoughts swirling, I missed the gentle rapping. I spring with all the agility of an overly-doped Olympian and launch myself on the door, peering through the little spy hole to the corridor outside.

The corridor looks empty, but it's hard to tell with the circular distortion. I angle my head, trying to see to the left, then the right.

Shit! I think I may have just cricked my neck. I grab the doorknob, and I'm about to open it—I mean, wouldn't it be an awful waste if he was just standing there and I never knew it—but I stop.

Enna! Are you thirteen years old?

Of course not. Good reminder. Good.

And all twenty-six hours seem to weigh on my shoulders and my eyelids as I thud back to the enormously empty bed. I'm going to sleep; I am. I'll worry about how to prove myself to Cole, which credit card I will put this unexpected hotel stay on, and how much I totally screwed the pooch on my *Dynasty*-esque life, tomorrow.

I am going to sleep; I promise. I lie within the white sheets, still chilled, eyes open and staring into the blackness. I neither sink into the mattress nor float on the airy cushion-top. The swirl of thoughts keeps me stiffly separate and unyielding. Sleeping in a suit of armor might be more comfortable.

What more could I have said? Should I have just hugged him and not let go? Should I have burst into his house and confronted her? And said what exactly? I was the one who left. He loved me, and I left.

It wasn't supposed to be like this.

A few fugitive tears make a run for it, trickling across my cheek and into the pristine pillow. Exhaustion finally beats my conscious mind.

Scranton is as I remember it: a city elegantly neglected—a Miss Haversham, if a city could be a literary character. The historic buildings around the square stand as a reminder of the Electric City's former glory, of a time when coal was king and this northeastern city thrived. There are some new additions, however, peppering a bit of color into the gray. I turn from Lackawanna Avenue, admiring the new red brick condominiums, onto Adams, and then Spruce.

I walk quickly, in spite of my computer bag—why am I again plagued by unwieldy baggage—pumping out carbon dioxide exhaust like a diesel truck. It is so friggin' cold here. Now, England gets cold. England can be bloomin' miserable, but holy frostbite, Batman, I don't think Blighty could get this cold and unfeeling.

Across the square are the verdigris triangular peaks of the Electric City Building, its famous roof-top light bulb sign, dormant now, waiting to light up the night and shine down on Scranton. In fact, when you look, when you really look, the buildings are quite beautiful, each a little different in masonry, color, architecture, but all stone giants standing resolute as transient life plays out.

Northern Lights! Thank you, sweet baby Jesus! I barrel into the cozy coffee shop and stand by the doorway heater, waiting for the blood to return to my extremities. I am not sure I can actually move my lips and form coherent words. I have a strong suspicion I need to wipe my nose. I'm pretty sure my fingers won't bend to actually hold a tissue, let alone a coffee mug. I should donate myself to medical science.

Ladies and Gentlemen, Mesdames et Messieurs, presenting... Cryogenic Girl! She has amazing powers of romantically fucking up, not thinking, thinking too much, and not packing an adequate wardrobe! Yay!

Applause.

I should have packed gloves, a scarf, a decent jacket. But I was not thinking of the Siberian welcome when I hurriedly squeezed as much of my English wardrobe as would fit into two suitcases. I was just thinking of the arms around me, holding me in front of the fireplace, the marble surround an emerald green and white, freckled with chunks of pink that we had chosen together, one of our "projects" when life was good and, I thought, settled.

Never would I have dreamed of swapping my prized Karen Millen black cloth three-quarter length jacket, with gorgeous embroidery and funky buttons, to join the legion of Pennsylvanians who warmly walk around hooded and insulated like vertical caterpillars. Eminently practical, fashionably illogical.

"I'll have a tall regular with room for milk—"

"'Cuse me." The man in front of me turns around, his hot foamy coffee in hand, and almost knocks me off my feet.

I reel backward, more from surprise than force, and he catches my hand with his right hand, his coffee well-secured in his left—it's just a quick movement. It's not a big scene, but his hand feels warm and this brief second of human touch is, oddly, comforting.

"Apologies, *bella*." He smiles with his dark brown eyes and cuts through the line with ease, exchanging "hellos" with various coffee sippers before disappearing through a side door into the adjoining building.

"Ma'am?"

"Yes?"

"That's two forty-nine."

I take the mug and trail away from the counter, taking up residence with my laptop in the corner. The machine whirrs and I sip in silence, watching the parade of puffy, insulated people converse and caffeinate. Most people know somebody; buying a coffee is not a simple in-and-out transaction. I forgot this about Scranton. With the bustle and focus of Ashtead life, a coffee run would literally be a run, not an amble with a five minute catch up. Maybe this coffee community was there; I just never took time to notice. There was much I didn't notice after all.

Eyes open. Come on, Enna. Let's right this shituation. And it is a shituation, isn't it?

How do you prove that you are trustworthy? How do you win someone's trust when you have lost it?

I fire up Google. I sip slowly. I may be here a long time, and God knows, if they kick me out from here, where will I go next? I'll probably be found by some Scranton junkie, frozen to death in an alley.

Shamed theater director found frozen, ironically on doorstep of Scranton Life building. Sources say her jacket was very stylish.

I wiggle my fingers. The heat from the coffee mug has revived them somewhat, and I click through various pages. Everyone has an opinion on trust. Of course they do. Writers; philosophers; psychologists; crazy, wacko, PVC-wearing pop stars:

"Trust: the most important element in a relationship…"

"Trust. Once it has gone, you can never get it back…"

"I'm not upset that you lied to me; I'm upset that from now on I can't believe you." Oh, Nietzsche, you know how to sting.

Is that how Cole feels? Is that what he is thinking? Is that why he was so reticent on the doorstep, because he couldn't believe that I still loved him? *But I do!*

Where are all the Hallmark quotes about forgiveness, making mistakes and moving on? What about that? After all, Cole did lie to me, telling me I would be the new director of the Scranton Theater, and maybe I made a big fuss at the time. Maybe I happened to return to England and negate my costly visa, but *shit*, we all make mistakes!

"The best way to find out if you can trust somebody is to trust them." Yes, Ernest Hemingway. True. It may take time. But if I stay in America for as long as I can, and if I believe he will remember all the good things about us, maybe he will learn to trust me again.

And, frankly, what have I to lose?

I cup the mug in both hands and sit back. It's a release, as if my muscles have, for the last thirty-six hours, been held hostage by adrenaline, and finally, finally, this resolution to stay, to fight, to earn his trust, has met the ransom and I can relax. Three months inappropriately dressed in a freezing Pennsylvania? I'll do it!

I sit up straight again, alert with a barrage of new thoughts: maybe I can extend my visitors' visa to more than three months? Maybe I could get a cash job waiting tables, or I could learn how to work one of those elaborate coffee machines and create arty swirls and hearts on peoples' foam.

An optimistic click to my automatic banking is a little sobering. I shall have to find alternative accommodation. *Bugger.* The thought of traipsing to some chewing-gum-white-sheeted motel that smells of smoke and exhibits questionable mattress stains is not appealing. I've seen Coen brothers films, and motel-dwelling never seems to turn out well. *Non, merci.*

Maybe I could speak with the Radisson people and ask for a long-term stay discount? It's winter. Are there tourists in Scranton in winter? Surely they have rooms just sitting there empty. Maybe I'll ask for a job at the Radisson in exchange for a room.

I will not fly back to England; I will find a way to stay. I click on my Facebook account, wondering if any of the friends I made through Cole might take me in, just while I get myself sorted out. My pride shrivels a little at the thought. Must I ask someone I don't really know, whose allegiance is elsewhere and who could have been told all sorts of things about me, if they will take me in? *www.notappealing.com.*

But what other option do I have? Going to Cole's friends? Negative.

Going to Cole's family? Nnnnnnnnnegative.

Going to Cole? I have to give him time.

Oh Jesus, why don't I have friends?

And then I remember: Tara!

Chapter 3

Tara and I share much in common: love of hummus and theater, dread of squatting, and weirdy bullshit adaptations of Shakespeare. Thus, our friendship is a strong one. Strong but infrequent, like a really compelling but limited tour that you wish you could see more of, but time, distance and circumstance always prevented. In fact, it must be at least fifteen years since Tara and I spent the summer in north London at the National Youth Theatre, squatting in a circle, shrieking in strange made-up languages, moving together in a group, a mob of fifteen-year-olds getting louder and louder and louder. The morning squat drill was a short course in torture. We bonded over the thigh burn and its complete uselessness for any role other than that of a circus performer or porn star, neither of which we were really aiming for, thank you very much.

We lost touch, then through the powers of Facebook, reunited. Tara graduated from the prestigious Bristol Old Vic Theatre School, had some bit parts on *Casualty* and some other BBC drama about ghost hunting — lots of shrieking — before she moved to New York and nabbed a small role in an off-Broadway musical. She had never returned, booking all sorts of short indie films, commercials, HBO background work on *Boardwalk Empire* — though she never met Steve Buscemi — voiceovers, and touring theater/musical theater projects. She said she had that "classic canvas," that she could be a "laundry commercial mum one day and nineteen-twenties East European whore the next," but for neither had she utilized her great squatting skills!

I drain my coffee mug and click over to my Facebook page and type in her name. There she is, her "classic canvas" and new shorter bob. *Twelve inches*, she typed in one message. Twelve inches she had donated to Locks of Love to make wigs for cancer patients. That's the type of person Tara is, truly someone who would help a friend in need if she could. Well, I am definitely a friend in need.

I rattle off a quick message with the broad strokes of the shituation.

> Hi T! I know this is completely random — SURPRISE — but I am, in fact, in Scranton, Pennsylvania! I am marooned here without a place to stay and...erm...fiancé-less. (It's a long story.) Anyhoo, I hate, Hate, HATE to be cheeky and ask, but is there any way that I could come and visit and maybe sleep on your sofa or something? I wouldn't ask if I didn't need your help. I am clean. I can be quiet. I can help you run lines. And I make a killer vegetarian risotto.
>
> Much love and many squats,
> E.

I wait for a few minutes, staring at the screen, willing her to reply. Wouldn't staying with Tara rather defeat the object of being on Cole's doorstep? Two hours away might as well be the seven it takes to get back to England. How am I going to just run into him at the grocery store, the casino, his old, familiar haunts? I wouldn't, would I? But I could still visit. Maybe he'd come out to the city, like he did when we were dating. Maybe this is exactly what we need, to date again, to be in a place we only associate with happy memories.

Bing!

Oh, I love technology!

> Mon petit canard!

I truly can't remember how this evolved, but that summer on Hampstead Heath, sipping on cider and running around in purple Converse trainers, high on Shakespeare, everyone was *mon petit* or *ma petite* pig/horse/dog/fish/cat. The more random, the better. After all these years, after so many miles, the reply from a friendly voice, the familiar memory of our pigeon French in this somewhat alien environment, makes me want to cry and kiss strangers simultaneously.

I pause, looking up at the coffee shop that is consumed with chat, with steam from machines, with nodding silently or tapping feverishly to the beat in their headphones, and, unnoticed, the stranger with the British accent in the corner, I dive into her message.

> How bloody lovely to hear from you! Sooooo many questions! Who, why, how, etc., but I suppose that will keep and be a better tale in person. Relief! Truly, I could kiss strangers right now! BUT, and here's the fly in the soup, or ointment, or whatever, my apartment is a teensy weensy bit on the small side (think: cupboard), so you may not find it the most comfortable, or maybe you will enjoy the free education I can give you on contortion. You know, another circus skill to add to your repertoire! Tee hee.
>
> The other slight pain is your stay might be très limited.☺ I found out yesterday that I will be performing aboard the good ship Lollipop! For real! I shit you not! Well, it's not really called the good ship Lollipop, but you get the idea. I booked a tour with a cruise line!! Well, I actually booked a show with a company in England, and they sold the production, costumes, cast, etc. to the cruise line. Too much info…my head is going to explode…but fun in the sun! Huzzah! I'm subletting to another actor here, but fret not, we will figure something the fuck out. You will not be homeless on city streets! I will make it my mission to see that this is so!
>
> I have an audition today at 4pm midtown for some voiceover stuff. I can be at Penn Bus Authority by 5pm. There's a 2pm bus from Scranton. You should get your skinny Minnie little arse on it!
>
> This is my cell…

Oh, she uses "cell" now, not "mobile." Thoroughly accustomed and Americanized. It'd be nice to be with a Brit who has navigated these waters and found these subtle differences before. I may be the alien — this is the Ex-files — but I am not alone. I'm sure that there's a joke in there somewhere.

I am relieved. I am so, so grateful. But — *does there always have to be a "but," Enna?* — Leaving today? This afternoon? Surely, I should linger for as long as my bank balance allows and give Cole the chance to rethink, to recall, to remember all the good he is letting drift away?

On the other hand, I put it all out there. Maybe I need to remove myself so he can mull it over and miss me. Do men mull? Is Cole a muller, or is he a react and forget about it type? He is black or white, in or out. He makes a decision and sticks to it. He is stubborn. He is hurt.

My fingers hover over the keys. Do I seem ungrateful if I ask for extra time?

The door opens and with it another chill from the Polar Vortex. A woman swaddled in her sleeping bag coat waddles in, the hood of her coat firmly tied, leaving a circle of pink, tear-streaked face. She looks around desperately until she catches the eyes of the man in the suit at the table in front of me. He stands and opens his arms to her. The pink face lights up with bright white teeth and gums and happy kisses.

"I am so sorry I'm late! So, God! I was held up at work, and then the boss called me in and I —"

"Hey!" He gathers her into his arms and rubs her back soothingly. His voice is deep and carries to my ears through the gargle and whirr of the milk frother. "It's okay. It's all okay." He chuckles. "I would have waited. I've waited thirty-six years for you. What's a couple of hours more?" He kisses her forehead and ushers her to the counter to order.

I strike the keys with assurance.

> Tara, you're an angel! I really can't thank you enough. I'll be on that bus. See you after 5. I'll loiter by the main Port Authority entrance. Here's my number…but I don't have international roaming on it yet, so it'll cost a rental payment for you to call it and for me to call. So let's try and meet old style, without calling! This is so appreciated. Can't wait to see you!
>
> Enna. x

I press send and sit back, watching the woman in the puffy cocoon shrug it off and nestle on the sofa with the man who had waited. How will I tell Cole I'm leaving? *Cheerio, I'm off! Tally ho and miss me muchly!* I look at the scrolling screen in front of me, the Facebook world constantly updating. People shift, scratch, shuffle, cough, slurp, shiver, inhale, exhale in my line of vision. The business-man who had caught my hand hours earlier walks past the window next to my table. He looks toward the glass, whether to see inside or to check his own reflection, I don't know. He greets an incoming woman — his secretary? Co-worker? Girlfriend maybe? Wife? They don't linger. Maybe they would in the summer, but this weather is bloody anti-social. They exchange cheek kisses. I can make out a *"Ciao! Ciao!"* and these Scranton characters tighten their coats about them and disappear into the vortex. All this day-to-day life continuing around me, and I feel paralyzed with unknowing, waiting, hoping and trusting he will come back to me. I must go. I must make myself move. The unimpeded clockwork glockenspiel dance of life continues.

Instead of moving, I order another coffee. It does look bloody cold out, after all. I have enough time before the bus comes. I tap out a few necessary messages to the parentals, to my brother Leo, and to Lucy who, after our friends-who-take-advantage-of-business-trips adventure in Munich is, I discover from Facebook, currently researching a piece for her travel guide in Thailand. I let them know I am alive but say little as to the underwhelming reception. Why worry them, right? *Yes, good decision.* The part of me that is burning to spill my guts and just regurgitate every word that passed between Cole and I, like some kind of verbal bulimia, will have to wait until I see Tara.

I replay my late-night departure: the cheek kiss, the whispering in his ear, the kiss again. He could have so easily stopped me, turned his lips toward mine. He could have made the effort if he wanted to.

The door opens, producing another thickly-coated Scrantonian and a blast of minus temperatures so shocking that I'm immediately extracted from my critique. Is this how an ice bath feels? Or when you see pictures of those crazies who plunge into ice holes on New Year's just for fun? FYI: that does not look fun. It looks bananas. *Sure, you go get 'em, nutjob! Take your pasty limbs, last year's bikini that has faded and lost some, if not all, of its elasticity, and smile for the camera! You're a champ! Enjoy your short flirtation with pneumonia; it's going to be swell!*

I really am going to need to buy a thick jacket. The cross-street winds of Manhattan are sure to be brutal. Not that Carrie Bradshaw and crew ever seemed to mind. She would always have put fashion first!

She's fictional, Enna.

Ah, yes. I shall buy a coat as soon as possible.

The Lincoln Tunnel is a bitch. The traffic converges together at the mouth of the tunnel and forms a scrum of metal, pushing forward with little care or awareness for anyone else. I hear the grunts of the big bus engine, clearly exhibiting its mighty right to enter the tunnel before all the other vehicles which were in front. The driver obliviously charges on. It's precarious sitting up front here. I can see the bus perilously close to crushing a Mini Cooper trying to defend her position in front. There is no orderly queue; it's *charge!* and fuck you.

The traffic belches forward again and my head strikes the window. Is this a lesson? Is the universe trying to tell me something? That being polite, that waiting my turn, is a loser mentality? That someone will always jump in and take my spot at the head of the queue? Like Will?

Oh, you just had to bring him up.

The rat bastard who single-handedly swept his way into my life and swindled his way out. I can almost hear him say it with his singular cocky charm, "It's survival of the fittest, my dearest," thinking he's so Darwinian, so erudite. Of course, he is. He'd be right at the front, cutting down anyone in his way. Is being at the front so important anyway? I suppose it used to be, but where, oh where did that get me?

Last night, this morning, early this afternoon, I was so pumped with adrenaline. Jet lag didn't have a chance; now, it has most definitely struck. The soporific sway of the bus as we lull in the underground docking bay, the engine idling as the wheelchair platform is lowered, makes me so utterly heavy. I pretty much could sleep upright at this point.

The doors finally open, and the rush of people surging for the door and flowing out into Port Authority is a flash flood of color onto the curb, flowing up the escalator and away in various directions. The flow sweeps me up with it only after the first few steps. I am fully awake, the elbow-rubbing transference, or maybe alertness to a potential human stampede, makes my legs move faster than I thought possible at this stage of transatlantic exhaustion. I've had a shot of hormonal espresso. It's just as well; I'm handicapped by two wheely cases, a handbag, and a computer bag. And if I don't keep up, this rush hour current might pull me under, or trample me, or some other fate too ghastly to contemplate, so I keep my head up and my bags close.

Where is she? Where is she? Where is she? My head swivels in long-necked meerkat fashion. The crowd sweeps me along—an invisible riptide. I'm dragged away from the entrance, but crossing the flow to the side seems impossible.

"Excuse me. Sorry. Err...Can I just...? Sorry. Pardon me. I just want to..."

"Enna! ENNA!" The voice comes from behind. There can only be one Enna on Thirty-Fourth Street right now. I feel the release of the case in my left hand as the owner of the voice simultaneously guides me through the human rapids to the corner.

"Tara!"

"Enna!"

"*Mon petit poisson!*"

"Bon-bloody-jour!"

The fifteen years since our last meeting flash away, and we greet each other with those same excited smiles, the way they were before they had learned to become guarded, reserved, sometimes jaded. We hug an almighty, bone-crunching hug. Sure, we are probably getting in some peoples' way; certainly, there is every chance the cases at our ankles will be stolen, but I need an actual tangible hug right now, and this hug is a meaningful one. It's a hug that in its solidity and length communicates, at least to me, sorrow for not keeping in touch and for missing these middle years, relief at finding each other, and delight in seeing this face opposite, whose dreams and wonder at the world had once mirrored mine exactly.

"It's so, *so* good to see you!" And it is! It's an instantaneous weight off. I don't have to be the face of the theater, constantly biting my tongue, pressured to say the right thing. I don't have to be apologetic and think of ways to appease her. I can just be me: ridiculous, clumsy, flawed Enna.

"Food? Drink? Sleep?"

"Please!" I nod gratefully.

"Okay, well, clearly the subway might be a challenge at five p.m. carrying the closet of Imelda Marcos. How long did you think you were staying?" She bugs her eyes at my luggage. "Seriously, these two cases are bigger than my bathroom!" She must see my look of contrition as she rubs my arm and gives me another side-squeeze. "Fret not. We will figure it out." And with that, she strides into the street, hand aloft, and practically dives in front of the first yellow vehicle she sees.

We lug the luggage into the boot—the "trunk," I should remember to call it now, I suppose. I slide appreciatively into the warmth and listen to Tara chatter away, giving directions like she was a bona fide, born and raised New Yorker. It's a far cry from her quiet rural upbringing in Ditchling, Sussex; that's for sure.

"So, let me take a look at you." She grabs my cold fingers, holds them clasped between her warm palms, and turns her soft brown eyes on mine. "You look great. Awesome! I would have known that face anywhere."

"I know!" I reply, stifling a giggle to hear this Americanized version of Tara.

A burst of Katy Perry's "Firework" rings out, and from pocket-to-ear in less than three seconds, Tara is all business.

"Hello, this is Tara." She turns to me, mouthing a silent pantomimed, "Sorry."

I look out the cab window as we start and stop our way down the West Side Highway. The lights from the buildings on my left shine brightly, even at five twenty in the evening. The Hudson on my right sparkles like freshly poured tarmac. This is a very "shiny" city. We turn left somewhere—is this Bowery?—and cross town, my eyes searching for familiar landmarks.

I am happily quite, quite lost, until we turn onto Canal Street, and finally I know exactly where we are. This is where Cole took me on one shopping trip. He was so out of his element in his suit and tie. He belonged in Macy's or Bloomingdale's; instead, I was dragging him to these seedy little Chinese purse stores, feeling the faux leather on the plastic no-name bags, waiting for the assistant to show me the real fake purses.

"You wan Gucci? You wan Coach? Here some Coach!"

I was excited by this back room dealing; Cole was not, but he stood beside me anyway, probably wishing he were at a bar watching the New York Rangers. I chose the Louis Vuitton bowling bag handbag, gorgeous in its bulbous shape. Cole paid in cash. I thought it such a prize, and me a proper New Yorker with a grown up purse! The stitching came apart and the lining frayed within a month.

He laughed when I showed him, my bottom lip in full pout, and he told me, "You get what you pay for." The next day he surprised me with a Coach purse—the real thing, not a knockoff. He'd driven down to Tannersville. His secretary had told him it was there. He knew it wasn't the same, but he hoped I liked it anyway. I loved it. Really, the name meant nothing to me, but the thought of him going through handbags in a shop surrounded by women shoppers tickled me.

Woof! The unleashed memory is bitter-sweet. *How could I have thought for one second that I should be without this man?*

In spite of the big chill in the Big Apple, the street life on Canal Street is ever-bustling. The street vendors are bundled up like Eskimos—I really need a jacket—and the steam rises from the pavement—no, sidewalk—from the gratings, the vents, manhole covers, the food carts proffering tacos, kebabs, and nuts.

I am, officially, faaaammmished! Just the sight of caramelized cashews and almonds shoveled into a little paper cone is enough to get me close to foodgasm.

I've never been good at eating when work or angst-focused; hunger's body rebellion is always a bit of a surprise. I forget meals and then, KABAM, the cloud of migraine descends on my brain, takes hold and squeezes it so I cannot function. It was missing meals, going way beyond that level of cellular hunger than is healthy, that caused my last almighty migraine attack. I should eat something. And soon.

I had been counseled in the hospital. The nurse worked predominantly with anorexics, bulimics, men as well as women. I didn't have a problem, I assured her. I was just focused. I loved food! I had the appetite of a sumo wrestler in disguise! She said she'd like to talk anyway. So I listened.

"There are different levels of hunger," she explained sweetly. *"First, there's eye hunger: seeing something that looks so good you want it. But you're not really hungry. Then there is the smell: hunger that is aroused by the aroma of something. Next, mouth hunger: wanting the feel of something in your mouth; it's comforting. Then there is taste: you roll that ball of food around, and you know you like the flavors, the textures. Stomach hunger is the real flag. The other precursors can fool you into thinking you have an appetite, but you don't. That empty feeling in your stomach is how you know you are hungry.*

"I think, Enna, you do a good job of ignoring all of these. Maybe as a punishment, or as a strict control, but that is how you get to the sixth level of hunger: cellular hunger. Actually, I think you go far beyond that, and that's when your brain and body start to shut down on you. These migraines you have experienced, the vomiting, the lack of vision — these are all due to severe cellular hunger. And there is one level left: that's heart hunger. That's when people eat to comfort themselves, to heal their heart. No food will ever mend a broken heart. The trick is to face the issue that hurts, so you may deal with it, and be happy."

It's funny the nuggets of knowledge, the snippets of conversation that come back three thousand miles later, sitting in the traffic in Chinatown, streets from Little Italy, the Financial District, Soho, West Village, the Meat-Packing District, East Village, Chelsea, Midtown, Hell's Kitchen, Uptown. Manhattan is a city that is all about food *and* focus.

Chapter 4

Finally free of traffic, we cross the Manhattan Bridge. The view is spectacular — the suspension cables lit up in the dark sky, the Williamsburg Bridge to my left and Brooklyn Bridge to my right, the lights, the traffic, the action!

We flow up Flatbush Avenue, passing college buildings, an outdoor market, a stadium, before Tara leans toward the Plexiglas that divides us from our driver. "Can you let us out here please? Here, at the corner. That's it. Sixth Avenue. Perfect."

I reel at the cab fee and dig my wallet from my handbag.

"No, don't you dare!" Tara snaps my purse shut. "This is my treat tonight. The cab, dinner, maybe another bottle of wine on the way home. It's mine, you hear? You can treat me another night. Deal?"

Is this a fair deal? Aren't I the one staying at her apartment? Shouldn't I be paying? But the firm grip she has on my handbag makes me realize it would be churlish to refuse.

I put my bag on my shoulder.

"Good girl," she says, pleased.

We leave the cases by the front door. The hostess beams broadly. "Sure. Sure. They will be safe. I will personally keep my eyes out on them," she says in her thick accent.

I smile at Tara, imagining the hostess plucking her eyes out and placing them on my cases like some weird deleted scene from *Beetlejuice*.

"We'll have two *caipirinhas* to start, please," Tara trills before I have even opened my menu. "Trust me." She levels her bright eyes at mine. "You'll love a *caipirinha*! And by the looks of things you need five, but all in good time."

She watches as I bob my eyes up from my menu again to check that my luggage is still by the door. Jesus, I know I didn't pack an adequate wardrobe, but the thought of someone stealing it would just be the limit.

"You don't have to worry about a thing here. I've been in this neighborhood for five years now, and I have never felt so settled. It's just got a great vibe, a community, a heart. Take this place; Café Cubana is one of my favorites. So stop worrying about your bags and relax. The hostess has got them. Now, what are you going to eat? Everything is good here."

It's just as well, because the dishes listed swim before my eyes—ugh. I hope this doesn't mean I'm getting a migraine. I close my eyes and point at the menu a few times before my fingertip hits a description I completely understand. Have I ever had a yucca before? What an unfortunate name for a vegetable.

I decide on the pulled pork. It's really the whipped plantains that sell it for me. Oh, and the beans, and the Rioja wine gravy. I'll get that! Exhaustion settles heavily on my shoulders. I want to be done with decision-making for the day.

I stretch out in the seat, tensing my muscles and rolling my neck in a circle. *Click, click, click.* The gasses fire off in the joints, making that distinctive cracking sound, like loading a weapon.

"You look done in, lovey. Oh! Look, here's your *caipirinha*. It's restorative. Well, not exactly, but it does have sugar and alcohol in it, so this will give you a jolt!"

I take a tentative sip, then another, then a gulp. She's right; this is just the pick-me-up I need. We order, clear the menus, talk of her audition—a featured role in *Orange is the New Black*.

"Stop! Wait. *O.I.T.N.B*? Did you get it?"

"I don't know. I should hear pretty quickly. It's just one episode. Just a few lines. They're shooting next week."

"Wow. That's really cool."

"You watch the show?"

"Well, no. Not technically."

"Not technically?"

"But I have heard of it!"

"You're too cute."

"I'm sure I'd like it. I would watch it, especially with you in it, but, well, the theater rather excluded television watching. I've heard great things though. It's big. Congratulations!"

"Well, I haven't got it yet. LOL."

We both take a sip. I replace my glass on the table. Am I *that* tired? Did she just say...

"Did you just 'LOL' me?"

"It was an ironic 'LOL'!" She throws her napkin at me, narrowly missing my drink, and we laugh and continue to swap terribly delightful and delightfully terrible audition stories from the last fifteen years. How could so much time pass so quickly?

There's a long pause, where eyes harden from their glossy dance of joint remembrance, a pause that can no longer be filled with sips or amusing anecdotes; it's that clearly defined point that says...*so, what's your story, Enna?*

I sigh and shrug my shoulders. "It wasn't supposed to be like this."

She reaches across the table and captures my wrist in her hand. "You don't have to tell me. You're welcome here. You don't have to say a thing if you don't want."

But curiously, now that we have reached this point, I do want to share, and not for validation or congratulation, but just to tell someone. And so I launch into the whole sorrowful saga of the last year: the visa hoop-jumping; the pressure to leave the theater that I was desperate to save; the promise of the Scranton Theater position; the terrible disappointment to learn I couldn't, in fact, work for a year; the argument; my midnight visa-negating flight back to England; the breakup; Will; the plan to save my theater; saving my theater; Will swindling my theater (I leave out the bit about him swindling my heart); the search; the hunger and attendant explosive headache; the accidental overdose; Cole finding and rescuing me; recuperation and realization; surprise flight back to PA; the doorstep heart-in-mouth monologue; the leggy blonde; the hotel; the loss of trust. The End.

I have, in fact, talked the whole way through dinner, shoveling in hungry mouthfuls of shredded pork and sweet plantains during the pauses for punctuation. My straw makes that awful slurp sound as I reach the end of my third *caipirinha*. Holy sugar, Batman.

"Damn!" she says finally with a long drawn out "am." She sits back in her chair, straightening from her attentive listener hunch, and balls up her napkin. "I think that's just about the saddest thing I've ever heard. You were just trying your best. Oh, Enna! *Mon poisson!* Cole's not a theater person. He would never understand why you did what you did. I get it. I do. And he's hurt—of course he's hurt—but to leave you on the doorstep, to leave you stranded in Scranton? Shit. I'm usually pretty great at advice, level-headed, but I think the best I can do tonight is…Tequila?"

And for lack of a better one, it seems a good idea. We go through the sticky back-of-hand routine and pull the same gummy faces as we suck the air through our teeth.

She slams her glass down on the table. "Rrrrah!" She opens her eyes wide. "We'll take another!" she hollers at the attentive hostess.

Since recuperating at home, I really haven't been drinking. *Caipirinhas*, tequilas, jet lag, emotional state—this could all go horribly wrong, but we continue drinking and talking regardless.

"I think what you've got to do is stay here for a while. Let him know you aren't a flight risk."

"But how? Where? On what?"

"Whaddya mean?" Her British consonants, which had sharpened during the last two hours, are starting to fade again with the alcohol. I suppose one of the perks of being an actress and a dual citizen is never having to commit to one accent. Instant American accent: just add tequila!

"I mean, A: how *can* I stay when you are going away? B: how can I survive when I can't legally work, and I don't have a nice whopping trust fund I can live off? And C…I don't know a C, but don't things always sound better in threes?"

"Meh…semantics. You can fix this. Those are just little hurdles, and you're giving in to them. Reclaim your power. You're not a victim. This is Brooklyn. This is America! Land of opportunities and posshibil—" *hic* "—ities and a million restaurants that will pay you cash tips."

"But that's not…"

"Sshhhhhhhhhhh!" She puts her index finger to her lips, or tries to — it's really more a weird cheek-hover that almost pokes her eye out — but I get the intended direction. "Then all you need to do is find a way to keep in contact with Cole without being stalkerish, but showing your undying commitment and make him realize what he is missshing!"

"Well, if that'sss all."

"No problem. You can do it! You're awesome!"

"Huzzah!" I cheer rather too loudly, believing Tara's positive spin.

"Sshhhhhhhhhhh!" She misses her mouth again. "Ooh. I think we oughta get home soon." She grasps the bill on the table — *the check, Enna, the check* — keeping it from my eyes, and folds a number of bills in it.

"Thanks again, Tara. I really mean it."

"S'nothing! Oh! Drinkies, drinkies, naughty little drinkies! I'm going to sound and feel like a toad in the morning."

"Ish better than looking like one!" I rejoin, realizing as I get to my feet that three *caipirinhas* and two tequilas, *and* jet lag, have had more of an effect than I thought. Naughty little drinkies!

We wheel out along Sixth Avenue, tripping on the tree-root-lifted paving stones, laughing and tripping again, and then up to Seventh. The cool air blows in my face, a bracing, sobering, pleasant rallying of the senses and faculties. It's only nine p.m. in Park Slope, and the lights are bright, the traffic constant, the restaurants packed. Nine p.m. and we are off home to bed. Rockstars! Yet, the weight of worry and loneliness feels less. We link arms and walk in step, just as we did up and down Highgate Hill so many years ago. It's not so hopeless, cold, or unfeeling with a good friend at your side.

Tara was not wrong when she wrote that we might be so crammed we would become contortionists. As I emerge from the bathroom, which I immediately christen the "basin room," I squeeze my frame between the bookcase loaded two books deep and the bed, then skirt the footboard and the wall to the square foot of open space where my inflatable mattress lies. I say "open space"; there's no actual open space now even to walk the perimeter of the mattress, so I toss my toiletries bag toward the pillow end and gingerly paw my way, on all fours, onto the airbed. This would be a challenging *Mission Impossible* obstacle course sober, let alone tiddly.

The two of us shuffling past each other in this teeny tiny little space reminds me of the figures rotating around a glockenspiel clock, going about our bedtime business in this fixed loop. It's like a toy version of an apartment, truly only meant for one. And yet, Tara opened her door to me anyway. Over a decade of communicatory silence, Facebook discovery, request and a few exchanged messages, "likes" and status comments and…here we are. I'm flooded with amazement by her generosity of spirit. I hope I would have done the same. If she needed somewhere to stay and I didn't have room to swing a microbe, would I have been that selfless?

The "kitchen" is through a midget doorway off the room, the opposite end to the bathroom. That's it. That's all. Three rooms and it probably costs more to rent this for the month than my whole mort-gage payment for the Ashtead house. I stare at the high ceiling — the only thing generous about this room is the wasted head room, not that it is wasted; the Victorian moldings and cornices that decorate the ceiling are quite beautiful — and I listen to Tara potter and hum.

In spite of the tequila, her humming is soft now. She explained in loud stage whispers on the stone stoop outside, before she aimed her key at the lock and missed five times, that her apartment was actually "in ssssomeone's house. So we have to be very quiet!"

Once through the outer door and through the heavy wooden and glass inner door — with yet another stubborn lock — we tiptoed up the stairs cartoonishly. I stifled the urge to do my best Elmer Fudd impression — *Be verwy, vwerwy quiet!* — yet it looped like a mental soundtrack as I hit every creaky step possible, paused, giggled, got *"sssshed,"* and repeated for four flights.

So now, lying in "bed," trying tremendously hard not to make a noise, I suddenly have even more appreciation of Anne Frank *en famille* in the attic. It's really hard not to creak, clunk or close doors that are just a hair tight in their frames and desperately cry out for WD-40. Everything I do, no matter how careful, I make noise. Tara seems to be used to it.

"I've got Earl Grey," she whispers enthusiastically, her head whip-ping around the side of the doorjamb.

"Earl Grey tastes like potpourri. I'll pass, but thank you."

Her head reappears. "How about Tetley? PG Tips? There's a Brit-ish store in the West Village, Soho area I guess. I'll have to take you there. It has Scotch eggs and Quality Street chocolates!" *These two food items should never be mentioned in the same sentence to someone who has just imbibed quantities of alcohol.* I think she must either be drunker than I thought or forgetful that I was in the UK forty-eight hours ago, so the promise of proper British tea is not exactly the thing of wonder it might be in three months or three years.

"I've cleaned my teeth. But thank you."

"A glass of water then?"

"Tara, stop. You needn't kill yourself to run around after me. Just pretend I'm not here. Have your potpourri tea, and I promise, if I need anything else, I'll ask."

"Okey dokey." Her head snaps back behind the door frame.

What am I doing here? I'm in the way. Clearly, I am in the way. Maybe I should just go back. Tell my parents I was too late, get a job filing or answering phones or something. Slowly die inside.

Enna, stop! Think of Cole! Do you really want to prove him right and just skulk off back to England again?

No.

Well, then.

I wonder what Cole is doing now. Is he alone? Is he with Patricia? Cozied up in each other's arms? Does she fit in the nook next to him, under his shoulder? Does he kiss her like he would kiss me? Hard, warm lips melting into mine. What does he call her? Patty? Pat? Trish? Tricia? Pickle? Relish? Sauerkraut?

I shoot up, sitting bolt upright. What if he came back to the Radisson to talk to me? Oh God! This sudden unthought-of throws me.

Crapola. I should have left a note or something. I'll message him tomorrow. Right? After all, teeth cleaning has had a great sobering effect, but I really shouldn't write to anyone after cocktails and shots. Maybe his worrying where I am would be good. Perhaps it will make him see that he wants to be with me after all and not…her. Right?

Oh, aren't relationships supposed to be easy? Isn't everything supposed to just fall into place and not be such a fight? Cole and I never played the typical dating games. I called him when I wanted, regardless of turn. Well, prior to the horrendous disengagement and my transatlantic runaway bride bit, that is.

At the beginning, before the bullshit, the paperwork, the visa interviews, the stress — when everything caused an energy power surge and wide-eyed wonder — he would leave me messages every day. Whether e-mail or Facebook or voice mail, his few words had never failed to make me smile, regardless of nineteen-hour work days.

"Ms. Peterson, have I told you today how much I miss you?"

"Hello, Enna's voice mail, I was calling to speak to the love of my life. I think you may know her…"

When had that disappeared? When had he stopped saying it? I nestle back into the mattress and close my eyes, scanning the microfiche of memory. When? When? When? I think it got lost between the small print and the black-boxed answers of the visa applications. I think when I started to become resentful for the endless and demanding form-filling. I think, no, I know I took it out on him, and his familiar loving messages just…evaporated. I want it back! I want *him* back! If I'm going to earn his trust, we have to start again. We have to get back to that: the basics of us, being a good team, sans bullshit. I will tell him in the morning. After a coffee.

"We are very hip, you know. Brits in Brooklyn, baby!" Tara exclaims with an ironic eyebrow lift. She is dressed neatly in her robe, Earl Grey in hand, shuffling past the bed and bookcase on her glockenspiel track to the bedside, placing her mug down safely on the coaster.

"Indeed," I whisper, popping up from my blanketed cocoon on the floor. "Hipsters always use coasters."

"We're not hipsters. We're…Britsters?…Hipstains?"

"Hipstains? You actually want to call us hipstains? This is, I believe, the part where I call Mensa and ask them to revoke your membership."

"It's hipster mixed with Britains!" We laugh and "shush" and agree never to refer to the other as a "hipster" or "hipstain." Ever.

It's not even ten p.m. and we are in bed, Tara sipping tea, dressed like my mother, and me on the floor, feeling as if I am twelve years old or younger.

"What's on the agenda for tomorrow?" she asks at a normal volume, her tequila-ed American fading back to crisper Brit. She seems just merry now and not a bit concerned about volume and that people sleep or read or watch TV somewhere floors below.

"Well…" I rest my chin on the corner of her comforter. "I think there are three immediate things to do: get myself a coat so I don't turn into a human icicle, let Cole know I am safe in Brooklyn, and work out how I am going to live indefinitely."

"We'd all like to live indefinitely." She sets her cup back down.

"You know what I mean—living in America."

"Hmm…not sure how much I can help with the last two, but the first thing, abso-bloody-lutely! I bet my stuff will fit you. It might be a bit baggy, but a couple of good Brooklyn bagels, and you'll be back to fine fighting fettle." She sweeps her covers aside, and from an almost James Bond-esque hidden panel, she starts tossing clothes in my direction.

"I couldn't. Tara, please!" I say as a brightly colored piece of fabric lands over my face and head. I lay it aside as another material missile flies past my ear. "Look, Tara. You've already been so kind. I really can't take your things."

She stops pulling hangers from the rail, the wind taken out of her sails a little. "But this will be fun. I'll feel good about helping you, and you will feel warm. I have little enough to give, but it's yours. Okay?" She continues to sort through her closet again. "Besides, didn't everyone say at National Youth Theater that we were like sisters? Well, now it's almost as if I'm helping my fucked up little sister! Joke!" She throws another garment toward me, laughing. Maybe she shouldn't have had those tequilas!

She pauses at the rail and takes an emerald green wrap-around dress off its hanger and extends it to me. "This one! This is perfect. This would look phenomenal on you. Try it."

"Okay." I capitulate. Emerald green always did get me. My mind and my hand immediately leap to the mighty chunk of gem, the ring fastened on a chain around my neck—his ring, the one I threw away then lost the right to wear. I feel it heavy on my sternum now. I like the ever-present weight of this stone that glows from within like kryptonite. This dress would be the perfect meeting-Cole-again dress. I wrap the jersey material over my negligee; even my choice of packed nightwear is woefully inappropriate.

Did I bring anything useful at all? A bloody negligee?! Like I would have been wearing anything lying next to Cole. We'd be skin to skin, a tangle of indivisible limbs, my head on his chest listening to his heart pound and feeling his chest rise up and down, up and down.

Come on, Enna! Focus!

"I knew it! It's perfect. Well, except for the lumpy boob thing you have got going there with that lacy shit, but with a proper bra, it'd be swell. Get it? Swell? No?"

I nod sadly. "Hello, this is the pun police…"

"Oh, stop moping. I'm too wired to go to bed. Try this one on."
She tosses another brightly colored garment at me.

"Is this a shirt or a jacket?"

"I call it a shacket."

"Novel. Is this like your Britsters nomenclature? Do you spend
your days finding new words to weld together?"

"You betcha! See, aren't you having fun? This is just like *What
Not to Wear*, or dress-up Barbie or something."

"Dress up Barbie," I mutter into the folds of something that smells
so clean and comforting. As my head emerges from the neckline,
she beams, and I'm unable to keep a wry smile from spreading over
my face. I have to admit, it beats torturing myself with thoughts of
Cole. It's retail therapy without actually costing me a penny. I love it!

Some garments are a bit loose—after all that has happened, I
don't think anyone would be surprised—but Tara says nothing and so
I carry on, trying on this, pulling off that. We do look similar—the
height and shape obviously, but the same fine nose peppered with
freckles, the bright eyes, the full brows that most would over-pluck
to nothingness. The features that mask the similarities are the mouth,
Tara's fuller, as if she has a natural lip liner indelibly embossed, and her
hair, the same color but much thicker and shorter. My hair brushes
my waist; hers barely grazes her earlobes.

I finally peel off the last item—a canary yellow cashmere twin-set
she bought, she tells me, from a consignment store somewhere in the
East Village. It's deliciously soft and warm and smells of meadows.
I hug it to me.

"Oh, it is made for you! Enna, seriously…with jeans and a popping yellow stiletto…or maybe a flesh colored heel…or with a simple
black skirt for a more professional look. You must take that one to
keep. It suits you."

Her generosity really is so touching. I fear I might cry again.
"Well, thank you. Are you sure I don't look like a giant blob of custard,
or jaundiced, or some kind of Teletubby?"

"You look great."

"I just feel like it's too much! You bought me dinner. You're giving me house space. I feel bad taking the clothes off your back too."

"*Mon petit!* They are not on my back. I won't need these in Bermuda. Will you please just enjoy and stop worrying?"

"What's your agenda tomorrow?" I ask, nestling back into my cocoon.

"Oh, busy work. The usual trawl through websites to see what castings are afoot, sending headshots and résumés."

"You're not getting tired of the constant push? You can't leave it to your agent?"

"If I'd have left it to my agent, I would have starved on the streets many years ago. Sure, I get tired. I have no retirement plan, and some months are hand-to-mouth, but I am still doing something I love. It's exciting. I think you have to pursue your passions or it's selling out."

I will not go back to an office job. I will not answer phones. I will not sell out!

Chapter 5

Park Slope is quite a different place in the morning. It's loud. Not that it was mute last night, but just kind of mellow. Or maybe that was the *caipirinha*-tequila fog muffling the nocturnal sound of the city. Now, the streets jostle with people: men in grubby sweatshirts throwing open the grated holes in the sidewalk to the underground kitchens, thrusting up the delivery truck's metal gating, crashing down the tail-lift and unloading or loading produce to the stores; people in scrubs and trainers — sneakers! — filing in or out of the hospital; kids weaving in and out of the foot traffic, loud, hearty; belligerent looking traffic wardens prowling for first blood; chic men and women, Bluetooth inserted and café latte in hand; mums wrapped up in their thickest dark coats, holding hands with the miniature version of themselves, the mini topped with some pink, fluffy hat with ear flaps; and the morning joggers heading to or from Prospect Park — in this cold, I question their sanity. It is, however, a beautiful morning, frigid to be sure — great plumes of breath make human dragons of us — but it's bright and crisp.

Tara gives me the nickel tour. It is mainly to do with food, the exception being the direction of Steve Buscemi's stoop. I know now where to buy bagels (Bagel Market), pizza (Smiling Pizza), fresh pasta, arrancini, and homemade pasta sauce (Russi's), fresh produce (The Co-op, but I might not be allowed in there; she'll check the rules). She directs me to a great cheese selection (Union Market), the best hangover breakfast sandwiches and the feta-est Greek omelettes around (Purity), and — I scowled at this — the best date place (Talde). Clearly, in Park Slope I will never starve. I might die of cold but not from lack of dining options or conveniences.

Actually, it's only the tips of my fingers that are pounding, red, raw, which fits my color scheme quite, quite well. Tara's wrapped me up in her woolen red duffel coat with toggle buttons, a royal blue hat and matching blue fingerless gloves. I feel something between a superhero and Paddington Bear. Tara is in pea green with a long white scarf trailing down her back, white hat, gloves and boots. Park Slope's dynamic duo: Tenacious Tara with powers of auditioning endurance, and Enna the Erroneous with her amazing powers of being mistaken and royally fucking up everything. Duh duh daaaa!

"Here's a cool place for you to hang out. You know, when the apartment starts to feel like the walls are collapsing in on you. It's called The Tea Lounge."

I expect some kind of Park Slope Starbucks — Ikea furniture and Michael Bublé on repeat — but this is quite, quite different. The space is huge. I've never seen a coffee shop so big, and even at nine thirty in the morning, it is a hive of chilled activity. The hodgepodge of kitsch sofas, tables, and chairs are largely filled by men and women typing away, headphones on or ear plugs in, nodding away to their silent beat. The right side deliciously displays a refrigerated cabinet full of cheesecakes, muffins, scones and granola-topped yogurt. On the counter above, an array of caffeine paraphernalia, including all the regular grinding, percolating, and spurting machines which sweep down to the bar area which is exhibiting drafts and three-tiered shelves of booze in front of a blackboard chalked with drink specials. It's clearly a writer's haven. Coffee before noon; after then, who knows?

The nostril-tingling aroma of good coffee awakens my senses even more than the morning air. Or rather, awakens my appetite!

"I vote we caffeinate!" I exclaim far too perkily to be cool. And this place is *cool*. It doesn't have the battery hen, cooped and processed conveyor belt feel, but a free range, organic vibe. There's no dress code, but there is a uniform here: laptop and an air of mindfulness and co-existence. No overly-loud cell phone talk; calls are hushed or taken outside. Conversation is quiet, intimate. Also in the air, as the waft of coffee ground fades, I detect traces of cigarettes and stale alcohol — ah, the dark side. It's urban shabby chic.

We order nonfat lattes—it seems the thing to do, being healthily unhealthy—and a sandwich to share: peanut butter, banana, and honey on wheat. It is on all-organic. *Look at me. I'm so Brooklyn!*

We find an empty innocuous beige couch. Its fabric is pilled, dressed up with a few turquoise cushions, and there we plant ourselves.

Tara has been distinctly quiet this morning. I realize now she just needed her first morning coffee before chattiness resumed. She practically inhales her coffee; she drinks it so fast, cupping it in her hands, handle in line with her nose and *glug, glug.* I enjoy taking this all in: the man in the corduroys with the underbite, tapping his foot and nibbling his nails whilst intently reading the screen; the girl with her mug a measured distance from her computer, her banana and apple laid out neatly as if some kind of trophy or reward; the woman with the bright red hair, arms inked with elaborate designs, face buried in *The Science of Yoga.*

How funny that I should be here, taking this in, eating and drinking and smelling, tasting, and living in a place I never expected to be, in circumstances so far removed from those I thought would be mine. Twenty-four hours, just twenty-four hours ago, I sat hopeless in Scranton; forty-eight hours ago I was hopeful on a flight from London, Heathrow; seventy-two hours ago I was bundled up at my parents' house, glancing at an e-mail.

"You look worried. Stop looking worried."

"Of course I'm worried. I've always worked for a living. How did you do it at first, when you moved over?" *God, this sweet, nutty banana goodness is divine.*

"God, it was so long ago now, and pre-9/11, so it was all very simple. I have dual citizenship because of my mum, so…Sorry. I know that doesn't help you at all."

"Bugger."

Tara finishes her last bite of the toastie, licks the escapee peanut butter off her fingertip and thumb, and we sit in silent contemplation.

"I know financially I can't afford to just do nothing. Legally, I can't afford to do anything. I can't work because I am not a permanent resident or a citizen with a social security card. I am just an alien tourist."

"You have two options then."

"Yes?" I try to sound hopeful and heave myself up from the quicksand cushions.

"Option one: go home where you can work and earn money legally."

"That's giving up and selling out."

"Option two: stay here and get a job that pays in cash."

"That *is* illegal, you know."

"Oh, I know. So you have to weigh up what is more important to you — if staying to try to win Cole back is worth the risk of being caught, found an alien criminal and deported forever!"

"You don't have to put it like that!"

"Okay, I take it back. Doing something that is a teeny weeny bit wrong in the eyes of the law, all in the name of love."

"Better much," I agree, taking a comforting, milky slurp. "And, I mean, who would know, right? What are the chances of getting caught? You'd have to be a complete moron or very careless to get caught."

Tara eyeballs me and doesn't reply.

"Seriously," I ramble on, "you're an actress. I was an actress. It'll be like taking on a role. How many times have you been paid in cash for doing a promo this, or photo shoot that, or tips from waitressing? It's cash. Nobody knows about it."

"Agh, you're heading down a murky path there, *mon petit.* I got audited last year, and it was the worst kind of torture, the ninth circle of Hell, the financial abyss. I cannot explain to you how emotionally and physically draining it was. I account for ev-er-y-thing. Period."

Fuck. I think of the financial crisis at the theater when Will cleared out the account. I was in the hospital, which may have been a lucky escape. The police and forensic accountants were left to go through ev-er-y-thing.

Could I break the rules? Is Cole worth the risk?

Abso-fucking-lutely.

We Eskimo back up and finish our tour, looping down onto Fifth and along, passing various shop windows I glance at without seeing. Conversation has evaporated, and I keep my words in my head.

Back in the Anne Frank attic, in the severe daylight, I am even more aware of the lack of space and the ability to make noise. I must sound like a sumo wrestler in a bad mood.

With just a kitchen(ette), a basin room, and a bedroom, there is no space for an office or desk. Tara lies stomach down, legs crisscrossed behind her school-girlishly as she scours her sites for more casting calls. I tiptoe-shuffle around the bed, so conscious of being in her space.

I lower myself to the airbed and fire up the laptop for lack of anywhere else to go. Maybe I could e-mail from the bath? Or whilst standing in the table-and-chair-less kitchen?

This is not a problem. She has said that you are welcome. You do not need to feel like a complete imposition. She's like an American now: they are free and easy and do not measure or limit hospitality, generosity, and friendships like you are used to.

American standard check: don't use her last tea bag; do replenish her hummus and maintain her stock of wine; don't sleep with her boyfriend, or fart during sleep. Check, check, checkety, check. I'll be fine!

We both tippy tappy type away. Tara looks very industrious, wirelessly printing this side and that e-mail. I trawl Facebook as I try to find the right words. Of course, I click on every post and every photograph on Cole's Facebook page. He's never really been interested in participating in the daily time-consuming ritual: the status updating, the parade of photos, the "liking," the "Happy Birthday-ing." I remember I had to beg him to join, telling him that he was old and crotchety if he didn't.

"But I see the people who are important to me. Why do I have to have all my private stuff in a public space?" he'd asked.

"But you don't see me all the time," I said through three thousand miles of telephone connection. "I can share things with you. Photographs and things."

"Can't you just e-mail?"

"Facebook's easier."

"Why is it easier?"

I was stumped at that.

"I don't know! Will you just do this for me, please?"

And he had, dutifully. His page now is fairly unattended. He is tagged in a few photographs, and there are a few posts from old school friends who have obviously just reconnected, the old, *"Hey, Cole! So good to see you on FB! How's life? What are you up to?"*

Of course, I click on the comments to read his response, holding my breath with illusions of grandeur that he would allude to me. *"Oh, you know, I was quite happy until this British bitch broke my heart..."*

Instead, he replies, typical Cole, *"All good, buddy. Work, family. No complaints. Beers soon."*

Cole, about as wordy and full of emotion as a lump of…I know that's bravado. I know that's the stony surround. I know that there's a vulnerable heart in there, and I hope it hasn't hardened against me.

I click over to e-mail. He'll check e-mail more. He'll take e-mail more seriously.

~~My darling Cole,~~

~~Hey Sweetie,~~

~~Hi!~~

Cole,

So much I want to tell you. I am so glad you found me at the Radisson. I know I lost your trust. I know I hurt you, and you hurt me too. But I want you to know that I am committed to you. The theater is not my priority. You are.

I couldn't afford a long stay at the Radisson — and by long, I mean more than one night! So, I am safe. I am staying with an old girlfriend in NY. I think I mentioned Tara to you. Yes, this puts me a little distance from you, but maybe that's okay. Maybe it would be more normal if we could see each other without a transatlantic flight at either end. Maybe you can come here, or I can visit you?

I think of all the good times, the fun we had, the adventures. We made a great team. I know our history has been tainted, but I want you. I hope that you want me too, because that's what is really important, you know?

Love,

E.

I want to type more. I think of all those little incidences when he filled me with wonder, but that's not Cole. He likes straight to the point. He doesn't want odes or prose. I press send and adjust the sound so I will hear when an e-mail is returned.

Ugh, the thought of never having that genuine closeness with him again is…I just can't; I won't imagine it. The thought of never waking up to that face, not the most beautiful but his, flawed and scarred and mine.

My stomach gurgles audibly. "Pardon," I throw over my shoulder to the industrious Tara.

She's engrossed.

I know I shouldn't focus on this, on him, on us, but replaying scenes from our history, reminding me of what we had, is somehow comforting. I can picture his face, cheek cupped by the white linen, a shading of stubble peppering his jaw around his lips, the crust of sleep around those eyes, the blinks, the daylight calibration and focus. And then he saw me, my cheek cupped by matching white linen pillow, a body in mirror image. He smiled, eyes fixed, and pulled me toward him, legs sliding in between the other, sandwiching thigh-to-thigh, wrapped in each other, rapt in each other, crotches touching, chests touching, faces so close that words were whispers, and vision blurred and refocused again. His hazel eyes looked at me to see me, not a trophy to admire or an object to own, but someone to connect with, to understand, to adore.

I close my eyes to savor that capsule of memory—his face, his look. I want to frame it, crystallize it, box and bottle it. If I could imprint it on the back of my eyelids, I would.

Like a 3D movie image it whooshes toward me, zooming in and displacing the memory of Cole's face, replaced instead with the consuming look of Will's hungry, amber eyes. I feel my body tighten and try to block him from my thoughts.

"You okay?" Tara leans over the side of her bed/office.

"Fine. Good."

How did I not notice he was only interested in himself? How did I not pick up on the fact he looked at me just to see a reflection of himself? My stomach churns again, and a bitter aftertaste of betrayal gurgles up my throat. I am not sure I have ever truly hated anyone as much as I do Will. He played me like a puppet. But it's weird, isn't it? To feel this loathing and remember such intimacy. I cannot unsee them; they are scenes from my life I cannot delete, or edit, or retake. You only get one take. Every day, every hour, every minute—you get just once.

You were a mug. Duped. Taken for a ride.

How could I have done that? How could I have been so thick? How could I have given up on those memories with Cole? How could I have replaced that face on the pillow, those hands around me?

Self-preservation. If you had no one else to take your mind off him, to make you feel special, you would have wallowed and tortured yourself for longer. You got on with it, Enna. Stop twisting the knife.

And maybe it was possible to let Will in because I was angry with Cole, because I was so incensed that he'd lied to me about the visa terms and the ability to work immediately, because he'd lost *my* trust.

And I'd lost his.

I'll get a cash job. I'll visit him in Scranton, and we'll create new memory capsules. What's the alternative? Trailing back to England, heart and money spent, selling my share of the Ashtead house, moving back in with my parents, no job, bugger-all opportunities, and a futile cycle of dating men who will never dislodge Cole's hold on my heart.

And if Cole still doesn't want you? If he still can't trust you?

It's unthinkable, but as I wait in silence for my e-mail to be received, read and replied to, I have to swallow the sorrowful lump cresting my throat. If he doesn't want me, maybe time will make things fade. Maybe I'll stop looking for e-mails or typing his name in the Facebook search bar. I'll probably forget the words he used, the expressions on his face. Maybe I won't even be able to picture that face on the back of my eyelids, but surely, surely I could never forget how he made me feel.

Ten minutes pass. An hour. I scour the classifieds online — Craigslist is apparently not just for psycho killers — but I think time has been paralyzed, the minute hand crawling along to reach the hour.

"I can't do this anymore. I need to get out of here and breathe."

Tara looks up from her screen. "I told you the walls start to cave in on you. I'm sorry. No response from Cole?"

"Nada. Waiting around for someone, doing nothing, is the singular most exhausting thing in the world. God, what if I have to wait, suspended like this for the entire three months? I'll go fruit loop, batshit, monkey nuts mental."

"Why don't you go for a walk? A run in Prospect Park even? I can lend you my spare sneakers and —"

"Thanks but I'd get frostbite. If I don't get raped and murdered, I'll almost certainly freeze to death."

"Prospect Park is fine! Okay, would I say go jogging there on your own at night in hot pants? Probably not. But if you stay to the running track, there are so many other people around; you are fine."

"Thanks," I repeat, "but I'll pass."

"Ooooh!" Tara sets her laptop on the bed and jumps up.

"What are you doing?"

"Now, where did I put it?"

"Put what?" It beats me how anyone could lose track of anything in this place; it's all right here.

She searches under piles of papers, resolutely not listening, mumbling under her breath. "Gotcha!" She brandishes a piece of paper victoriously.

"What? What is it?" I'm standing now. Why do two standing bodies seem to take up so much more of this space than two sitting bodies?

"Okay," she says, one hand clasping the paper and one hand splayed, halting me like a scared horse or something. What's with the gentle, gentle? Is she going to propose we get matching tattoos? "I have an idea. So, hear me out."

Gingerly, I sit on the end of the bed. Why do I think I am not going to like this?

"Last year, when Bob and I — he was the dicktard who was knobbing the stage manager at the same time as 'exclusively' dating me; I think I vented, maybe fumed, on Facebook a number of times. We were finally, categorically, catastrophically done, done, done. I was pretty stinkin' damaged. Meh, spade a spade; I was fucked up. I know you see me now, a stable, carefree, happy-go-lucky ducky, but once, yes, things were pretty bleak."

I don't know whether to laugh or sympathize, so I rub her non-paper-clutching hand and stretch a thin-lipped pouty smile on my face. Where is she going with this? Are we going to shave our heads in a statement of dating rebellion? Is this why she donated her long, thick locks last year?

"Anyway, it's a long story…yada yada…a friend picked me up off the floor. She had to like seriously scrape me from my pool of despair on the carpet and take me to this place."

Oh God. She's going to take me to church. Or counseling. Some weirdy therapy with people who don't use deodorant. Maybe a help group. Arseholes Anonymous? *Hello, my name is Enna, and I'm an Arseaholic.*

"The irony being, I really wasn't so devastated about him. Well, I wasn't heartbroken-heartbroken, more just really pissed off at myself for being sucked in by a fellow cast member who I trusted, you know?"

Oh, I know. I hear you loud and clear.

"Cast members having flings — ugh — all so cliché anyway, but I didn't see it coming. Others knew. Fuck, I think everyone in the cast knew. There I was telling everyone how happy I was in the dressing room; meanwhile he's schtupping her in the green room. So humiliating. Mortifying. So that's when I cut my hair and cut him off. He always said he loved my hair, so it felt cleansing."

I knew it! Oh no, she does want me to cut my hair.

"But anyway, I digress. Cassie took me to this." She turns the dog-eared paper over.

Jaya Yoga Schedule.

"Yoga? Like organic-yummy-mummies-in-gratuitous-amounts-of-Spandex-with-their-arses-in-the-air-and-driving-Range-Rovers yoga?"

"Umm, that sounds dangerous. I don't recommend driving in a downward dog, no. It's physical and mental exercise. It brings peace, calming, self-love and enlightenment."

"Oh, well then."

"Seriously, I think Enna needs enlightenment. I think Enna needs to give herself a little bit of love." She wraps her arms around me and gives one of those awkward half hugs, right arm around the back and the left stretching like Mr. Fantastic elastic to reach around the front. I'm glad it's awkward as it gives me a chance to laugh rather than cry. No doubt a full force power hug would bring on tears in zero-point-five seconds.

Another closet raid, three e-mail checks, and we are bundled up again to leave.

I'm walking. My feet are moving. My brain is resisting, but there is definite bipedal movement. I could win Olympic gold for talking and mal-coordination, but neither are skills used in stretchy stuff and shit. To add to my general trepidation, the amount of black yoga capri pants and sporty reinforced bra tops that Tara owns suggests she does this a lot. Seriously.

I will fall over. I will sweat and pass out. Or vomit. Or tangle myself and get stuck like I did in drunken Twister at university.

"Okay?" Tara checks with me, rubbing my arm vigorously as we walk up the stone steps to the beautiful brownstone with the Jaya sign flying like a flag from the building.

"Oh!" I can hardly renege on the woman who is being so hospitable. "I'm —" I search for the word " — peachy."

"Good. You are going to love this. I don't know why I didn't think of this before. Awesome."

She opens the door and welcomes me through. The reception we walk into is bare: honeyed wooden floor boards bathed in pools of buttery light where the overhead bulbs shine softly. The air is scented, an unplaceable mix of…what? Sunday lunch? No…not lamb; it's rosemary. It perfumes the air and inflates my nostrils.

There is a neat line of shoes by the front door. The lineup is a mixed spread of Hunter wellies and Ugg boots. There are at least ten other bodies here, but you wouldn't know it from the silence.

The white walls and lack of furniture make the space seem far larger. Where are all the people? I peel off my shoes and a bare-footed figure is standing there as I rise.

Tara seems delighted to do the introductions. "Mallory, this is my dear, dear old friend from England, Enna."

"Hello, Enna. Welcome to Jaya." Mallory clasps my hand and gives a warm double-hand squeeze.

"Nice to meet you."

She smiles this incredibly white, beatific smile, and her dark eyes burrow right into me, as if she knows the answers to everything.

I wobble, finally pulling Tara's too-small boot off my foot.

She steadies me as I regain both feet. "Have you taken yoga before?" she asks, appraising this obvious novice.

"Sorry, no."

"No need to be sorry. We were all new once." She turns, her long hair swinging at her waist. "Oh, do you need a mat, Enna?"

I look at Tara as if I need a translator.

"Yes. Yes, she does."

"Great, well, go through with Tara, grab one of the black mats, and find a spot. Class is starting in one minute."

The moment we walk into the studio room behind reception and out of Mallory's calming circle, my performance anxiety goes into overdrive. I am not sure I can do this. I was terrible, *terrible*, at ballet after all.

I follow Tara, picking through the patchwork pattern of mats already positioned and incumbent with a Spandexed person pretzeling herself.

Not the front! Please, PULLEEZE not the front.

Tara turns to me and whispers. Her yoga whisper is far more quiet and sedate then her tequila whisper. "How is over there?" She points to the side, where the candle flickers in its glass vase.

Oh, wonderful! Not only will I humiliate myself, I will go down in a ball of flames too. Peachy.

Tara places her mat down in front of me. At least I can watch her, and she can't see me be pathetic and fail entirely at this. She goes through an intimidating routine of standing up and folding over and jumping back and — from the back, at least — something I term "humping her mat" all while doing this perverted breathing thing.

I look around. *One thing here is not like the other.* I am sitting on my mat, hoping it will fly me away from humiliation. Everyone else is supine, in the fetal position or with their legs bent to the side or folded into their chests.

Mayday! Mayday! I am surrounded by origami people.

I don't even know the rules, and that Cuban dinner last night might really make an embarrassing cameo in my yoga debut. I clench my cheeks tightly. *Those* cheeks.

Mallory quietly closes the door, turns out the dim lights so we are solely illuminated by candlelight and the red glow from the fireplace at the head of the room. With her foot, she repositions the draft excluder to block out the light from outside, and she makes her way to the mat at the front of the room, her feet making little kisses with the floor.

"Let's all start out in a comfortable seat. Find those sitz bones."

In my peripheral vision, I see the room wiggle as bones root to the mat and connect with the earth.

"Now, close your eyes and find your breath."

Find it? Isn't the perk of being a human that breathing is automatic? How does one find it? How does one lose it?

Everyone is still, and those I can see through this dim glow have their eyes tightly shut. I reluctantly close mine too. It is strange to be in a room full of strangers with my eyes closed and myself vulnerable. And it's then that it starts, in the heat and the darkness, my echoing thoughts crashing through the silence, the creeping feeling of emotion ballooning with each rib-expanding inhalation.

I shouldn't be here, in this class in Park Slope this afternoon. I should be at his side.

He's not going to answer. He doesn't trust me anymore.

The first fugitive tear squeezes through between my lids and makes a run for it.

I shouldn't be here. I shouldn't be here. I shouldn't be here.

Shit, and I don't have tissues, and I'm not even wearing sleeves! I snatch little sniffs and hope they are audible to my ears only.

Jesus! I am a fucking human geyser. Stop crying. Stop crying.

"Empty your minds, ladies. Focus on your intention," Mallory gently coos.

I try and block the domino rally of thoughts running rampant through my mind. *How does one just stop thinking? I came for a workout, not a lobotomy!*

"Think of someone or something…"

Oh, so now we are allowed to think?

"…you want to dedicate your practice to tonight."

Dedicate my practice? Like a book dedication? This — what's it called — "downward dog" is dedicated to…that's ridiculous.

The silence is a bullhorn for my thoughts.

Okay, okay! I'd do it for him, of course. I'd dedicate everything to him.

Only, what's the point? He doesn't trust me. If there isn't trust, there is nothing.

"Don't tell me that I'm a bad guy and that I don't care. I have a hard time believing you right now. And I don't honestly know if I can ever forgive you. The trust is gone."

I picture him now, in that last whiskey haze of the Radisson bar, his words flicking rapidly like steel, julienning my hopeful heart like a whipping épée through an apple. Touché.

"Let go of the week. Let go of the 'to do' list. All the worries and concerns of the day — just let them drift," soothes the yogi in her melodic, mellifluous tones, flat-footed, calm and effortlessly beautiful.

Fat fucking chance! I am not supposed to be here!

I wiggle deeper, opening one eye that catches Mallory's sparkling irises. I squeeze them shut again. I am trying to focus. I'm not itching, or drumming my fingers, or twisting and squirming. I am still, but my mind is the torture victim of thought. As I am rolling my head in slow circles — "Don't forget your breathing" — the back of my eyelids play the movie montage of Us, a rough cut edit jumping from scene to scene: Us locked in thirsty kisses as clothing was tossed to the trees on the back of the quad in the woods; cut to Us in his kitchen making spinach and ricotta gnocchi and laughing—oh, his glorious, uninhibited laugh—as he wrapped his arms around me, squashed my gnocchi babies with his fist and reformed them; the film splices to Us in his bathroom, me in scanties, sitting on the lip of the double basin, patting his freshly shaved skin with the cologne I had bought for him, bow tie straightening, cuff link fastening, lint-rolling, lip sucking—I see all those little tasks I had imagined I would do for him through his forties, fifties, sixties, seventies, eighties and beyond; and Us together, Us as a team as we cut through the crowd at the Christmas charity gala, shaking hands with the people I pretended to remember, the glossy grins, the wine glasses imprinted with red lipstick, the bloody filet mignon, the starched collars, the feel of the thick cloth under my fingertips as I danced with him. These kaleidoscope images are branded on the back of my eyelids.

I am listening. I am rolling my head, stretching in a seated arch left and then right, then into some spine stretching positions on all fours called "cat" and "cow." This is all very animal. I go through the motions. I follow the instructions, but it is impossible to escape these and a thousand other unignorables, these memories of a life that could have been, drifting away from me.

Stop! Come back!

I move on cue to my first downward dog, my mat squeaking with hot tears.

How could I adore someone so completely, but he could just close the door? How could he cast me aside like a snotty tissue?

Because you cast him aside, moron.

"Inhale. Exhale. Inhale. Step your right leg forward, left heel down at an angle. Rise up to warrior one, foundation core expression."

Oh, I'm standing. I'm wobbling.

"Cartwheel your arms, frame your foot, and *vinyasa*, flow."

Already? I only just got up here!

I watch Tara do a slow push-up through to a lifted worm-like position. Oh, "cobra," or "upward dog," I realize, as Mallory rattles off these positions like she's saying the rosary, so quickly, so automatic, so meditatively. We go through a few rounds of this, the repetition fusing these, at first, separate halting movements together so that they meld.

We sweep through a round of awkward movements, twists, lunges, balances, all with complex and unfathomable names. It's like some weird game of Simon Says, as Mallory cues the class and I try copying a few sweaty seconds later. I follow Tara, leaning back as if sitting on an invisible chair, and twist to the side.

"This is detoxing you, ladies. You're wringing out all those toxins, all that stress, all that junk, everything that does not serve you. Don't give up on yourself! One more breath. You can do anything for one more breath."

I am not just leaking emotion, memories, and toxic damage; I am sweating like a beast. I can feel the heat radiate from inside, and the sweat rolls down my arms as I twist to the side and flower open my arms like Tara.

"Twist, twist, twist, ladies! Detox to retox."

Those bastard, mutinous drops unashamedly roll down my face. I'm not sure which are tears and which are bona fide beads of sweat. Every flurry carves a new course down my foundation. Perhaps, if I never stop crying, I can just erode away. The water will melt me to nothing but a pile of clothes. Not even shoes!

Hidden in the candlelight, a new downpour comes with every movement. I don't know why it is so uncontrollable. The music shifts from a classical piece that reminds me of Rachmaninoff, and in the silent interlude, the *plink* sounds as loud in my ears as the crunch of a solo chip-eater. "Let It Be" piano chords follow.

"Concentrate on your *ujjayi* breathing. That's your victorious breath. In through the nose, out through the nose, so I hear that Darth Vader sound, ladies."

I follow the cue through another round of poses, trying to make my breathing louder than the sound of my tears. Sir Paul Mc-Fucking-Cartney is not helping. Back to downward dog.

This is supposed to be the restful position?

My upper arms burn as they hold my body weight up. We shift forward into something called plank—an extended press-up. I have found my nemesis. Who invented this terrible pose? It's torture.

"And, hold it. Five breaths."

Oh my God. I am going to die.

"You can do it. One. Breathe through the 'uncomfortability.' That's a Malloryism; get used to it. Two. Shut off all those messages screaming in your brain to stop. Three. Just breathe. Engage your core. Don't let your butt collapse. Four. You are a fighter, you are a warrior, you are strong, and you don't give up. Five. Release down slowly, slowly, and flow."

I don't flow. There is no movement flowing but sweat and tears as I press my cheek against the rubber.

"I honestly don't know if I can ever forgive you," his bass echoes as I feel my heart pumping into the mat.

No, Sir Paul, I will not let it be. Thank you very much.

We invert. We twist some more. We stand like warriors until I think my arms might drop off. We appear to become a number of animals: pigeon, eagle, tortoise, camel. I may be the whole fucking zoo; I am pretty sure I smell like one.

We "rest" in this knot of limbs, with legs bent at the knees, folded like a nesting bird and our heads resting on the mat. As we stop moving, the reel of thoughts plays again.

I see him shut the door. I imagine *her*…in his house. I see her in my place: touching our things; in front of our fireplace; watching the shows we watched together, maybe the ones that I DVRed.

What the fuck? What the fuck? WHAT THE FUCK? Has Goldilocks been sleeping in my bed? Has she slept with him? Have I been completely replaced?

Mallory has said something; it's all just noise, so I follow Tara, sitting back on my heels and then bending backward.

It's harder than it looks, and my head drops back behind, clouting the mat.

Mallory rushes to the side of my mat, those shining eyes appearing above me. "Are you okay?" Her eyes sparkle even in the candlelight.

"I'm fine. Fine. Really." Though it feels as if his big giant hands—the hands that would always catch me—just disappeared. Literally and figuratively.

"Camel can be an intense pose for your first time. Rest back now. Class, it's time for *shavasana*, your final resting pose, or corpse pose."

The fluid movement of the room stills. Mallory blows out the candles, and for a moment, just a brief, blessed moment, I forget that my heart has been trampled and crushed by Will, saved and then rejected by Cole. I am instead just breathing. Individually. By myself. I lick my top lip and enjoy the salty taste of hard work.

"Thank yourself for coming to your mat this afternoon. You probably could have done a thousand other things, but the universe brought you here."

Residual tears and beads of sweat — I am not sure which is which — slowly trickle, traversing my temples, welling in my ears. It's a really weird sensation, as if I am underwater.

"Everything is temporary. We often find no end in sight when we are in a cloud, but it will pass. Remember, 'the universe is unfolding as it should.'"

My heart lurches. I imagine you can see a fist-sized muscle smash at my ribs like the bars of a cage, desperate to be set free, to find him.

The track finishes, and I follow instructions, with one eye peeking, back to cross-legged.

"The divine in me bows to the divine in you. *Namaste*."

"*Namaste*," the rest of the class choruses.

Bent over in this seated position, other bodies start to move, to roll up their mats. I stay down, savoring the last final moments and covering my, what must be, mascara-streaked face. I can't just jump into action, back into the niceties and Howdy Doodys of being. I unsteeple my hands and wipe the last lingering trail of tears and sweat from my face.

"Not-this-day," I whisper to myself.

Chapter 6

"So?" Tara is chatting with Mallory in the honey butter reception area, glistening with sweat and an expectant smile.

"Yes, yes, good. I think." Apparently, the heat has evaporated my adjectives. "I mean, I didn't fall over" —*or fart*— "so I'll take it as a positive. I sweated buckets! It's more wet yoga than hot yoga."

Mallory extends her arms open toward me and with her right clasps my shoulder. She doesn't rub my arm or envelop me; it's just a touch, but a firm grasp that underlines her words. "You did very well. Very well. The heated class is a tough one for a beginner, and you kept up. You didn't give up. How do you feel?"

"Exhausted," I reply automatically. Then, after a second of actual thought, I add, "And oddly energized."

"Good. Self-study—*svadhyaya* in Sanskrit—will make you more aware of yourself and what you need. Sometimes, most times, we are all so busy going through the motions, running the rat race, doing what we think we should do, rather than what is good for us." She unclasps my arm and smiles brightly, her eyes twinkling again. "Hope to see you again, Enna." Then Mallory, this warm, fuchsia-topped energy ripples past us to speak to a yogini pulling on her Uggs.

Putting on layers of Eskimo attire after sweating in a ninety-three-degree heated yoga studio just feels wrong. I still feel really warm in spite of the cool down.

"Wowser, that was hot," I say to Tara whilst chicken-winging my arms.

"What are you doing, *mon petit* moron?"

I suppose I might look a wee bit strange. "I'm drying my sweat." It is completely logical to me. I don't want to put on my borrowed Paddington Bear/Superhero duffel coat and sweat into the lining. Next time, if there is a next time, note to self: bring a towel or a baby wipe.

"It gets hotter, you know. That was just heated *vinyasa* yoga. The *bikram* is wild hot. Africa hot. In a heat wave."

Just the thought of it makes me feel slightly nauseous.

We leave arm-in-arm down the stone steps.

"I am *très, très* famished. I knew we shouldn't have shared that toastie. All I could think of in *shavasana*—"

"Which one was that?"

"The corpse pose. At the end. The one where we just lie there—"

"Oh, I nailed that one."

"Good. I'm proud of you," she says, pausing as we walk to give me her sarcastic little grin. "Well, all I could think was, 'what are we going to eat?'"

Strangely, the heat or the excursion has dissolved my appetite. I know I should be hungry, but I am not aware of feeling hungry, just kind of…less anxious, energized, erm…grateful?

"Hello! Enna, concentrate! I'm talking about food. This is important!"

The space that should be filled with hunger, temporarily occupied by yoga afterglow, swells instead to thoughts of the e-mail I sent to Cole…three hours ago.

"I've got to get back for Cole's e-mail."

Tara stops our momentum again—the very opposite of what my comment intended—and turns her serious face on me. "Enna, stop. It's an e-mail. It will be there when we return. You are not waiting on it to pack up and head back to Scranton, are you?"

"I…"

"Well, are you?"

"No. I suppose not."

"Well then, what's the urgency? His answer can wait. And you should make him wait for you to read it and respond. I think you should take advantage of this little space you have, this breathing room, to really focus on what you want and *why* you want it.

"Is it because he makes you a better person? Or do you just want him because it seems the *right* thing after he came to England, saved you, yada yada? Because, Enna, doing what we *think* is right and doing what is *really* right for us is not always the same."

She waits. For an answer.

"You know, I am only saying this because sometimes being an outsider looking in, you see more. But it seems that you fling yourself with almost wild masochism on these men, so maybe you should ask yourself *why?*"

Okay, the afterglow has now completely evaporated. I'm cold and—bless her—I wish she would just stop talking.

She's taken you in, Enna. Do not argue.

"Okay, fine. Where do you want to eat?" It just seems easier.

She pauses, working her lips from side-to-side, the shifting pout that I know I do when debating options. Whether she wants to say more or not, she opts for food too. She puts her arm through mine again, and we walk quickly in the direction of Seventh Avenue.

We decide to do some shopping—groceries!—at the famous Co-op and just make a healthy salad for a late lunch/early dinner. Then, maybe later we'll nibble on hummus and wine and have quite the carpet picnic. "We" is really just Tara. I go along with it like a lemming because I don't want to invite any further sidewalk psychology.

The Co-op is bustling and quite the distraction. This community store of fresh, locally grown, organic goodies is a hub of the crunchy granola folk in Park Slope.

Tara has her membership and works there a couple of hours a month, so she knows where all the items she needs are kept. She talks as she gropes vegetables and bags up foliage. "Kale is so good for you. Really. It's the single most important part of my diet." Perhaps it's because it's not her life choices she has just criticized that she finds it easy to swing back into the benefits of leafy greens.

I'm struggling. I am. I've never had kale. It looks rough and unpalatable, and I'd rather eat liver.

Enna, look interested! She is explaining the health benefits of kale. You should listen.

But what did she say? That I "fling" myself on men! I don't fling. I have never flung!

"You'll bruise that apple if you don't stop." Tara takes the Granny Smith from my hand and smiles gently. "It'll be okay, you know. I didn't mean anything by it. I was just trying to point out that giving yourself a break and time for yourself might be just what you need."

"Don't buy that apple." I take it back from her, this strange produce pass-the-parcel. "It's a little bashed there. Here, this one is better. How many should we get?"

It's funny this sudden female domestication. Buying the house in Ashtead with Leo and basically living alone because he was always elsewhere, followed by my short sojourn with Cole, I had never lived in a house as an adult with a female. Tara is so capable, knows exactly what she is getting, and how much she can carry home without the bags breaking or cutting into her fingerless gloves.

She's right. Space, time—I've never really had those valuable commodities. The whole time juggle of running the theater, producing shows, maintaining a transatlantic relationship, filling in visa forms so complicated one really needs a degree in Immigration—I always felt pressured, under a deadline. Time was always a scary thing, the wolf at the door—tick-tock tick-tock —always so much to accomplish in such a small, twice daily rotation of black hands. And now here, in the city that never sleeps, I truly have nothing but time.

Three months. I have three months to prove myself. I've probably never had so long to fulfill a goal. It should be plenty of time, yet these empty days waiting seem so daunting.

We tiptoe up to the attic apartment, Tara saying "hello" to some shadow on the first floor I don't even see until I have passed. The kitchenette is too tight for both of us to be fussing in; slow dancing is about all two bodies could do in there. I plonk the bags on the side with a sigh and look at her for release.

"Oh, okay. Go check your e-mails. Jesus, why do I feel like your mother?"

"Sure? I can wait and help with the salad first." I'm lying.

"I can do this. You go do what you need to do."

The laptop takes an age to come to life. I try to find advanced excuses for him as a "Get Out of Jail Free" card: maybe he is out with a client on some emergency aggregate business; perhaps his phone is not receiving reception and he is not in front of his computer; maybe he is already on his way down the I-80 to find me and bring me back?

As the screen lights up, I pounce on the finger pad and scroll through the inbox senders, mostly a virtual shopping mall of mass marketing: Victoria Secret bras, Caché dresses, Madewell cardigans, BCBG shoes, Visa, MasterCard offers, Cheap Tickets, CheapOair, cheap, cheap, cheap, but there it is! He did write.

OhthankGod! OhthankGod!

> I really can't believe this. No. I guess I can. You sweep in unannounced, drop a bomb, and then get out of town? What kind of escape artist are you? Run, Enna, run. Clearly PA is not good enough for you.

My eyes swim. I sit motionless, cross-legged on my mattress, reading and re-reading and trying to interpret how I could have been so misinterpreted.

"That's not what I meant!" I gasp out loud to the screen.

Tara's head immediately pops around the doorjamb. I don't look up; I can just sense her there—she's only feet from me, after all. "Oh, honey!"

The screen becomes a blur, and then her Spandexed body wraps around me and squeezes me tightly. We've never been this close before. There were hugs when we were teenagers, tears when we had to say goodbye, but never this cling-on need, like a barnacle to a rock, anchoring its holdfast as the waves coming crashing down. She doesn't say anything. We just hug. Eventually, I shrug myself free and give the screen for her to read.

"Ah. Well, a simple mistake needs a simple explanation. That's all. Tell him you had nowhere to go. Tell him you thought he needed space. Tell him New York seemed a damn sight closer than England!"

I want to say all of those things, but if he is determined to misinterpret me, what is the point? "I think I need to call him. I think I need to get myself to Verizon or Sprint or wherever and find some kind of plan that they can add to my phone. Then, we can speak and not continue to do this to each other." I grab my coat and handbag.

"But what about the salad?"

"It won't get cold. I'll have it when I get back."

"You should eat! You haven't had anything since breakfast. Enna, just have a quick bite? Take a Luna bar."

"I'm fine." Again, I'm lying. I am not fine. "I'm not that hungry. This has rather nuked my appetite. I'll be back soon."

"But you don't know where you're going!"

"Yes, I do. I saw it when we walked back this morning." Was that just this morning? *Woof.* "It was on Fifth Avenue and something."

"And Ninth Street. Good eyes. Okay, here's a key. Here is my card, with my number. Try not to get lost. Okay, give me a hug."

Perhaps it's the bloodshot eyes and strawberried face; perhaps it's the British accent, but the store assistant looks at me like I am a Martian. He is probably only nineteen or twenty, phoning it in—pun intended—for a paycheck.

I have to explain about ten times that I have a phone "from Eng-gal-land" and that it works perfectly well; I just need to make it work here. This is, apparently, rocket science.

He calls the manager over, so I regurgitate the shituation all over again.

"Ma'am, what you should do is call your service provider in Great Britain or the United Kingdom and extend your coverage to international coverage," the funkily-cropped and overly-pierced blond manager explains. The goofy teenage assistant hovers. Holy fucking ineptitude, do they not hear me? I *need* to speak to Cole. My phone works. *Why* is this so difficult?

Maybe it is the fact that my body is operating on fumes right now, maybe the jet lag, maybe delayed emotional release from heated yoga, but…erm…I go a bit mental.

"I CAN'T *FUCKING* PHONE MY *FUCKING* SERVICE PRO-VIDER!"

The air from the showroom is sucked up in a unison of gasps.

"Ma'am, that's—"

Cole, Will, the theater, my life…I've fucked *everything* up. I just need to use the phone!

I bury my head in my hands and sob. "How can I call when I have no service?" I ask, slump shouldered, defeated. My knees seem to have melted, and I can barely stand.

I suppose I must look rather piqued, as the manager's demeanor changes. She puts her arm on my shoulder and guides me to a seat in the customer service waiting area. I practically cave into the chair. "Now, let's see if we can sort this mess out for you, shall we?" A response that completely contradicts her hard, holey look.

"I'm sorry. It's so pathetic, only, I traveled from England. I had it all planned out, and I was supposed to be with my unfiancé — you don't need to know this. I don't know what I'm saying. Anyway, he closed the door in my face. Literally. I mean, like closed it, actually shut on its hinges. And I came here to stay with my friend, but I need to use this." I hold out the useless object. "I need to call him. And I don't expect you to understand or give a fuck, but it's really, really important."

My mother, with her stiff upper lip, would disown me right about now. Oh God, what it is to be such a disappointment to everyone.

The pierced manager — her badge says, "Hello, my name is Beth" — crouches to eye level. "Look, maybe you can get a new phone. A pay-as-you-go phone. That might be easier for you. Or you could get a SIM card, or, you know, I probably shouldn't say this." She looks over her shoulders and then whispers, "There's always Skype. Have you thought of that?"

It is as if the sun has appeared, bright and warm and beautiful from behind a swarming black pall.

"Skype?" And I hear my voice in my ears, saying the word like "Narnia?" "Eden?" "All-expenses-paid trip to Maui?" This word inspires such wonder. Of course! Skype! I wipe my face with the back of my hand and, ta da, composure restored. I'll Skype. Much better he sees me. Text and e-mail are never clear. He has to hear my voice. He has to see my face, otherwise all intention, all intonation, is lost, wasted, flushed into the cyberspace loo.

I take Beth's hand as she hovers beside me, nearly unbalancing her but with the best of over-enthusiastic intentions, and I do catch her before she stacks it to the ground. There's a moment of awkward jostling while she rights herself. Then, I give her hand a squeeze and say, "Thank you."

She looks fairly puzzled, like I am absolutely barking, bananas, batshit crazy, but what do I care; I've got Skype! I practically skip up Ninth Street and along Seventh Avenue.

Back in the attic, I pull my duffel coat and gloves off before I even get in the door.

"What happened? Is everything okay?" Tara looks up from her office/bed.

"Peachy! I can Skype! What a donkey to not think of this before! Why is the obvious so easy to miss?"

"Because you are too busy, too frantic, too go, go, go! If you go back to yoga—and I really think you should—you become more aware, I guess. Slow down, breathe, take a moment."

"I'll take a moment when I speak to him. I need to clear up this miscommunication."

"No."

I stop mid-crawl to the laptop on my air mattress.

"You have to eat something first. Seriously, you don't want to be that cry-y, whiney girl, right?"

Oops, have I been cry-y and whiney?

"You really need some energy that comes from fuel, not adrenaline. Please? Ten minutes?"

So, I eat her bowl of weirdy tough kale mixed with other leaves, butternut squash, and dried cranberries. There's a zesty kick in the dressing, and she's right; a few mouthfuls, accustoming myself to this unusual texture and flavor, and I do feel different, fortified. I also feel a bit like a cow, like I need one of those bovine jaw sockets that chew side-to-side as well as up and down. This kale chomping takes work.

"Kale helps with brain function and tons of other things." It's rather off-putting, her watching with chatty commentary as I demolish the bowlful. But in such close quarters, where else am I going to eat? "It's good, right?"

"Ahumms, 'svery…" 'Svery bloody hard to speak through a mouth of roughage.

"Yoga and kale in one day! You're going to be like…Super Human by the time you leave here. And so enlightened. Seriously. You need yoga. Big time. Maybe tomorrow I'll take you to restorative…the poses are longer, deeper, but really allow for that emotional release."

Like I need extra help with that!

I spear a chunk of roasted butternut squash. "Tara, don't take this the wrong way, but how long am I staying here? When do you… what's the word…embark! When do you embark?"

"Five days. I have to report to Cape Liberty. That's in New Jersey, so at least I don't have to fly. Adam is the actor I am subletting to, but—isn't the universe mysterious—he e-mailed me this morning. He's been booked for a nationwide tour of *Annie*—"

"Oh! What part?"

"That's not really the point! I don't know. Drake the butler, I think. He has great singer-dancer talent. That's too much work for me. Besides, I'm too old."

"Hush your mouth! You are not too old! How can you be too old? And you certainly have energy. You killed those positions in yoga today."

"They are called *asanas*."

"Well, then, you killed those *asanas*. You were like…badassana!"

"You're too cute. I know it's sad to think of thirty as over the hill, but for a dancer on tour, it's up there. For a dancer on a cruise ship, is like geri-fucking-atric! Fortunately, when I auditioned, I was cast as a singer, not a singer-dancer. So I just get to do vocal acrobatics, wear sequins, change costumes ten times in one sixty-minute production, and sway, pirouette, and box-step elegantly."

I nod, chomping on my roughage, taking in all this new information.

"It's hard work even without the dancing bit. We have a show five nights a week, two performances a day. We have workouts — there's a lot of food about, and I have costumes to squeeze into — then run-through and prop setting, dinner at lunch time, hair and makeup, perform, reset, perform. It's work. It's not glamorous. But it's work."

"Well, I think it sounds jolly fucking exciting! And Bermuda! Ber. Mew. Da!"

"Yes. I will get a nanosecond every week to sail into port, and maybe in the seven months, I will have enough time to see the entire island, or at least learn where the best restaurants and pink sand beaches are."

"This kale is a real jaw workout."

"Well, it is supposed to marinate and soften in the lemon juice and olive oil for a couple of hours, but I figured you'd be hungry and that with enough cranberries and squash, you might not notice."

I stop mid-chomp. "I noticed."

"See! You're already becoming more aware! So, back to Adam! He is going to be on tour. I would look for another subletter, but honestly, at this late stage in the game, I don't want the aggro. So… my palace is yours!"

I spit out the leaf flapping between my lips and catch it in the bowl. "No."

"Yes."

"Nooooo!"

"Yessssss."

"But I can't afford this. I'm not working."

"I thought of that. But here it is…while you were gone, I called Mallory."

It takes a second. "Oh, Mallory. Yogi Mallory?"

"How many Mallorys do you know? Look, don't answer that. She needs someone to sign in the yogis, light the candles, sweep the floor. Little stuff. It's not highly paid, but it'll give you something in cash and unlimited yoga classes. And the sublet is just half of the rent."

"Really?" Cash and a home! I'm not proud. "I'll do it."

"Obviously, she's doing this as a *huge* favor to me. So, no fucking up."

"Got it. No fucking up."

"Now, she has someone for the weekends, so maybe that is when you can schedule to go to Scranton and see Cole, but as you saw today, she is pretty much a one-woman band and needs to have someone at the door, greeting, taking payments, and directing traffic."

"Easy! I ran a theater, Tara. I can run a yoga studio standing on my head."

"Remind me what happened to the theater?"

I throw her a scowl. *Cheeky!* But a job. That was easy.

"Time to Skype," she says authoritatively, taking my salad bowl. Back to business.

I turn to the humming techno-portal dormant on my mattress. I gulp. It's not kale stuck in my throat, but a rising fear. I have this vision of him: this man, always immaculate, not a hair out of place, the epitome of success and, I thought, love. How could he have moved her in so quickly? He said she was "nothing," but nothing usually amounts to something. Did he erase all traces of me first? Are the clothes still hanging in the walk-in wardrobe he built for me? I forgot that. He hung the slatted folding doors and made a room for me in the space that used to have his steamer, his weights, some torture contraption for bicep crunches and leg lifts—a room out of his sacred bachelor pad. He painted three walls a sunny yellow and hung floor-to-ceiling mirrors on the fourth wall. He was so delighted to unveil it to me. What had become of my sunny closet area? The photos we had hung? My books on the shelves? Had he trashed the artificial flowers I had bought in *Michaels*, genus unknown, with petals tipped in glitter? I feel sick.

What was that yoga breath? In through the nose and out through the nose. I close my eyes and sniff hard.

"No more crying. You are strong. You can Skype," Tara says, poking her head in from the kitchenette. "I'm going to run out to the post office unless you need me here. You don't need me here, do you?"

I'm rather relieved, no audience to remember my terrible verbal diarrhea. "I'm not crying. My eyes are just sweating. Joking! I was trying to do that yoga breathing—"

"*Ujjayi* breath. That's your victorious breath. Well remembered. You're a yogi in the making!" She bangs the door—it's old, and fits in its frame rather like the ugly sister's foot in a glass slipper—with much force.

I close my eyes again and take a deep breath, in through the nose, the chest, the ribs, the belly; out through the nose, the belly, the ribs, the chest. I do this a couple of times. Can you get high from too much oxygen? I am at altitude in this attic. No. I feel far too low to be high.

In the reflection of the computer screen, I check my teeth for trapped foliage; how funny if the camera had been switched on all the time. NO! What am I thinking? I get up, shuffle quickly to the basin room, check my teeth, and reposition myself. I smile at the camera. Lip gloss! I uncross my legs, pop up and dash-shuffle for my lip gloss. There. Beautifully globbed with sticky glitter! Maybe the sparkle on my lips will detract from the pink puffiness of my eyes.

I settle once more, critiquing this little mirrored version of me from shoulders up. Clothes! I'm still in a sweat-dried yoga sports top with slightly crumpled cups and yoga pants. I opt for the canary cashmere cardy, force my fuzzy yoga/mad-Verizon-meltdown hair into elastic band submission and am ready for my close-up.

I check the time on the screen: 4:11 p.m. He'll still have his laptop open. He could be on a customer visit, but those tended to be before or just after lunch, so Cole or his clients could rack up their expenses. I feel sure he is there. I can picture him sitting at attention in his vast black leather swivel chair, squeezing his signed baseball, and reading quotes or trade news on his big screen computer; his secretary, the ever wide-eyed and bubbly Merrie—what an apt name—coming in with a pile of papers for his signature, or approval, or whatever.

Is my photograph still on his desk?

I press the turquoise S highlighted at the bottom of my screen and click to his name there at the top of my contacts. I only have a few, Skype never being a favorite of mine…until now. Before now, until two days and a continent ago, who had time for Skype? That type of conversation meant having to engage and not multitask while talking—a ridiculous idea! Who just sits there on the phone doing nothing? No one! You accomplish things. You get shit done! From picking the nail varnish off your toenails, to eating—not with toe-nail hands—to writing your "to do" list. No one just sits. Except for Skype. All you do is sit. Two disengaged people engaging. I readjust my hair, taking it down after all—a ponytail can look so severe—and I press Video Call.

It rings for what seems like minutes, long minutes that contain many more than sixty seconds. All the while, I breathe in and out and try not to hyperventilate.

The rings stop, and the spot on the screen goes black before I hear a gruff, "Hello." It's the voice I know, heavy on the O, like he is very important and being disturbed. Insert annoyance and a sprinkling of impatience. The black patch of screen pixelates, and there he is. Tie loosened, blue shirt, leaning in to the screen so all I can see is his torso. Oh, how I want to nestle next to that chest.

"Hi! Hey!" I say, adding a dash of Americana. "Surprise! I thought this would be easier. I—"

"Well—"

"Hope—"

"You coulda—"

"Oh! Sorry. You go."

"No. Ladies first."

"You have a lovely chest. But can I talk to your face?"

"Sorry." He angles the screen away. He is in his office. I get a limited browse as the camera focuses in and out: the white walls, the desk furniture, the leather chair, the display case, the golfing pictures, the decanters of something the color of runny honey.

He's there. He's framed. He does look aggravated.

"Cole." I pause to gather the words, but each syllable melts off my tongue like rice paper, a Quaver crisp, the communion sacrament, fizzing with potential but leaving nothing substantial.

"Enna, I have a meeting in five minutes."

"Well, I just wanted to say that…I think we miscommunicated. I think we misinterpreted, misunderstood. Actually, since the whole visa fuckeroo, I think we have had a major communication breakdown, and I feel that every time I open my mouth or type you a line, you misunderstand me."

"What's to misunderstand?" He lifts a tumbler from out of frame and takes a sip.

"I—"

"You were here in Pennsylvania. We had a chance. We had a great shot at happiness, but you ran away to England. Then you come back, and you run away to New York. I don't think that can really be misinterpreted. I don't think one thing—I don't think a *commitment* to one thing—is possible for you. The grass is always going to be greener for you."

The muscles in my jaw go slack. Where did this come from?

"And I don't think—" he sips again "—that I can live with someone, devote my life to someone, give them my whole heart, when I don't know if in five months or five years down the line, they will be looking elsewhere, devoting themselves to something else or someone else. I want guarantees, and frankly, I don't think you are capable of giving them."

"I *am* committed, Cole! You are judging me based on a unique situation."

"Isn't everyone's situation unique to them?"

"You know what I mean! I was under enormous pressure from you, and the theater, and I was torn—"

"That's my point! There! You shouldn't have been. I should have been enough for you. But I don't think you can sit still and be content. I don't think you will ever be my girl in blue jeans, happy to grab a beer and watch the game. And honestly, I'm old. I'm sick of this shit. I don't want the constant Enna drama."

What is happening here? What is this? Why is Cole behaving like this?

In through the nose, out through the nose. I feel a single tear stream down my cheek.

Oh dear Christ, Enna, suck it up!

"I think that is unfair. I gave up everything—"

"And don't you throw that in my face...every...single...time?"

Mayday, mayday! How do I save this conversation? How can I haul us back onto the tracks?

"I've admitted I was sorry. I've told you at your door, in the hotel, in the e-mail, that I am here to make this work, because I remember the good times. All you seem to focus on is the shit. Don't you remember all the good about us? The laughs, the wonder, the little everyday things?"

He is quiet now, not so finger-on-the-trigger with his responses. Maybe he is listening.

"I didn't run away, Cole. I just had nowhere else to go. I booked my ticket, packed and journeyed to you without ever imagining I would be anywhere else but in your arms. But with...Patricia there" — I try to say it quickly without sneering — "you didn't even offer me a place to stay. I lost a lot of my savings in the theater nightmare, and I hadn't accounted for staying in a hotel."

"Ugh!" He lets out a deep sigh, drags his hands over his face. I hear the rasp of his stubble over the microphone. "I would have found you somewhere. I wasn't going to leave you on the street."

"I know you wouldn't have done that, but...what? I was going to stay the night at your family's house, at your friends'?"

"They were your friends too."

"No, they weren't. Everything was yours. The only things, the only allies that I had were in England."

"Oh Jesus, we are not talking war!"

"No. But I feel now that I am fighting for us, and you are fighting against. And that makes me really, really sad."

"Pickl—" he starts to say, then corrects himself, "Enna, I don't want to fight."

I gasp and lean in to the camera, shielding my face from his sight. He has had it. He is done. All of this effort and love, he is throwing it away.

"I don't want the drama. I just want us to be normal, and content with normal. I just really don't think you can do normal."

My chest heaves.

Why is this so difficult? What the fuck is normal?

"Well, how normal is actually going on a date?"

"You are in New York."

"Yes. New York. It's not the Serengeti. We've had dates in New York before."

"You don't get it. I don't want the whole glitzy-carriage-ride-honeymoon kind of dating, where there is always something new to look at and to talk about. That's what we did the first round of dating, and you know what? It meant that the normal, the everyday, the being at home and cooking, grocery shopping, visiting my parents, being 'real,' wasn't you."

"But the quad! The back of the quad!"

"What?"

"In Montrose, under the trees." The kaleidoscope of flesh and foliage replays again. His hands…his big, mighty hands touching me, lifting me up and thrusting me down. "Don't you remember?"

When did my life turn into a weepy Adele song?

"No. We never went to Montrose," he barks, taking a long, thirsty swallow.

"But…?"

He doesn't remember? Is he joking? The single most crystallized memory of us — the sex, the skin, the passion — and he doesn't even remember?

The air is sucked out of my lungs. My chest is caving in, and for a second I feel as confused as I was while watching *Inception*.

"It happened, Cole. I did not dream it."

I watch him take another slurp and nonchalantly shrug his shoulders. He loosens his tie further.

What is the point? Why is he being such an almighty dick? Do men just shut off, switch off, turn the channel?

He says nothing.

"Well, let's do something normal. No frills. I'll get the bus. I'll come to you."

"I have plans Friday."

Plans? With her?

"With…" No. Better I don't know. "Okay, how about Saturday?"

He closes his eyes again, holding his temples in his hands now. "I'll let you know."

I'll let you know? I'LL LET YOU KNOW?

I bite my lips and draw them across my face in my impression of a delighted person. My mouth feels crowded. "Okay." What else is there to say?

"I'll e-mail you."

"Okay."

"Have a good week."

"Okay."

The square of Cole de-pixelates, and I am left alone. Well, that was about as satisfying as a dry heave. Bereft of tears, I will instead steep myself in bitter sarcasm. I will brew like a tea bag and be strong and stiff and completely unpalatable.

I lie back on the mattress and hold the pillow over my face. Whether or not the person downstairs hears my muffled scream, I neither know nor care. This is not what I had planned.

Chapter 7

Tara's imminent departure and my new role as yoga gopher is a great distraction. I spend the next two days in a whirl of bikini-shopping-second-opinion giving, wedge-heeled-espadrille seeking, yoga studio sweeping, computer system learning, class taking, and kale chomping.

After this, I'd better be so enlightened, I'll glow.

The poses are getting easier, the routine, the flow, becoming more familiar. I feel so smug when Mallory cues an *asana* and I know what she means before she even demonstrates it.

I'm learning!

Mallory smiles knowingly, and her eyes gleam with mischief whenever she cues *navasana*. I call it "boat pose," not being too *au fait* with the ol' Sanskrit yet. It's funny; she always seems to look over at me for our little boat ride.

"Embrace the uncomfortability, ladies!"

"Fire yourself up from the core. You can!"

"Power through! You've got the determination, the boldness, the spirit! You've got this." She's talking to everyone, of course, but it's as if it's for me, as if she reads my thoughts and answers them.

As sore as three classes a day for the last four days has made me, it's a happy kind of sore. My practice—yes, I have a practice!—is becoming far less teary and far more sweaty. Mallory said I should take it easy, but honestly, the physical exertion gives me a focus, a point to my day, counting down the hours until I travel back to Scranton. It's more than just a mental distraction; it's a redirection. It feels good to sweat, to see how far my body can go, how much my body can take. Stronger, deeper, further. Stronger, clearer, simpler.

Perhaps the aspect I like best, though, is not actually the practice, the calming flow, the challenge, the satisfying slick of sweat; it's the people. The same ladies check in like clockwork every day. They pull off their Uggs or, on nicer weather days, slip out of their Toms and greet Mallory with a *do I have stories for you* expression. And then they greet me! They actually acknowledge my existence and remember my name.

"Maria, this is Enna. British Tara's friend. She's going to be helping out."

"Katie, this is…"

"Cat, this is…"

"Leah, this is…"

"Lacey, this is…"

"Sandi, this is…"

And, boom, I'm accepted. It's a little yoga community, so different from the nameless stranger-passing in the street below, the subway side looks and avoided stares. In here, within the white walls and honeyed floors of this tropically heated studio, it's a vacuum of quiet, contagious contentment.

It's also a great relief to be out from under Tara's feet. I leave her to pack, clothes laid out over my mattress, her mattress, hooked onto the bookcase, along the door frame; the small room is a canvas of violent primary colors. It's like living in a packet of M&Ms.

The studio is, by contrast, restful in its un-forceful monochromatic shades.

Mallory is out to lunch as I refold the towels. It's rather nice not having the go-go-go pressure of owning the theater and desperately trying to save it. It is nice to do something fun and without repercussions or consequences. Something I can't possibly fuck up.

I wipe down the black spongy yoga mats. Most people bring their own. Who wants to do the hump thing—wait…that's…cowerbunga… cowerchunder…*chaturanga!* Yes, that's it. *Chaturanga!* Who wants to do *chaturanga*, press-up or press-down to get nose-to-mat, where others dripped their sweat before? Not this yogini! I scrub with the disinfectant wipes a little harder. Singing as I work—I always was a terrible whistler—I get the job done and am rolling up the last mat to the un-serene lyrics of The Foo Fighters' "Walk." Of course, Dave Grohl's gravelly intensity doesn't sound quite the same when sung in whispers, but I surprise myself by how the lyrics fit my shituation so perfectly.

Mallory stands in the door, and I look up before she coughs lightly. "Don't stop! I just wanted to let you know I was back. Didn't want to startle you."

I'm getting better at that. Will used to crop up behind here, around there, and frighten the living bejesus out of me. I seem to be more aware now. Maybe that is intuition. Maybe it is having less work-wise to completely preoccupy and rob me of my senses. "It's okay. I've just finished anyway. How long until the five p.m. class?"

"Forty minutes. The keen beans will start arriving soon to meditate and warm up. Why don't you bring a bolster." It's not a question. It's an invitation.

"What? Sorry? Pardon?" I reply, feeling incredibly English in my Hugh Grant buffoonery. We've chatted. Mallory has told me what my duties are, but the last four days have all been business. Now, with mats sanitized and no business left to do, she has a different tone entirely.

"Here." She pads around me and grabs two large, black bolster cushions. "Take a seat."

So, there we sit, cross-legged—well, me in crisscross, Mallory in lotus—in the middle of the cleaned studio floor.

Mallory closes her eyes and circles her head, as if it orbits her neck and shoulders. Is she giving me instruction? Am I supposed to follow suit? I wait a second or two then join in. The little bones and cartilage click, click, click, like a weapon being loaded and primed. I level my head and open my eyes. Hers beam expectantly.

"You have delightful energy. Really delightful."

Erm. "Thanks." Awkward pause. "I've been working very hard on it," I add to break up the awkwardness. It doesn't.

"You've lost something, and you are searching for it."

Yes, apparently the ability to tell jokes.

"Just focus on you, and you will find it."

I clamp my lips between my teeth before I let any other trite response escape and just nod.

"Many of the women who come here are in the same position as you. Maybe the specifics are different, but the outlook is the same. Their hearts ache for something or someone, and they find yoga to be some kind of heart rehab."

How much has Tara told her?

"You know, the thing of it is, yoga can make you stronger and more focused. But make sure that you are focused on the right thing." She opens her eyes wider. "That ring around your neck, don't you ever take it off?"

"This?" I clutch the gem. "I like it close to my heart."

"It's an emerald, right? Emeralds symbolize hope. They are healing stones. Green is the color of the heart *chakra*. Perhaps you wear it there where few will see it, to remind yourself, to keep yourself focused. Just a thought."

"I…don't really know. I've never thought about it much before."

"Maybe you ought." She says it so easily, so naturally, not in a teacher-pupil way, but just as a friendly suggestion.

Hope.

I hold the ring and tuck it back behind my yoga top, like some vestigial lump. It's funny; I rather like the fact she noticed it, that she asked questions, that she told me something new, something hopeful.

"You know that movie with Tom Cruise and Renée Zellweger? The one about the sports agent?"

"*Jerry Maguire?*"

"Yes. Yes, *Jerry Maguire*. You know what? I hate that movie."

"Oh…" I shift on the bolster.

"You're surprised. I know. I'm a yogini. I should be all 'peace and love and *namaste*,' but that movie gets me really fired up, because it sells people this schmaltzy romantic ideal that you need to find a man, or a woman, who is your 'other half,' who 'completes you.' Bullshit. No man can complete you! If you have a hole in your heart, fill it yourself. Don't be dependent on someone else for your happiness. You make you happy. And that starts with a choice. Life is all about choices. You can choose to be happy or you choose to be sad. You follow?"

The words fall from her lips. She's impassioned but nonchalantly so, as if she's passing a box of chocolates to share with me and doesn't give a damn if I take one or not. God, she's so self-assured. *Life is all about choices.* I nod, lips still clamped. I remember that scene; I always thought it a rather lovely scene.

I always liked the idea that Cole and I were two parts of a whole. Even our bodies fit together, that space under his arm that was designed just to accommodate me. The knowledge that, together, we made each other better was reassuring. Only lately, maybe that's not so true. Lately, it seems I merely serve to aggravate him. He seems to be a different person.

"In rehab, you learn you have to teach yourself, your mind, and your body not to be dependent, addicted to particular substances. Men can be just as addictive as drugs or alcohol. You know, they can give you that great high, but conversely they can take you to that real low, and you acknowledge the low. You don't like the low, but still you take it because a high might be just around the corner. And you spend your time trying desperately to scrabble back up to that heart-soaring high. Tara did tell me the broad strokes of your situation, and I want you to know that you are welcome here, no question; but if you are here seeking sanctuary, or you're trying out a stint of rehab with the sole intention that you will go back for more, then please look for what you need and what makes you happy inside of you, not other people or things. Because you don't need anyone to complete you; *you* complete you."

Shooting her bolster to one side, she places her palms on either side of her and pushes herself up, levitating with her legs crossed. For a petite lady, she is mighty.

"There's really no way of getting out of this gracefully." But she does anyway, tucking her crossed legs under her and jumping back to plank and flowing through an impromptu sun salutation. The sequence is so natural and effortless. "We better get out there and unlock the door," she says and hovers out of the studio, her footfalls so light over the floor.

I pile the bolsters back in the corner and, with the studio floorboards empty and beckoning, I cartwheel to the door, rub my hands, and walk out to man the front desk.

The now familiar faces flow in, and I go through the usual "hellos" and "howdy dos" rather automatically. Honestly, I'm bothered.

I should be focusing on me. Instead, I'm trying to recall the plot line of *Jerry Maguire* and making more links than I want to. A reel of images flicks through my brain. I see the underdog who is so passionate about what he does, but it *is* him; it consumes him, and he loses Dorothy because he puts his job first—just like I had with Cole.

And I'm peeved because I had wanted the romantic ideal of someone completing me. I was suckered in by that. It sounded so... united. Maybe it is not a case of someone completing, but adding to an already completed and content, stable person, to become an even more fabulous, positive, achieving-more couple?

Was I addicted to Cole? *Am* I addicted to Cole?

Had I been addicted to Will? Maybe. He was certainly toxic. He was certainly bad for me. Shit, he didn't "add" to me; he took away.

The class starts. I wait five minutes for any late-comers before locking the door and taking up my position at the back of the studio. I've missed the meditation, the brain-calming and deep breathing. I try and find it for myself as Mallory cues us through the first postures, but clearing my brain is particularly difficult now. Mallory's words really percolate, like the morning coffee, awakening the senses with every drip, drip, drip. I glide through to upward dog, enjoying the click of the back stretch, and pull back into the restfulness of downward dog.

I *am* an addict. Clearly. This is what I do. What I have been doing. I've been chasing a high...hurling myself at Cole, trying to scramble back from this low to that pinnacle we once found. Once. It seems so long ago, and yet yesterday. How can that be possible?

I stretch back up, my lower back aching for mercy. That time with Cole was such a high, but if he can't go back up, I can't carry him. I can't claw my way back without him. The sweat rolls off me as we turn in to side plank, like the slates of a blind turning in unison. If I have been focusing on men, on the theater, addicted to them like drugs, what the fuck do I need to make me happy just as I am?

I try to find it through the rest of the class. *What do I need? What do I want? What will make me complete and fulfilled without being dependent on someone else?* I ask myself in the shower, dressing in the studio cubicle, on the F train, out into the cold at West Fourth Street, through the streetlamp-lit, bundled-up bustle of the West Village to Bleecker, as I pass the shop windows that would usually warrant some pause or rubber-necking, and into the restaurant at which

Tara had requested we meet. The constant replay of questions with no answer is tedious. Where is the light bulb, the thunder bolt, the sudden realization? I just don't know.

I sit at the table, waiting for Tara, and, apparently, an answer to my woes, snapping off the top of a breadstick and crunching it with mindless mindfulness. Toasted crumbs scatter over the white tablecloth, and I smash them to powder with my fingertips and brush them on the floor. I will not ruin Tara's last night on land with my thoughts. I will not be selfish and vomit all these new revelations up on her. Absolutely no way, no how.

"Do you think I am a man addict? Like a drug addict, but with men and penises?"

She halts her forkful of steaming white risotto inches from her mouth. A clump of globbed rice grains takes a dive and lands on the table between us.

"Men and penises? Or men with penises? Or just penises belonging to men?"

"I…err…"

"I'm just teasing. Interesting thought though. Prompted by…" She replaces her fork and steeples her fingers.

"Mallory."

Risotteria is a cute, cozy little risotto restaurant on the corner of Bleecker and Morton. The windows steam up with risotto fog, laughter, our carbon dioxide. We huddle at our little table now, the pressure of waiting diners, who stand anxious to be seated, hanging over us. Tara faces the street. I face the chef behind the glass creating a seemingly endless stream of custom risotto dishes.

"I'm not saying" —I lean closer into the table— "I'm, you know, addicted to sex. That's different entirely. I am not Michael Douglas. But, maybe the highs and lows? I think there might be something in it."

Tara nods ambivalently as I plough another furrow through the mound of rice.

Perhaps she doesn't want to talk about this. Maybe I am shanghaiing her last night. Maybe I should just shut up. Or change the subject. I stab a chunk of chicken and courgette to enjoy the flavors in one mouthful. It is divine: sticky, starchy, cling-to-the-roof-of-my-mouth, divine. Another crescent of courgette is unearthed, its skin a bright green against the creamy mounds.

Her edible silence sparks another round of thought.

"Courgette is such a nice word. Corr-jette! Why the need to call it 'zucchini' here? Why do Americans pronounce it riz-o-toe, not ris-otto? Why do I…" I trail off as my gaze follows the steaming saffron risotto placed in front of the diner an arm's distance from me. "Crave what I can't have?" I can smell it. I am almost uncomfortably full and yet could elbow him out of the way to taste the steaming bowlful.

"Perhaps that's your problem entirely. Stop groking!"

"What?"

"Stop staring at that person's dinner. It's embarrassing."

"Sorry. It's just smells so…"

"Enna, seriously. This is you. You want what you can't have!" She chortles, not a mocking laugh exactly, but a lightly amused one. She leans and extends her fork for a swipe at the rice left on my dish. "From what you've told me this last week about Cole and about Will, you do seem to have this pattern of intense, all-or-nothing relation-ships. You had Cole, yet you wanted the theater and Will. You had the theater and Will — or not — and you wanted Cole back." She gulps down the forkful as I consider. "Ohh, yours is good! Try mine." She pushes her bowl toward me with her left and holds her right in front of her mouth, continuing to dissect my choices. "It's like you have relationship ADD. Who is to say that if you got Cole back you wouldn't be in exactly the same position a year from now? Someone artistic and unexpected will come along and blow your doors off—"

"It wouldn't happen. I'm committed now. I know what is truly *important* now. Where I want to be and with whom."

"Really? Because I think that if someone came along who you connected with, *really* connected with — the type of man who always made you feel on that special high, the kind of man who would just look at you and you'd want his babies — you'd be as noncommittal as a Kardashian marriage."

I gasp and almost choke on my mouthful of risotto.

"Enna, listen, I'm not saying all this to upset you. You're here and you're lost, and I want to help. Maybe Mallory is right. From what you have told me over the last few days, Cole and Will are very different men. The pattern is not there, but both, in spite of their differences, were very similar in their approach to you. Both made you feel special because they hounded you. Both forced their attention on you. That's what you became addicted to. They pushed it, and you got hooked. And they both—apologies here—but both treated you like complete shit and left you wanting more. So I do get the addiction analogy."

Oh. I shuffle back from her conspiratorial lean. I don't like that. "Cole really didn't treat me like shit, you know."

"Enna, he shut the door on you. You had traveled three thousand miles, and he didn't even let you in!"

"Well, that's not fair. I didn't ask."

"Well, he should have insisted you stay! Honestly, if I had been in that position and he had left me on the curb, that would have been it. Sayonara and goodnight! That's not what you do to someone you love."

"But he was surprised! He was blindsided because Patricia was there. He came to find me at the hotel as soon as his head was on straight."

"Too late! Too fucking late."

Is she drunk already?

"I'm sorry, Enna. Maybe I've been living on my own for too long, but you make all these excuses for him. It was a shitty thing to leave you on his doorstep. Shitty. And now, here you are, stranded, clinging to this idea of him as if it were a life raft. But you can let go, you know. You *should* let it go and see what happens."

"That's very *Eat, Pray, Love* of you," I say, perhaps a little defensive.

"Really? I was kinda going for Idina Menzel in *Frozen.*" She sings quietly, animatedly at the table and I can't resist a giggle.

"I don't know about letting it go, but I am certainly sweating it go with all this yoga."

She extends her hand and squeezes mine, resting, replete, next to the nearly empty bowl. "Yoga feels good, right?"

"It's weird. It's more than just a physical exercise. It's like…I don't know how to describe it. And good diversionary tactic, by the way."

"It helps focus. Sweat it go! Bwaha! I like it. Mallory will love that! But seriously, Enna, let things unfold. If it's him, it will happen. If it's not, it won't."

I know she is trying to be supportive here, like she's the Spanx of friends, lifting me up and keeping me perky, but as I smile sadly, stretching the muscles across my face as I should, I feel the barrier come down, the shield that protects the nugget of hope that is me and Cole. I shan't talk of him again to her. I will keep it to myself. Well, I guess I won't have to; she'll be floating away tomorrow.

We discuss the ins and outs of her embarkation, her worries, her excitement. Seven months at sea sounds an unfathomable stretch of time.

"Crikey, I could almost get knocked up and deliver by the time you return."

"That's a terrible idea, and if that's what you're thinking with Cole, don't lasso him that way."

I wasn't, actually. Terrible idea. Emotional blackmail. I will not even give it a moment of thought.

He is a sometime Catholic though, Enna. He would absolutely be a gentleman. He would insist. Without a doubt. So…if we were to have a horizontal tussle for old time's sake and…

I'm not thinking about this. Not thinking…

"So, any mail that looks important…"

But if I am to remind him of the good times, sex would certainly have to be involved…

"And then just e-mail me. Regarding the rent, we'll have to…"

This time tomorrow, I'll be in Scranton. This time tomorrow, I could be sitting across the table from him, sharing the porterhouse for two at Carl Von Luger's, or maybe beside him as we sit at Osaka, the overly-enthusiastic hibachi chef twirling and tossing his knives, hurling a teriyaki shrimp in my general direction for me to catch like a performing seal—I won't; it will be sure to go in my eye. Maybe we'll just grab drinks at one of the sardine-crushed bars on Linden Street. I hope not. I hope he talks to me. I hope this is a fresh dating start where he leaves his disappointments at the door.

"Of course, you can look after the apartment until you have to return to the UK."

Maybe he'll take me to one of the restaurants in Clarks Summit for a bit of intimacy…

"Enna?"

I remember those nights, knee to knee, at Blu Wasabi—

"You're not listening!"

"Sorry. Yes! Pardon?"

"You know, you should probably look into extending your visa. I'm pretty sure you can extend it to six months these days. If you can't, liaise with my landlady Margaret downstairs, and maybe you and she can find a trustworthy subletter after you go. It's Park Slope. Apartments are a hot commodity."

Oh God. Responsibility.

"Don't look so aghast. You just put a postcard up advertising the sublet in the Co-op. I promise you, you will get a flurry of interested e-mails. Just check they are not a psycho. Perhaps vet them with Margaret—she has overall say-so; it's her house after all—and then you can pass off the key when you leave. Perfect!"

It doesn't sound perfect. It sounds horribly complicated. It sounds like responsibility. What if I can't find a suitable tenant? Will I pay for the remaining four months? Oh, blimey!

She squeezes my hand again reassuringly. "Don't look so worried. You've got plenty of time. Whatever happens, embrace it. Onward! Now, let's pay the bill and get out of here."

Good decision. If I eat any more, in ten minutes my stomach will officially hate me.

Chapter 8

Is it actually possible to go near a cruise ship and *not* think of *Titantic*? I stand at a distance from the massive floating hotel and hum strains of "My Heart Will Go On" as Tara fishes her paperwork out.

"That's not funny."

My hums get louder and I squeeze her in my arms. The idea of being alone in Park Slope, of navigating my own vessel through this shituation, is alarming and exciting all at once. I hold fast to her. It's hard to believe that we've been living together for fewer days than I have fingers, the short hours reinforced and lengthened by that teen bond of theater, that shared history that pulls together two diverging paths, spinning the threads together again. It seems rather brutal to be yanked apart.

Tara bubbles with energy. She's nervous. I haven't really seen her nervous before. She's been so in control and carefree, so sisterly! "Okay, okay! Don't hug me so hard you break me!"

I let go and hold her passport-ready hands in mine. "Thank you so much. I don't know what I would have done without you. Really. You've been just so kind and so generous."

"It was nothing." She fusses with the buttons on her coat, a juggle of passport, purse and person.

"It was everything. Thank you."

She looks up from her fumbling and holds my stare for a few seconds before a quick dismissive nod, and she says, "Now, what are you going to remember?"

Ooh! Ooh! I know this!

"To extend my visa?"

"Yes. And?"

"Find a subletter who is *not* a psycho?" I sing-song, parroting by rote just as Tara has been demanding for the last two days.

"Yes. And?"

"To…eat kale, and *chaturanga*, and sweat it go?"

"Naturally, that goes without saying."

My frown crumples inwardly and puckers. "I'm out. What?"

She hitches one bag with a mighty heft over her shoulder, and with her case on wheels behind her, she turns around and flows toward the embarkation tent.

"What?" I repeat. Is this some test?

Without stopping, she shouts into the distance. This is *very* annoying. "You'll figure it out!" And there she filters through a sea of security guards who eye every bag and crew member suspiciously.

I swallow the sadness cresting in my throat. I want to say, "Come back!" I want to tell her that being reunited after so long was providence, fate, destiny! I want to go with her and jump on board as her long-lost sister! I want to demand that she tell me what I am supposed to remember. But I don't do or say any of those things. I rub my hands and jump on the spot, determined not to die of frostbite. I suppose what it is I shall have to remember will stew until it bubbles to the surface of my brain. It'll be one of the four a.m. morning thought eurekas.

She turns around again in the mouth of the cavernous embarkation area and waves, and for a second, a heartbeat, I recall Cole as he stood so many months ago, having just proposed and waving to say goodbye, mouthing he loved me as he ducked into the machine that went *ping* and shuffled through the TSA line. Little did I realize then that our relationship, with visa-wrangles, theater pressures, and then meeting Will, would never be the same.

And the idea, the reality of seeing Cole again tonight, on his territory, fills me with excited terror. Terror-tory.

What if this is it, where I realize I cannot save this? What if Mallory and Tara were right, and now I'll see that he's not so good for me after all? What if he is careless, effortless, mean? What if it's my fault and I made him this way? What if it was my negligence, my callous, head-up-arse and in-theater attitude that turned a wonderful man into this?

"People who hurt will hurt people," I recall reading somewhere once, maybe in one of mum's *Woman's World* or *Woman's Own* magazines, or the *You* supplement from the *Daily Mail*. Maybe that was it. Cole was a hurt man, hurting.

I take a gushing inhalation, in through the nose, out through the nose, and close my eyes to the harbor-side wind.

Just concentrate on breathing, Enna.

In through the nose, out through the nose.

"Are you going to stand there all day?" The aggravated Brooklyn "forget-about-it" tones carve through my breath. "The meter's running, y'know."

Yes, the meter always seems to be running, the clock always ticking. Why does life seem to be an episode of *24*, and I'm always running against the clock? I take another breath, half amazed at myself for making the time to do so, and slip into the yellow cab.

We zoom back across the Hudson, weaving death-defyingly in and out of traffic. Clearly, cabs do not believe in stopping-distances or indicating any intention of the last minute swerve and lane change. I sit in the back, closing my eyes, trying to clear my head of thoughts of imminent death and the imaginings of what the night will bring. I even combine the two: what would Cole do if I were injured in some horrid taxi head-on collision and I missed our date? Would he even care?

I repeat silently, like some yogic mantra, *"He flew to England! He found me on the bathroom floor! He wouldn't give up on me now."* And all the colorful blood-caked visions of yellow metal squashed like an empty Coke can around me, Cole drumming his fingertips on the linen table cloth, waiting…waiting…waiting…cannot be dispelled by the breathing or the internal hopeful whispers.

The yellow cab spits me out at Port Authority—I'm sure I could have rented a car for that amount—and without the burden of the two wheely cases, just an overnight bag tossed over my shoulder, I dodge through the crowds of questionably smelling bodies. I retrace my footsteps of nine days before with a wider, bolder stride. I just have to get to the bus. I just have to plonk myself down and be delivered there and let the cards fall. I just have to get there and stop thinking. Perfunctory. That's the word. All these steps are just perfunctory movements, legs moving automatically, sailing, getting me to my destination. Bodies passing uncomfortably close are faceless blurs of brown, of beige, the odd red scarf or Yankees cap—a noisy, smelly blur. Just breathe and move and get to the bus.

The woman behind her shield of reinforced Plexiglas grunts into the little circle of holes between us and shoves a ticket and receipt into the trough. Her leathered fingertips don't even touch my royal blue gloved ones, but even so, she pumps the anti-bacterial sanitizer next to the window and rubs her hands voraciously before pointing in the direction of gate thirteen, the bus to Scranton.

There is only one bus to Scranton. Less chance of me getting on the wrong one, but still I read the illuminated destinations above each doorway to each bus slip with paranoid attention. I won't—I can't—miss this. Cole will be waiting. Or will he? I rushed off an e-mail between yoga classes yesterday, telling him the 3:15 p.m. from Port Authority would pull into Scranton at five forty-five.

All I received in return was a loaded "Fine."

Fine. Fine! *Fine.* Four letters that together could be interpreted so differently. Couldn't he just say, "That sounds fine, pickle"? Would those extra syllables have cost him so much? I didn't even need the term of endearment. He could keep his "pickle," but the buffering of the preceding words, the ten letters, would have made a difference. His communications have all been so abrupt, so monosyllabic. This from the man I could hardly get off the phone when he was calling from the States to tell me about this visa form, or that affidavit. *Fine.*

I am thinking too much. In through the nose, out through the nose. Breathe, be present, stop worrying. Fat chance! Slim chance! Whatever moderately, well-proportioned chance! There's got to be *some* chance. Why would he even bother with a "fine"? Why communicate if there is no chance? I have to believe that there is some part, some fiber, some molecule in that square-jawed, familiar face that wants to save this.

Oh God, I will go mad. Stop thinking!

There's a line from the doorway that snakes into the bus. There are many of us bound in a northwesterly direction, I see, and it seems to take forever for me to process from the door, past the uniformed man I hand my ticket to, and up into the stale smell of the bus. By stale, I really mean urine-scented. I position myself as far from the bus toilet as possible. Seriously, who uses those things? I would have to be dying. And, it seems like someone was, or more accurately, someone did.

If only I could sleep to mute these conversations, but the smell, the anxiety, and the frequent head smacking into the window as we roll through another pot-hole makes that just about impossible.

My hand rests on the bump on my sternum, the nugget of green nestling underneath the violet scarf. I'm wearing the emerald wrap-around dress — Tara's idea — with a mish-mash of Tara's winter wardrobe complete with *Fame*-reject purple legwarmers. She said they are all the fashion. I wouldn't know. I haven't picked up a *Cosmo* or a *Vogue*, or flicked on the TV for what must be months. I wanted to feel confident, to feel sexy. As I survey my green and purple ensemble, I am instead the personification of Mardi Gras.

I get restless, looking out of the window, my head on a swivel as we take the 81 exit ramp. I must look rather like the dog in the passenger seat when they sense they are close to home. *Home.* Funny that that word has so changed in meaning for me. Where is home if Cole doesn't want me anymore?

Don't think of that. It's going to be fine.

There. Fine! Fine is a good thing! A *fine* thing. The Martz bus slows as it makes its way down the expressway and into Center City, turning left on Lackawanna and passing the Radisson, its sign already lit up in the five-forty-in-the-evening dusk. Every traffic light halts us at red. I wish I had gum. Or a Listerine breath strip. I breathe into my cupped hand. I think the general stench of "stale" has nuked my senses. I rinse my teeth with my tongue for good measure and add a coat of lip gloss. If in doubt, add lip gloss!

We pass Wyoming, Washington, Penn. I wasn't half this nervous a week ago when I last descended on Scranton. *Surprise!*

I guess the surprise was on me.

Breathe.

A right turn, and the bus halts, hums, sinks, and lowers. I scan expectant, red-nosed and shiny-toothed faces from the window, up-turned and searching in return, welcoming their weekday warrior back to the Electric City. The cold glass fogs up. I trail my fingerprints across the cloud, desperate to see his strong jaw, his slightly too close together eyes, the frame that will stand shoulders above the crowd.

Each unrecognizable face is a little stab.

He's not here. He's not here. He's not here.

I stagger down the steps, as only the travel weary can, and head out of the cold and into the waiting room. Maybe he is here, in the warm slightly less cold waiting area?

He is not.

Maybe he is just late.

Why didn't I just buy a new phone?

Why was I so utterly dumb?

If he wanted to be here, he'd be here. He'd make the effort. Nothing would stop him.

What am I going to do?

Is he okay? Maybe he's not okay. Maybe he's hurt?

I start to envisage all the myriad ways Cole could be injured or worse.

The other travelers hug their awaiting loved ones. There are kisses, laughs, bags hoisted, and the procession of reunited partners slam car doors, disperse and scatter. I am alone on a Saturday evening at the Martz bus station. The counter is unmanned. There is no generic panpipe music, just a small TV mounted up high with some evening local news. The clock mocks me. It's six nineteen. He should have been here thirty-four minutes ago. He knew I was coming thirty-four minutes ago. I watch the minute hands and I shiver.

Chapter 9

The glass door from the parking lot swings open, a gust shooting in to freeze my ankles, and there he is: hands in pockets, long navy woolen coat over his suit, his tie a little skewed.

"Hey!" he says in his deep voice as I stand.

I feel like the naughty child outside the headmaster's office waiting for the parent to collect and reprimand.

Shouldn't he be the one feeling guilty?

He keeps his hands in his pockets but extends them slightly, like he wants to hug me, but thinks better of it or doesn't want to risk it. Safer that way, distant, unexposed. No one can cut you if you stand an arm's distance from everyone.

Oh, fucking risk it! What risk? What do you have to lose? You know I love you!

Seconds seem paralyzed as the space between us fills with unspoken thoughts like some verbal Tetris game.

Where have you been? Why did you take so long? You knew I'd be here waiting! Why won't you bloody hold me? I let rip with my frustration and silently shout up into his face, the built up recriminations coming faster and faster. I might choke on the words quickly swallowed before surfacing. Am I convulsing?

He just stands.

My chest heaves and the movement, slight though it is, lurches me a step forward into the gulf of dirty, tiled divide. His face is unreadable.

There is nothing to say. Haven't we said enough? Both doorstep deadlock and hotel bar standoff were words, disappointments, frustrations, guilt. I look from the filthy floor into his hazel eyes. They look black in this light and so hard. What can I say?

So I do what I have longed to do since freezing on his doorstep. I rush to him. I let my legs do the talking and cross the space thick with the unsaid between us and thud into him, wrapping my arms around him, nuzzling for the familiar comfort, the place for my head by his armpit that used to fit me so perfectly. His woolen coat, still icy from the air outside, is unforgiving next to my cheek. I squeeze my eyes tight shut.

Please hug me back! Please, oh dear God, hug me, you bloody fool.

His hard body, so stiff, does not hug me back. His hands remain in his pockets.

WHAT CAN I DO? What can I do? WhatcanIdoooooooo? I squeeze my eyelids even tighter, perhaps like a child found at hide-and-seek; if I keep them shut, rejection will not catch me.

His chest thaws, and suddenly the coat surrounds me, a human cloak of arms. I can feel his breath on my temple, a warm jet of air that has circulated through him. Then, the soft, warm pressure of his lips. Is he whispering something into my hair? I can't hear it. I can't help it; the tears are literally pumping from my eyes. I know he hates me crying, but his touch makes me convulse with relief.

THANK GOD! Thank God! ThankGod.

I stand in the deserted, seedy Martz waiting room, this pit of despair, where the soles of my boots stick to the flooring, and, engulfed in his arms, this is bliss. His hand, which is as big as my head, holds me closer to him. It has, I realize, been six months since we hugged like this. Half a year — that seems like a decade. And I have been so annoyed, upset, frustrated, but all of that anger evaporates. All logic, all reason, gone. I don't care. I just want to be in these arms. We had danced in the kitchen like this, close and slow, with the back of my head cradled in his hand. We turn a circle now, shuffling like penguins, and I finally open my eyes and raise them to his. He shifts his grip and holds my tear-streaked face in his hands.

"I didn't think you were coming!" I let out in hot gasps. Where is my controlled yogic breath?

"I almost didn't."

He must see his response visibly affects me.

"Now, don't…I didn't mean it like that. Enna…ugh! This is all so crazy. None of this is simple. I just want simple. Drama free. I want to go home, kick off my shoes, and drink a beer."

Clearly, it's not the romantic porterhouse for two at Carl Von Luger.

"I don't want the drama either, Cole. I just want to be with you."

"This time."

I rag-doll in his arms, those two acerbic words hacking me down.

"Come on, then." He releases my left hand for the overnight bag on the seat, and we walk out onto Lackawanna Avenue.

I turn as we start walking. "You're not in the parking lot?"

"No. No, I parked up on Linden."

"Linden? Why ever did you park on Linden?" Of course, it's not important. I should drop it and let it go, but Linden is blocks away, and in this fierce cold, surely parking closer would have made more sense. It's the city of Scranton, after all, not Manhattan. There's parking everywhere, meters gulping quarters for every spare inch of curbside.

He walks fast, holding his coat close against the wind. My hand, little in his, follows along with the rest of me as we skirt around the courthouse square and up to Linden which is now a hive of Saturday night activity. The food trucks jockey for position outside the strip of popular "young" bars — the ones with dentist chairs and bartenders able to withstand the Arctic conditions of bartending in a shirt that has about as much material as a handkerchief. A small one. For children.

His Suburban SUV gleams outside Von Luger's. I was right! He did want to take me somewhere special! I see the cake yellow light shine through the picture windows and exhibit the fun ol' time that the well-to-do, or the wannabe well-to-do, are having inside. There's some kind of celebration going on.

He unlocks his car from the fob in his pocket, takes my overnight bag, tosses it into the car, and relocks it with a series of musical beeps.

"Are we going in?" I ask, madly brushing my wind-swept tangle of hair through with my gloved yet numb fingers.

"Just quickly."

He leads the way in, greeting Bobbi at the door—Oh! A familiar face—and exchanging handshakes, back slaps and the odd kiss to the ladies. It's someone's birthday. There's a jazz band, and some tables have been cleared for dancing. The decibels are high, and the chances of us having an intimate dinner and discussion are about as likely as me being able to get a vegetarian option. It's okay! As long as we are together. We'll have fun. I will make the best of it and remind him of how compatible we are.

Bobbi takes my coat. There are a few stares as I am unshucked from the Eskimo-like coat. I'm glad I wore the emerald green wrap-around dress. I am less confident in the purple leg warmers. What is fashion-forward and cross-street-wind appropriate in New York is downright weird and bonkers in Scranton. I clasp the matching green ring hanging around my neck and turn from the coat check to enjoy the party, to enjoy being on Cole's arm. I know we make a great couple. I know it. Didn't people always comment we were like Barbie and Ken? This should be our comfort zone.

The niceties with others continue. I stand at his side, trying to listen and look interested as he nods and chortles, and a mustachioed man in a sports jacket puts a tumbler of whiskey into his hand.

"Hey! I thought you were never coming back!" His matching tumbler sways precariously. He's a little sloshed.

Coming back? He was here before? While I was waiting?

"Just something I had to do," he murmurs to Mustache, but I hear it and wither a little.

He was here before.

I stand, spare to the left of Cole. Nobody puts a drink in my hand.

"Ah, well, back now. You missed Judge Conway. He was here buying a round. Twisted old fucker. So…who is this?" Mustache asks with almost predatory intent. He takes my cold hand and paws it.

I take it back quickly and forget to smile and be charming.

"This is Enna. My British…"

I hold my breath, wondering what I will be.

"Friend."

My heart does not return to the place safely inside my ribcage, but it yo-yos from my mouth to my shoes in one short noun.

"British? Cole, you never told me you had a British one." He leers toward me, gesturing, and the contents of his glass sloshes up over the side—and, ta da, projectile liquid douses the emerald green wrap-around dress and gleaming ring. "Ooph! What a waste of good Johnny Walker, eh buddy?"

Cole sips his drink.

Mustache chortles, oblivious to my open-mouthed horror, and takes the napkin bunched in his hand toward me.

Oh dear God, he's…coming to wipe my…

"Stop!" I demand, slightly more loudly than intended and more desperate than I had hoped. Many nearby suits turn toward us.

I try to take the napkin from his hand, but he smiles with full teeth, biting thin air. He doesn't let go, and I pull harder. His grin grows. I don't want to play this game. Can Cole see this? *Cole!* I let go and he totters back slightly. The strains of jazz disappear with a sad brass whimper.

"Cole, you never told me what an arsehole friend you had," I reply, eyes locked on Mustache. I am sure I must be puce with fury. I break contact and look at Cole, his nose half in his tumbler.

The mustache bellows with laughter, and the surrounding listeners join in.

Oh, yes, it's all so bloody funny.

I wait for Cole to say something, to defend me, but he sips, re-raises his glass and says, "Only you, Johnny!"

They clap backs in some manly show of solidarity, and I slip off to the ladies room. Unimpeded, unhindered, Cole does not seem to notice or stop me. I rush so he can't, but I'm inwardly chanting, *"Please Stop Me! Please Stop Me! PleaseStopMe!"*

He doesn't.

In the privacy of the ladies room, the strains of the saxophone crooning once more, I stare at this sorry version of myself in the mirror. Hopeful romantic? Pathetic fool?

Where's your yoga warrior? I inhale deeply and let out an audible sigh. Cleansing breath, my arse! I need to be scrubbed with rock salt to feel clean right now. The sweat from striding to the bus, the grime from rubbing next to passengers jockeying for position in the line, the grubby filth of traveling, breathing and re-breathing other people's exhaust — the air of disappointment clings to me like the whiskey-soaked material. I can smell that distinctive stench of wood stain and disinfectant that whiskey always reminds me of.

I breathe deeply again, leaning my forehead against the mirror, trying to clear my nostrils of the acrid scent. The door swings open and I right myself to see Bobbi standing there with a handful of cloths and a Tide pen. "I thought maybe you could use a hand."

"Well, short of Air Force One to take me to England, a hand is much appreciated."

"What?" Bobbi says with a bemused laugh.

"Oh, nothing." I take the cloths and start soaking the whiskey patch. "Thanks for these."

"No problem. It's nice to see you again."

"Thanks, Bobbi."

"I was wondering where you went. If you'd gone back home. If we'd be seeing you again. Porterhouse for two, creamed spinach, and garlic mashed potatoes. See! I haven't forgotten. Always the same, you two."

"I'm flattered you remember."

"When he was in so much without you, I worried. Oh! Not that he was here with other girls. Don't worry; he wasn't. Just with those men, having a drink, or five. LOL!"

I stand there rinsing the alcohol off my chest and am speechless at this. I am not sure what worries me more: that Cole has clearly been here drinking a lot; or that someone over thirty actually said LOL out loud.

I stand in front of the hand drier. "I'll be back out in a moment, Bobbi. Don't worry about me. Thanks for the serviettes."

"The what?"

"Oh. The napkins. Thanks for the napkins."

"Any time!" The door swings behind her, and I press the air jet on and dry out my whiskeyed chest.

It is still early, just past seven p.m., and I estimate that three quarters of the bar are half cut. Sure, it's the weekend, but they must have started early. I weave through the swaying bodies in expensive suits and arrive at Cole's side.

"Better now?" he asks, leaning down to me.

Is he drunk? Bipolar? Schizophrenic? His character seems to change hourly. I don't know what to expect next, a heart-soaring hug or a derogatory smirk with his cronies. And when did he get cronies? Sure, there were the game night guys I had met, the golf partners, but these were new men in suits with egos and schooners the size of Texas.

"Erm…I'm fine." I search around for the mustache to check that he is out of earshot. "Who's the dicktard with the slug on his lip?" I say this mostly in jest. I say this because I think it might get Cole to laugh, and a laugh would really help us right now. But, apparently laughing at his friend's expense is not the way to make it happen.

"He's a good guy, Attorney Sawarski. Cut him some slack. It's his birthday."

"It's not my birthday, and I'm not an attorney, but I still have manners, Cole." I start counting off offenses on my fingers. "He soaked me, he didn't say sorry, he leered at me, and I'm fairly certain he would have gone for a full open-viewed boob-grope if I hadn't stopped him. He's a dicktard."

Before Cole can respond, another suit holds his elbow, and they exchange words I can't quite hear. I keep thinking that, any second, Cole will turn to me and introduce me. But he doesn't. I wait until my pride can stand no more, and I slither through the suits by the bar and nod to get the attention of the bartender. I don't remember him from the times we had dined here before, but he smiles regardless and mouths a "What can I get you?" with a calming reassurance. Someone notices me. Thank God.

"A chardonnay, please," I mouth widely back.

I see no one is, in fact, drinking wine. Should I swirl a dirty martini like the woman to my right, or sport a schooner full of amber who-knows-what like everyone else?

"Your chardonnay. That's eight dollars. Or do you want to start a tab?"

I ferret through my purse and draw out a ten dollar bill, flattening it on the bar counter. It's okay. I can pay for myself. I don't need Cole to rush to my elbow and tell the bartender to put it on his tab. I am perfectly able and empowered. I whip my head around for Cole, always the tallest and therefore easiest to find, but…there he is in a group of suits, laughing without reservation.

I sit and I sip. Alone, I study the cocktail menu with scholarly focus, the busy bustle of martinied swillers behind me. When I know every ingredient in all twenty of the listed specials, I begin to study my cuticles instead, pushing them back as I listen for his laugh.

"You got a drink? Good. Sorry, I got caught up." It's Cole finally at my side.

Finally, I exist. Finally, he is solicitous.

I take another sip.

He puts his arm around me. "Come on, our table's ready." He plants his hand back, spanning both shoulder blades, and without much pressure propels me into the front dining room. It's just as well; I feel decidedly tottery. It is less raucous in here than the bar and main dining room. With a few families and some older couples, this clearly is the room for those who don't want or need to be on show. Maybe we will be able to talk here after all. We sit. My linen napkin is flapped in the air, and like a magician's trick, we are linened, like a proper couple.

My British friend. Humph.

"I'll take another Johnny Walker," he says to the retreating waiter.

I smile. Is that the second or third since we got here? How many did he pound down before he remembered to collect me? I clamp my lips.

I will not be a demanding nag. Why does it matter that he was here before? Repeat, I will not ask. I will save it in the vault of disappointments. Has he even noticed the green gem dangling around my neck?

"So," he says.

"So," I reply.

And the square table between us seems to stretch much farther than its proportions.

"Your menus." Bobbi appears on cue, filling in the silence while we find our lines.

"Thank you."

"Thanks."

"Enjoy your meal."

"Thank you."

"Thanks."

Our server replaces her at the tableside. "Your Johnny Walker, sir. Would you like to hear the specials?"

"Yes—"

"No."

"Oh."

"Whatever she wants."

I smile but only politely. I don't feel like smiling. Why is this so difficult?

I pretend to listen as our server rattles off a list of meat.

What are we doing here?

Pretending to have fun.

Am I having fun?

Not really.

Isn't this the man who always made the extra-mile effort, who pursued me relentlessly over three thousand miles, who I can't, apparently, hold a conversation with?

Breathe. Be present.

The waiter gives us a moment.

"Sounds delicious, right?" I lean across the divide and touch the idle, non-drinking hand. "Are we getting the porterhouse?"

His fingers trail down the starched cloth and turn the page of his menu. "I thought I might just get the New York strip. You get what you want." And it's a harmless, generous enough statement, yet it stings. We always shared the porterhouse.

"Oh, okay."

We order. We eat. The conversation warms. I ask about his family, his work, his house projects. I recall Tara had told me on one of our walks to yoga that the best dinner party guest is not the one with all the stories but the one who asks all the questions, because that shows interest in others, and people automatically like you more for making them feel special.

I resist asking the questions that burn in my throat, the pills I just can't swallow: *Is my being here making any difference to you? Why don't you seem to give a damn?*

I tell him what I have been doing in Park Slope: the yoga, the healthy eating, my life minus theater. How life minus theater is a lot less stressful. I tell him of Café Cuban, Sweet Melissa, the Tea Lounge, The Co-op, the little Vietnamese café that makes bizarrely tasty bubble tea, and Russi's fresh pasta. I tell him of my deli debacle, where I asked the little wizened woman for hummus and she shouted across the store, "Sanj! Sanj! Do we have any homos?"

I forgot how much I love his laugh. The rich, round, booming laugh that should belong to a Shakespearian jokester like Falstaff or Sir Toby Belch.

He offers me a bite of his rib eye, and we compare with a bite of my filet mignon. Forks across the table, there is more leaning and laughing. When the dessert listing comes around, he eyes me first and asks if I'd like to share something.

Thank God! I'm full to bursting, but the mere offer of sharing, of acting like, no, *being* a normal couple, is soul-soaring.

Of course I devour far more of the crème brûlée than he, but by the time the check is brought to his side, I don't want the evening to end.

How to earn his trust? We must go forward and stop looking back. We must both stop the blame game and end the finger-pointing and recriminations. This is where we must move on from if we have any chance. For once, I have crystallized my yogic intention. Mallory would be pleased. My intention is to look forward, progress, proceed and breathe through the uncomfortable bits and the skin-crawling attorneys.

The suits have cleared out by the time we pass through the restaurant and bar. We wave various goodbyes, find our coats, and brace ourselves for the bitter wind. He unlocks the car from the vestibule and slips out ahead of me to get my door first. *This! This is the gentleman I remember!*

It's a less than graceful ascent—with skirt and heels getting to the passenger seat seems more of a mountain climb. We blast the heat, the sound humming as we sit in silence, safe in this reinforced tank. He shifts to drive and the Electric City passes behind the tinted glass.

"Where to? You want to get another drink?"

I am pretty sure we have both had enough. Does he really want another? Or is it that he doesn't want the night to end?

"I'm fine. Really. I mean, if you want, of course. It's just…" I see his arms stiffen as he grips the steering wheel. "Cole, we are both adults. We've been here before. Well, I mean, not the break up, re-union, non-reunion thing, but we've been together. I want to spend time with you. I'm hoping you want to spend time with me. I know not everything can be fixed with an apology and plastered over with a steak. I'm not pretending that everything *is* fine, but, I suppose, what I am really saying is that I want to try. I do. We still have a good time together, don't we? And if you want to take me back to the bus station now, that's fine. But, if you want to take me home, to have a nightcap there and—" it's now or never "—well…maybe go to bed and fuck the living daylights out of me, I'd prefer that."

He swerves a little. I'm not watching the road; I'm looking at him, but I feel the Suburban sailing across the median and the quick jerk back into our lane.

He pulls over into the next clear spot on Linden, jams the car into park, and turns to face me. I expect him to lean over and a frantic fumble of fabric to ensue. But he doesn't. It doesn't.

Instead, Cole looks away, back toward the windscreen, and clasps his head in his hands, thumping his forehead into the steering wheel.

I unclick the seat belt and shuffle forward toward him in this cavernous car. Why do I feel, even in the smallest spaces, so far away?

"Cole…Cole! Stop that!"

He thumps his head again. "You don't get it, Enna."

"What?"

"You just don't get it."

"So tell me!" I wrestle his hands from his temples and hold them between us, forcing him to look at me. "Cole, I am not a mind reader. Tell me what's going on. Please."

"I guess I'm just not as good at pretending as you. You're the actress. I guess I'm not as good at forgetting either. I see you smile and laugh and make small talk, and all I can think of is that other guy with his hands touching you, his mouth kissing you, your mouth around—"

"Cole! Stop!"

There's a silence, like the lull after a cymbal clash. I want to touch him. I can't predict this volatile Johnny Walker version of Cole.

"Cole, he is not important. It's done. It happened. I was duped. I took the bait, and I am so, so sorry about it. Are you going to hold that against me forever?"

He doesn't answer.

And in the awkward, heavy stillness, my mind flies through defense options. "Let's not forget you were getting pretty cozy with someone too."

He makes some guttural growl, but I continue, "And honestly, your keen sense of chivalry didn't stop you from giving Mustachioed Dicktard a free grope at the buffet."

"Oh, c'mon! It's not the same. He was just being friendly."

"Friendly? Cole, he would have licked me dry if he could. He's a pervert. And, no wonder, you gave him free rein! Carte blanche! Green light! She's available for drooling and grabbing. She's just my 'British friend!'"

"Well, what are you then?" he barks, our voices getting loud enough now for Saturday passersby to turn around, scouring for the voices behind the black glass.

"I don't know! I came here to be with you, to start our lives together again, and all you do is push me away."

"Can you blame me? I thought we had everything. I thought we were a team. One argument, you're back in England, shacked up with some other man."

"That's not how it happened, and you know it."

"You wonder why I hang back, Enna? It makes me shiver to think how quickly you jumped into his bed."

"That's not what happened. We didn't —"

"Have sex —"

"No! Why are you being like this?"

"Answer me! Did you have sex with him? Did he fuck you?"

"Cole!"

"Did he?"

I snatch a breath. "Yes, we had sex," I answer quietly, resignedly, through the tears. "We fucked. We fucked like animals, like deer rutting, and it was good. It was great. It helped me forget that across the ocean was the man I thought I loved. The one sitting across from me right now who I'm not sure was even worth it!" I swipe my face, sticky with tears and hair and snot.

He turns to the steering wheel and pounds the Chevron insignia with his fist, letting out an angry howl, then a wail and a sob. Despite his fury, I want to throw myself on his back, to wrap my arms around him and just take this all away. But I don't. I am frozen with pride and sadness; and so, I suppose, is he.

After a minute, he picks his head up from the steering wheel and stares at me.

"Cole," I say sadly, searching for the words to finally admit defeat for us. "Maybe we should —"

And he's there, in my face, his fingers clasping my head to his, a clash of teeth, a lick, a bite, ravenous kisses as we hunger for something we lost in the other. I feel weightlessly heavy, some half-drowned body on a beach held up in his arms, his air rushing into me, tears dropping on me, lips moving, whispering, breathing.

"I want to believe in you," he pleads between kisses, exchanging oxygen and carbon dioxide like he is trying to inflate my lungs with an air of trust that will revive us.

I want to believe that he wants to. If not, what's the point? And I kiss him back, clasping him to me and burrowing within the confines of his thick, woolen coat. It's a mad scrabble, the hand brake providing no end of problems, so he heaves me over and reclines his seat, and there, behind the tinted windows of the black Suburban on Linden Street on a Saturday in darkest winter, we unfetter belts, ties, and inhibitions. We move aside and rip apart underwear. And, as we find each other, as I slide onto him, I let go of the bitterness, the sadness, and grip him, pulsing and squeezing as if my life, the life of our relationship, depended on it.

The emerald around my neck beats into my sternum like a metronome with every rock backward and pound forward. There's no awkward repositioning or adjustment of rhythm; this is a tune we know, the beat I crave. I squeeze, clenching muscles, and this time, his palm smacks down on my buttock, driving me harder. We close our eyes and feel the tremors of pleasure twitch through us like some joint electrocution. I clench and brace and pant and come in a chorus of breathy sighs. Just as I finish, Cole unceremoniously exits, and Tara's green dress receives its second soaking of the evening.

"Oh!"

Never did my romantic fantasies end at the dry cleaner.

"You didn't have to," I say, appeasing, not aggravated, as I snatch a fistful of Kleenex from the box behind the passenger seat. Reliable Cole, always with a box of tissues in the car.

"I thought it better safe than sorry."

A rivulet of sweat and spunk run vertically. *Does he not trust that I'd be careful at least? Has that been affected too?* I wipe my skin and the cloth as best I can.

He lies with his eyes shut.

Stop over-thinking, Enna. Maybe it was a courtesy exit. Maybe it's a good thing that he doesn't assume.

"I am on the pill, you know."

He doesn't reply but pulls me to him, the triangular slither of skin from his neck to nape, exposed by my hasty shirt unbuttoning, is slick with sweat. I nestle there for a minute, listening to our breathing slow, his heart rate decrease, and my thoughts spin.

Did that just happen?

Jesus!

That just happened.

We humped in a car, and we are not eighteen years old.

"Better safe than sorry." What does that even mean?

"Well…"

"Well," I say. "Isn't the police station like…right across from here?"

He lifts his head so he can just see out of the tinted window. "Yeah. I guess so." He reclines again, pulling me to him.

I knuckle down and hug him tightly. I love this, the closeness. I abhor the distance. I just want to squeeze the old love back into him.

"Please, let's forget the bullshit," I say, looking up from that space on his chest that is molded to fit me.

"No bullshit."

"Can we go home now?"

"No. I think I'll drop you back at the bus station now."

I lift my head, a meerkat at attention.

"What?" Did this mean nothing?

"Of course you can stay. No bullshit, no hysterics, no drama. I don't mean you have to be on your best behavior, but I want to see the real Enna, not the phony-baloney one."

"When was I ever phony-baloney?"

"No bullshit. Now, hop over. My leg is starting to lose circulation."

Chapter 10

Getting back into the bucket-like seat is even less graceful than getting over it. As Cole drives through the streets, I locate my knickers and decorum.

Oh my God, Tara will never believe this.

I will have to buy her a new dress. How can I ever take this to the dry cleaners with my head held high? Is there a twenty-four-hour drop off? God! Lucy back home will never believe this. My mum will never...well, maybe I won't tell Mum. I have been expertly avoiding all communication with the motherland, knowing that they will ask how the reunion went. "*Not quite as planned!*"

But I am home. This is home—Scranton. Isn't that what the sign says at the exit ramp from the highway onto the expressway: Scranton, Pennsylvania. Welcome Home!

The journey to the white house with the dark green shutters and the candle lights glowing from each window is quick and silent. What relief that we touched, kissed, that our bodies were hungry for the other, that chemistry hadn't dissipated. Will had not tainted that, at least. It's not just physical; it's a mental connection, and Cole still has it. Or at least...I do.

So, what, I'm caught in the hallucinogenic afterglow of passionate, make-up, quickie sex that I forget the words before? I haven't forgotten. I will just choose not to remember or focus on negativity right now. Breathe. It's not avoidance; it's self-preservation. Cole won't forget the words before. Cole's memory is like an elephant. But if I rehash them, bring them up again, what will be achieved? Nothing has changed, because I can't change the past. I can't erase Will from my history any more than *her* from his.

Patricia. Trisha. Trish. Trash. Did they sleep together? Was she walking through the house that we had shared? Sleeping in our bed? Opening our fridge and playing "house" with him? It's like some twisted version of Goldilocks, but instead of porridge, chairs and beds, its territory, belongings, Cole. What did she touch? What did she break? Is everything covered in a film of her presence, her forensics?

Stop thinking. Stop thinking.

The garage door rolls up, and the Suburban fills the space snugly. My feet are decidedly wobbly as they reach for the ground, and my ankles turn slightly under me. Cole takes my overnight bag, and I follow him into the house. It's warm and inviting, in spite of her presence. I can't smell her. It smells like him, like home, like his Hermès cologne. I look around for differences, new photo frames, articles out of place, but all seems the usual Cole way: neat, minimal, without the outward show of some eager, décor-stamping female after a couponing frenzy at Michaels or Target.

The coast is clear of her presence. Maybe she visited only once. Maybe she had just popped by last week. Maybe she was just a friend coming to give him landscaping advice. At night. In the winter.

Stop thinking.

I unbutton my coat and fold it over the kitchen chair, still surveying the area.

Relax. Be calm. Be happy.

I perch and then slowly roll back into the cushy arms of the sofa. It's glorious to stretch out after the last week of tiptoeing and contorting myself around upstairs in the toy-sized attic room, and after the unexpected human-origami in the car. It's the little things. Who would have thought a sofa in an apartment would be necessary or missed?

"So? Nightcap?"

"Sure." I slough off my boots and curl up on the sofa. "Shall I put the fire on?" I call to his back retreating toward the bar. I don't hear his reply but hop up and kneel on the floor in front of the fireplace we built together. I say built…bought together. I watched and cheered as he installed. We chose the marble surround together. This is the one house project for which I can take some credit. Is that why I want to light it up now, even though the central heating is doing a grand job of toasting the house? Maybe. Maybe I want to remind him of our "togetherness," but it is jolly pretty.

"Vodka club." He holds the tumbler over my shoulder as I try to conjure the flames. *Yes, it appears we are indeed in the vodka club.*

How many clicks do I have to make before this comes on? *Think, Enna!*. I take the proffered drink and take a sip. I suck the air through my teeth. "Wow! Where's the club soda?" I replace the flammable liquid on the marble and continue clicking.

"That's not strong. Mine's the same."

"Well" —*click*— "maybe your 'strong'" —*click*— "and my 'strong' are two completely different things" —*click*.

"Ha!" he blasts, sitting back into the sofa. "Like your version of committed relationship and mine?"

I stop clicking and look back over my shoulder. "Really?"

"Move aside. You're going to blow up your eyebrows. I always liked your eyebrows."

An insult, a compliment. Is this how it is going to be now? Little jibes to protect himself: push her away, push her away, throw her a bone; push, push, throw; and repeat. I sit back on my heels and watch him click once, and the flames roar and dance like a Mexican wave over the lumps of fake coal.

How long will I have to withstand the constant reminders before he stops? Should I give him my dog-eared copy of *Eat, Pray, Love* and tell him to "let it go" whilst still holding onto me really tight? How do I bring us back to the same point? How do we meet somewhere in the middle, without turning the world on its axis and pretending to be something we aren't or think something we don't? Why can't we just hold each other in front of the fireplace and be content, flawed as we are?

We sit on the sofa, watching the flames cast their glow, their heat, their mesmeric dance; and slowly as we sit side by side, he melts against me, half-sitting, half-lying, with his head in my lap. I run my fingers through his hair, massaging his scalp. He nuzzles into my hands like a cat wanting more. I can't see a clock from where we sit, but I imagine five minutes or so pass before I peer over his shoulder and see that he is out cold. I continue tracing patterns through his hair, not exactly disappointed by the conclusion of the evening—at least we aren't shouting and hurting each other, anything but that—but I suppose I hoped I would sleep with his arms around me like a lover, not cradling his head like a mother.

When the ice in my undrinkable drink has all melted, I gently shimmy out from under him. He doesn't even stir. I pad to the fireplace and turn the gas off. The flames give a final bow and disappear, and he sleeps.

By the time I have brushed and scrubbed off the grime of the day, wiped the mascara traces and remainder of shimmer eye shadow, his legs have joined the rest of his body, and he lies flat out on the sofa.

It is a big sofa—everything in Cole's house is big—but so is he, and fitting me in the space he has left is not ideal. But the thought of going upstairs and sleeping alone is not either. Stashed in the ottoman, I find his New York Rangers blanket, bought the time he took me to see his beloved Rangers play at Madison Square Garden, and I dressed completely inappropriately in jeans and an off-the-shoulder jumper, not realizing it would be f-f-f-freezing. He disappeared at the end of the first period and then appeared with a steaming hot chocolate and a fleecy red, white, and mostly blue blanket. He handed me the Styrofoam cup and bundled the blanket around me. I had felt so loved.

I drape it over him now, switch the light off, and climb over him and cram myself in the empty space. I jam my legs and feet behind the cushions, and my torso and head lie next to his feet. A close, clinging depiction of love and lust, this is not. A Gustav Klimt *The Kiss* painting, this is not. I turn to the cushion and close my eyes.

At some stage in the night I suppose—though I am too fathom deep in sleep to wake—Cole must get up, perhaps visit the bathroom. He does not however resettle upstairs in the comfort of his California king-sized bed, but he returns to the sofa; and so when I do eventually wake, the daylight fighting through the darkness, his arm is surrounding me, his body behind me, folding in concert with mine, like two lone stackable chairs thrown to the side. I wriggle around so we are face to face. He scrunches up his nose and peers through that first light eye-sting.

"Good morning."

"Ugh. Good morning."

"How are you feeling?"

He opens both eyes and then closes them. "Shhh," he says and brings me closer to him in his arms, laying a kiss on my forehead. It's not the most comfortable position in the world, but, after a while, I feel numb to the discomfort and we slumber on.

Full, bright winter light streams between the slatted blinds when we finally, properly wake. I have to be back in Park Slope for the six a.m. yoga class on Monday, so I will have to leave tonight. This will be my only sleepover morning, and I am savoring every minute of it. How comforting it is to wake up in someone's arms. A complex tangle of intertwining flesh and bone, tissues and organs and blood, molecules and genes so similar yet so different.

"What are we going to do today?"

"Ummm…" He kisses my forehead again. "I thought pancakes at *The Glider* and…I don't know. We could run to the stores."

"Perhaps go to the movies?" I ask hopefully.

Another forehead kiss. "There's an Eagles game on this afternoon."

"Oh. Okay." I snuggle in tighter. "I have to catch the seven p.m. bus."

No response.

"I suppose we ought to talk at some stage."

He shifts. Silence.

"Don't you think?" Pause. "I mean, I don't know what all this means. I don't know where this puts us now."

"Shhh."

I shouldn't push. He obviously doesn't want to talk. Perhaps he wants to forget and let his fierce words last night fade with the daylight. But surely we should have some resolution? Some discussion on where we go from here? Do I just go back to Park Slope and wait until the next invitation to return? Isn't that like weird dating? We were engaged. Living together.

I lie still in his arms, simmering with questions, gagged by the fear of saying too much. But what if I say nothing? There has to be something.

"Do you want to come to Park Slope?"

Eyes open. "No. No, I don't want to go to Park Slope. I do not want to talk, and I do not want to go to Park Slope, okay?" He throws back the Rangers blanket, collects up his shoes and clothing that had been jettisoned during the course of the night, and heads upstairs.

I listen to every footfall above me, staring at the ceiling, waiting for the next thud. What am I doing here? Should I just get the earlier bus and leave now?

No. I can't give up. I can't. He just needs time.

Instead, I shower, unable to stop the playback of last night's argument. I dress. I line my eyes so it doesn't look like I've been crying—a thick line for less puff—and as I look at the reflection in the mirror, I see his face hovering in front of mine, reclined, eyes closed, sighing. How could our relationship be so…contradictory, changeable, two-faced, bipolar? Can relationships be bipolar, or just the people in them?

"Are you nearly ready, Enna?" he says outside the bathroom door.

He sounds so patient, so kind, so like the old Cole. How am I supposed to give up on someone who reminds me of what he can be?

The Glider, legendary in Scranton breakfasting options, is packed, the backroom as well as the front metal mobile home capsule. It's not the only diner around here that goes in for that slightly worn lunar module architecture. Inside the front pod, we slide into one of the booths, the split on the plastic seat a garish wound of yellow foam stuffing patched over with duct tape. I suppose it's shabby retro chic.

The waitress, who probably also dates from the nineteen fifties, or who perhaps has just had a hard life, holds the coffee pot in her hand.

"Can I get youse started with some coffee?"

"Yes, please."

"Yes, and I'll take an orange juice too." He scans the plastic sheathed menu fleetingly, tosses it away like he might a bad hand of cards, and drums his fingers on the table.

I can hear Mallory echoing through my brain. "*Work through the uncomfortability.*"

I did tell her, hoping I didn't seem like the greatest British arsehole, that, "*Really, Mal, I don't think that is a word. Discomfort. Discomfort is a word.*"

"*Don't 'dis' me! I like uncomfortability!*" she said. "*It has letters and you know what it means; therefore, it's a word. It's my word. Patent that, little yogini!*"

This morning's display of silent dispassion seems not to abate, even with a stack of pancakes doused in maple syrup and a pile of crispy bacon, which he picks up and chews on like licorice whips.

I am not being critical. I am not being critical. I love these quirks, don't I? So, I'd have a heart attack if he picked up whole pieces of bacon in England, but we are not in England, Enna.

I pick up my knife and fork and try to delicately cut the piece of bacon on my plate, and it shatters like glass, fracturing into pieces too small to stab with the tines.

He smirks. "Just pick it up."

"Well, I can't pick it up now, can I?"

He doesn't answer but watches intently as I try to press as many little shards of bacon to the tines of my fork. I force the pieces back together, clamping bits of bacon, hoping they will balance and stay on my fork, and I bite down. It tastes good, as only bacon can, and yet it tastes different served in such small, fractured splinters.

We mechanically pass through the day doing the things we should: breakfast, a stop at Lowes for something, a return at Macy's, a few groceries, unpacking the shopping, and then Cole returns to the sofa, sprawling like a well-fed dog. I sit at the edge of the sofa, watching the clock. He checks nothing but the score. I feign some interest at the game. I take off my shoes and snuggle to his side to try to recreate some closeness, but I am shrugged off as soon as the Eagles score and he jumps to his feet.

He settles back, but I am not repositioned. His arm does not reach for me or wrap around me again. I sit for the remainder of the very long and halting game, pretending to enjoy myself, wondering if we are possibly in "relationship time-out" and counting down the hours and minutes until he will take me to the bus station and kiss me goodbye.

I hold back the disappointed tears as I kiss him goodbye. He stands there firm, hands in his pockets as the driver stows my bag and I ascend the steps of the Martz bus.

I wave from the window, desperate for a mutual signal, some sign that I am not alone. My heart lurches at my sternum, like a bird flying into the bars of its cage again.

His hands remain, resolutely, in his pockets.

Chapter 11

I zombie my way through the pitch black five a.m. streets, my bright colors just grays and blacks in this darkness. I see a few bodies move in the darkness — night shift workers from the hospital, easy enough to spot. Some delivery men with milk, bagels, the day's fresh produce. The Park Slope uniform is the same; all of us zombie the streets in various shades of gray, clutching a paper or polystyrene cup in our right hand, each beverage giving off steam signals in the dark.

I climb the stairs of the porch, and Mallory is already there, lighting candles and adding color to my world. There she is, bright in her fuchsia yoga top and turquoise yoga leggings.

She smiles. How can someone's eyes twinkle so mischievously before six a.m.? "She returns!"

I smile and kick off my boots. "What needs to be done?"

"It's all taken care of. If you would check people in as they arrive, that would be fine."

"Sure."

Maria shuffles in. "I made it. Ugh. This girl needs some detox!"

I hand her a towel and her mat and check off her name.

"So, how was the big weekend?"

The question takes me aback a little, not just because it is hideously early in the morning, but because, sure, I'd shared a little between classes. I had given the requisite answer to the perennial question of "Where do you come from?" the mind-boggling, oft-asked, "Are you from Australia?" and the definitive "What brought you here?" Honestly, I didn't think anyone was listening or cared enough to notice the newbie foreigner's two-day absence.

"Oh, you know…quiet."

"You missed a hardcore heated class yesterday."

"Oh, I'm not sure I'm ready for that."

"Er…Hello! Girlfriend! I've been behind you a couple of times now. You're a natural."

I really like her.

"Thanks."

"Seriously, we should hang out some time. I know this great cheese and wine place. We sometimes go after class. You should come." Clearly, we have a lot in common.

"This morning?" Clearly, I am not fully awake.

"No! Heck no! I mean, I like my wine. I've often thought it's the motivation that brings me to my mat, but no, we don't drink at seven thirty in the morning. Usually Wednesday Happy Hour, after Ashtanga. You should totally come!"

I know this is just temporary. I know I'm not staying here, but it's so nice to feel welcomed, not an inconvenient distraction from a party, a drink, an Eagles game.

A few of the six a.m. regulars arrive, and I check them in. As per instructions, I wait five minutes after class has started, then I lock the door and find my way to my mat.

Mallory sits in lotus position, her "nemesis" as she calls it. "Sometimes, it's the poses you like least that are the ones you should practice most. But just breathe. Empty your mind and fill your lungs. You can get through this. Don't let your mind stray. Stay through the uncomfortability."

I snort at the repetition and reminder of her Malloryism and when last I used it.

How am I supposed to empty my mind when you keep reminding me of where it wants to go, Mallory! Are things with Cole uncomfortable, or are they painful?

"Don't forget to be gentle, ladies. It's early. You're not warm yet. Don't force your body somewhere just because you've been there before. Every day is new. Don't force it."

What kind of weirdy guru is she? Can she read my thoughts? Am I forcing things? Of course I have expectations of where things were supposed to go. We were engaged!

"Be present, ladies."

We cycle through sun salutations A and B. I know some of the names now and know which *asana* flows into the next. Sometimes I wobble, stumble, lose my footing, but mostly I feel solid. After this weekend of disappointment, it's almost a relief to hit the mat, to feel the rubber underfoot and stand in the warrior stance, my hamstrings active, my arms strong, my fingers reaching.

What am I reaching for?

I stare to the front, my gaze along my arm and over my middle finger, as my other hand stretches toward the back wall. How ironic: one hand reaching for the future, the other toward what is behind me. I am my own human tug-of-war.

"From warrior two, turn your front right foot to the side wall, so both feet are bent at the knee for goddess pose." It's like a wide-legged squat. "Now, for your hand position, your *mudra*, I want you to clasp thumbs and splay your fingers like you're making a little bird in front of your chest."

"Or jazz hands!" I say out loud, surprisingly.

"Yes, Enna." She smiles. She sparkles. "But inverse jazz hands. This is Garuda *mudra*, fingers together; fan *mudra*, fingers apart. This *mudra* builds focus on your balance. If you are stuck in an emotional wheel, this *mudra* gives a sense of freedom. Matched with your goddess pose which channels your boldness, strength and femininity, this makes you a badass yogi!"

I marvel at this discipline that is mental and physical and, dare I think it, spiritual; at the dedicated women who show up at five fifty in the morning to get to their mats; at the fact that there can be anything peaceful and calming in positions called warrior; that someone can empty their mind for an hour and change, and still be so mindful, so present and aware. I see all of that here, in this nucleus of all that is positive and empowering.

The yogis roll their mats away, and I clean up the studio. From the amount of hair I sweep from the studio floor, you'd think yogis have alopecia.

"Enna!" Mallory stands at the doorframe in tree pose, her foot resting above her knee.

"Is there something wrong?"

"No, not at all. But that can wait. Come with me."

I leave the still-tangled straps and unstacked bolsters and follow Mallory to the front of the studio. There's a little bench where the yogis can sit to put their shoes on. There are only two pairs of boots, one standing vertically at attention and the other pair horizontal. Mine and Mal's. The next class isn't until ten a.m.

"Pick a color!"

"What do you mean?"

She looks at me with eyebrows high and arched.

"Okay…blue."

"Blue? Interesting."

"Why?"

"Because…" She pops up and produces a blue yoga mat from behind the bench. "This is for you."

"For me?" I stare at this un-yogaed-upon roll of cobalt blue rubber. I hold it out in front of me, like Aladdin with his lamp, like Uma Thurman with her *Kill Bill* ceremonial sword. I hold it like a precious tool that contains such possibilities and significance. "This is for me? How did you know I'd pick blue?"

"Yoga magic! Nah, I had you down to blue or purple. There's a purple behind here too. Your energy seemed low when you arrived this morning. I thought maybe you needed some cheering up after your weekend." She holds my eyes for a second. "You want to talk about it?"

"Not really." I do, actually. I really, really would like to tell her *everything*, but I hardly know her.

She's your boss, Enna.

Yet, with her warmth, I feel I could tell her anything.

"Well, maybe this will help." She takes the roll from my outstretched arms and unfurls the cobalt blue mat with a magician's flourish. Ta da! The rubber smacks the floor boards, a sound so delicious to my fresh yogini ears. "The color is important, because each chakra is linked with a color. Blue is the throat *chakra*, for communication. Maybe this will help you better express what you want. You also have a color personality. Blue is for water, and like this pure element, is steady and unstoppable, purposeful and patient."

I bend over as if I aim to touch my toes, but instead I touch the rubber. It feels so different from the many-times-used black, foamy mats. The give of the rubber seems to push back. I inhale the scent of its freshness, this nascent rubber. From this forward fold, I look up at the turquoise and fuchsia guru by my side. "Mal, I am definitely not pure, and I'm certainly not patient."

"Very good. Maybe patience and purity, simplicity, is something you need to cultivate then. Blue also means *satya*. Truth. Truthfulness. *Satya* is not simply 'not to lie' — that's obvious — but that you must seek out the truth. Find a way to see the world as it really is, without ego, material things, or physical passions swaying you away from what is real."

I can't resist a laugh. How ironic that I pick this color, this meaning, when it's the very thing I lost with Cole. "Truth," just one consonant from "trust." Maybe if I can find one, I can gain the other.

I fold over again and feel the little ridges of grip kissing my palm. I remember that line in *Romeo and Juliet*, when the lovers first meet and hold steepled hands together.

"And palm to palm is holy palmer's kiss." It feels so different to connect with my own mat, like something devout, holy, like I'm making progress at something. My own little magic carpet! A rectangle of blue that is mine and mine alone to surf, to root down, to dig deep, to escape and to deal with.

"Thank you. I am really very grateful."

"I know you are. And I am grateful for you. If you do find your voice and you want to talk, I am here."

"How about I get us some coffees?" It seems such an unfair exchange, but it's something, a token of gratitude.

I head to the little French press coffee shop, my thoughts racing. Tara has only been gone forty-eight hours, and I wish I could talk to her. I wish I could tell someone.

Since when did Cole and I have nothing to talk about but the menu? Since when do I fuck in cars? This delayed walk of shame realization dawns on me as I follow the trail of business suits to the door of the popular Slope café. I shouldn't have let Cole treat me that way. I should have put my foot down and my knickers up! I should have demanded a little respect.

Why *did* I let him treat me that way? Perhaps to assuage guilt about Will? Maybe I was hoping deep down that enduring his neglect would somehow make us even? But should a good relationship be about point scoring and equalizing all the time? Can't we just be happy where we are, as we are, without mind games? Shit, he didn't even message when I got back to Park Slope last night. I could have been attacked by a pack of rabid bus-goers, and he wouldn't even know.

"Two regular coffees with room for skim or two percent, please."

The pastries send off their scent lure, like they fire invisible molecules of lusciousness attached to grapples that anchor up my nostrils and draw me to its source. I have been hijacked by my senses.

"And two croissants, please." Damn.

"You brought a studio picnic?" Mallory pops out from the green yoga room the second I walk in the door. My jaw must be agape at her powers of perception. "I have a diabolical sense of smell. I can smell pastries at fifty feet!"

"Well, it's the least I can do."

"Oh, a croissant!" she shouts gleefully, taking the transparent-lidded box from my hands and setting up a picnic blanket—really it's a yoga blanket, but I'll never tell—on the studio floor. "Sit! Sit!" She automatically pretzels her legs to lotus.

We sip the coffee and pull off strips of the warm, buttery croissant. A scattering of pastry showers the blanket. I shall have to clear that up later.

"Hmm! Just what I needed. It was a busy weekend here. I think the weekend classes in the winter are our busiest. How about you? Were you go, go, go?"

"Not really."

"Oh, you didn't do something fun?"

"We spent yesterday watching the Eagles game."

"The Eagles?" She coughs a little. "Sorry, flake just went down the wrong way. That's all you did, watch a football game?"

"Pretty much."

"No dinners? No lovin'?"

I don't know how comfortable I feel talking about this. Yes, it has reached the level of uncomfortability!

"There was food and there was…something—I am not sure you would class as *lovin'* or not—but, honestly, Mal, it was just…like he didn't care, like I was an annoyance even being there. I feel like I must tiptoe around him, suck up his moods and constantly apologize. He makes me feel…worthless and weak and disposable."

"Wait, wait, wait! Sorry about what? Why should you apologize?"

"It's a long story."

"I've got a coffee and croissant. I'm free. Open that throat *chakra*, girl."

And so I do, beginning to end, my truth, the flawed, rose-tinted kaleidoscope way I see it.

"Hmm." She sucks the dregs of her coffee through the little stirrer straw. "Have you told him that his attitude makes you feel like shit?"

"Not really."

"Yes or no?"

"No." Pause. "It should have been obvious."

"Nothing is obvious to men, Enna. You need to spell it out, play by play, moment by moment, or they don't understand you. You are acting and talking like a female and expecting him to interpret women's subtleties. What he needs to hear is, *'Stop being an asshole and show me attention. I will not put up with bullshit because I do not deserve it. I made a mistake. Deal with it and move on.'*"

"I know, but…"

"Enna, we all make mistakes. We're human. But it doesn't mean others can treat us badly. I have said it in class and I'll repeat it to you now, because I really think you need to hear this: Forgive yourself. Love yourself. Get rid of what doesn't serve you! You must progress, proceed. Be unstoppable like water!"

This isn't just a loss of trust. He's not just being defensive. The truth is that something else has changed.

"What color is your mat?" I ask, picking up the stray flakes.

She smiles her secret smile. "Green. The color of the heart *chakra*. And the color of hope."

I clutch the emerald, that notch pressing into my sternum.

"*Satya*, my grasshopper. *Satya*. Let's clean up."

Chapter 12

The next few days I spend as a dedicated yogini. It's rather gratifying in its virtue: waking to yoga, practicing yoga, talking yoga; cleansing my body, cleansing my spirit; being comfortable with the silence of thoughts, silencing thoughts; collapsing into the deepest of sleeps I have ever knowingly had; finding ways to make kale palatable. Mallory says I need to be aware, to check in with myself and self-study, or, *Svadhyaya*, one of the many Sanskrit words peppering into my daily language.

I practice at home too, in the small square foot of space where my inflatable mattress used to lie before I took over Tara's bed. I wonder if the landlady hears the crashes as I fall out of a balance pose, and if she is at all curious about the brightly colored, Spandexed figure that tiptoes down the stairs at five thirty in the morning and back up at nine thirty in the evening. I practice and practice to find…what? Some kind of peace of mind, some calm against the inner panic, some fulfillment, yet I am as confused as ever.

I dedicate every practice to him, to the memories of us. I'm sending out good energy. I press my hands together at prayer so much, it feels like my shoulder blades will sprout wings, and I still don't know the answer. How could someone's behavior change so radically? Why is he not trying? Should I pack up and return to England? Peace and love and *namaste*.

As I make my way up the stairs three steps at a time, hoping speed will make the creaky boards sound less, I get to my door and freeze like I'm about to be tasered.

I kneel down slowly to the rectangular brown package addressed to me.

It's from Cole. It's Cole's tight cursive. It's the script he forms when he is taking care, like the signatures on all those visa forms, those meticulous peaks and troughs that trail off into a snake after the first four letters of Krupski. He took care with this. He sent me a package! I pick it up, not gingerly now, but as if it were a long-lost ragdoll, and I hug it tightly. I hug and squeeze it and love it, without the slightest idea what it is.

Oh!

Maybe it's a "Dear John" letter and parting gift. I hold it away from me.

Oh God. It couldn't be, could it?

"Face your fears," I hear Mallory saying.

I focus.

I breathe.

I rip the packaging off in a frenzy.

Oh my God!

I immediately look up the ship's itinerary Tara e-mailed me. She'll be docked in King's Wharf, Bermuda, and her show will be down. I'll Skype her!

"YOU'LL NEVER BLOODY BELIEVE IT!" I shriek, before her face illuminates the screen.

"Sit still. I can't see you in the camera. What happened? Did you find a subletter?"

"No."

"Look, sit down! I can't talk to you jumping up and down like a toddler needing a pee!"

"Okay, okay." I sit crossed-legged and angle the laptop screen.

"Mallory e-mailed me that you were doing really well."

"She gave me a mat. My own mat, a really good make too. She just gave it to me! A blue one."

"True blue. Nice!"

"Truth! Exactly!" I laugh. Was the world of color and meaning hidden to me all this time? Was I so unaware working in the black box of artificial lighting and false walls and scripted lines that I just didn't see the real colors around me? How funny that, now I am looking, everything seems to have meaning, words and colors, poses and intentions.

"Well, you look happy. That's good. What's new?"

"I have news! Big, huge, shiny disco balls kind of news, but shit, you first! Are you seasick? How's the show going? What's Bermuda like?"

"Steady on, calm down. It's good. Hard, but good. The cast is great. They're all from England! I'm quite the novelty, living in New York. They cast the shows in the UK, so it's like a working holiday in England but with better weather."

"How come you got cast then?"

"Well, I still have an agent over there. I auditioned when I visited Mum at Christmas. Seriously, Enna, I have the best songs!"

"Originals or covers?"

"A mixture. Some covers with the lyrics poetically sliced and spliced to fit the show and mopped up to make it kiddy friendly. The shows are pretty impressive. Don't roll your eyes, Enna! Really! Okay, it's never going to win a Tony. It's not your Shakespeare or classic drama, but these shows are professional, put together, and on the ball. My costumes — I have five changes for most shows, and we do four big production shows. It's something! And dancing on deck. When the waves are buffeting, keeping your balance takes a lot of effort. I've got through the first week and my calves are killing! So, what's the big, exciting news?"

"Cole sent me a letter and a gift!"

"Just as well. I was so angry when I read your e-mail. You deserved better treatment than that."

"Yes, well, anyway, he wrote — like hand wrote, not typed and put through spell check but actual pen and actual paper. And guess what he bought me? A new cell phone and unlimited plan. Isn't that thoughtful?"

"It's just about the most romantic gift I ever heard of."

"Tara! Would you be serious for just one second? You're spoiling it."

"Okay. Okay, I promise I won't make fun. That was very thoughtful. Now he has no excuse not to call."

"It was really the letter that was so lovely. Listen."

En,

I'm real sorry about how the weekend turned out. I haven't been myself lately. I've been tired and irritable, and with all of this, I took it out on you, but that was not gentlemanly and so I'm sorry. I acted rudely and was mean. That's not me, Enna.

You know I love you. Of course, I do. I'm just really struggling with this. My head tells me that this is done. It's over. Yet I see your picture in my office, and I have never wanted to fight harder for something or someone.

Please accept this cell phone and calling plan. Things should be easier if we can communicate, right? I have no appetite for that Skype thing. I want to hear your voice and be able to watch ice hockey on mute! Kidding! Okay, call me when you get this.

C.

"Watch ice hockey?" Tara repeats incredulously.

"Oh! I knew you'd pick that out. Come on, give the man a break. He was just joking!" I do really hope he's joking. "He said he's sorry. Why are you so negative?"

"I'm glad he wrote, Enna, truly, and it is so nice to see you smile."

"Thank you!" I slow down for the first time since the Skype started and realize she looks a little wan. Maybe she's seasick. Maybe it's the screen. "Are you really okay? You look peaked."

"I'm fine. Fine. Mum's had to go in for some tests, that's all. It's nothing. She says it's nothing."

"What sort of tests?"

"Don't know much yet. She's playing it down, doesn't want me to worry, but how can I not?"

"You can't, I suppose. Oh, *mon petit lapin!*"

"It'll be fine. I know it will. She's an ox. She eats Marmite and walks five miles a day with the dogs, but I think it's being here, captive on board this ship. It just makes me worry."

Gah! I'm stumped for things to say. I can't imagine how anxious she must feel. "I'm here if you want to talk about it."

"Nah. It's just tests."

Mum writes almost daily, updating me with life in Ashtead. She and Dad seem to be hale and hearty; Mum gardening, shopping and drinking tea with the neighbors; Dad cooking, playing jazz, and shouting at customer service representatives on the phone. Their lives sound quite peaceful without the theater drama. Let's face it, mine is much more peaceful without the theater. The old shell is dark, of course — no one can afford to take that on, even the property developers, it seems — and until the police actually track Will down, I cannot even contemplate stepping foot inside the revolving glass door. How funny to be without the thing that defined me most.

"Seriously, Tara, I'm here for you any time you want to talk. Aside from when I'm at the studio, obviously."

"You're really becoming quite the yogini!"

"It's all about the *satya*."

"The what?"

"The *satya*. The truthfulness in the world."

Chapter 13

Another week in Park Slope. And another. I see there is a fixed routine rarely deviated from — a daily plan with yoga as the keystone about which everything hangs. It may sound devout, or dull even, but that's okay. I think I need that right now. No waves to knock me off course. Good. Just calm, untroubled waters.

"You were right, you know, about heart rehab."

Mallory pauses skeptically, her mouth mid-suck on her straw and her eyebrow up. It's one of her funny quirks, sipping hot coffee through a stirrer straw. She does have impressively white teeth; maybe this is why.

"Remember, you told me yoga is like rehab? Well, I didn't necessarily see that then, but I do now. Maybe it's not all breakups, breakdowns, and divorces, but I think we are searching for that inner strength so we can have the belief of mind and body to be able to be okay with things. To be self-reliant and love one's self without the need for any other validation. It's like your mat is a safe place to escape to, somewhere to deal and heal."

"That's very astute for a young yogini. Well done. And do you feel that you are strong enough to be okay with things?"

"I feel stronger, physically and mentally. Things are certainly better with Cole. We text back and forth. We chat some evenings, but it's still tough. It's slow."

"Sometimes slow is a good thing. Slow and steady, right? Like water, patient and purposeful."

"You know, the mistakes we made initially were where we rushed things. We were on such a high-pressure, fixed schedule: visa deadline, interview deadline, travel deadline. Nothing happened…organically. It was all so forced and rushed."

"You know you've been shopping at the Co-op too much when you start using 'organically' in sentences without vegetables."

"You know what I mean! Everything had a plan. I think I felt very pressured by that. Now, the only pressures are the deadlines I set myself. In two months, I have to return to the UK, or maybe I will extend and give us extra time, but if it's not fixed and tied up in a bow by then, guess what? I think that's okay. It doesn't mean it has to end. We have done this before. We have transatlantically dated and made it work."

"But are you wanting to make it work because you want to share the rest of your life with him, or because that was the original plan?"

The question hovers for a moment. She sucks on her coffee. I suck the air.

"Actually, I don't know. I think *I've* changed. Or maybe my appreciation of things has changed. Cole was always so impressive to me—his suits, his size, his cars, the gifts, the travel, the carefree fun—but I see now so many of those things were material. It wasn't *him.* I look at me, so much of what I was, who I was, revolved around the theater. That basically defined me. 'Oh, that's Enna with the theater.' Now, I don't have that anymore. I'm not that anymore. I'm just Enna."

"And what does Enna want?"

The door sweeps open, blasting in a winter gust that chills my bare toes and freezes my answer. It's the early birds for the midmorning class. I check them in and listen as they chatter about their weekend, as I contemplate Mal's question. *What do I want?*

What the yoginis like most is interaction with Mallory: an exchange, a few words, a reminder that she remembers who they are. I see it. I see them queue up, and the added bounce to their step when she repeats their name.

I realize, in here, we are without labels. I have no idea what Maria does for a living; I just like her. She has a loud, saucy laugh that I can hear from the front reception to the back studio room bathroom, and it makes me giggle. Most of the ladies walk here. I don't see what cars they drive, or even if they have a car. Some have an array of nice Lululemon yoga wear. Others come in the same black tee and yoga capris day in, day out. Some have well-maintained pedicures; others are a bit chipped and dry and cracked. I might notice these things, but they are without value. I can't tot up a price tag. I know nothing but that these women—and Jerry, the occasional CrossFit instructor who likes to come once a week to stretch it out—are dedicated to self-improvement, and for that reason, if nothing else, I like them. I like that constant effort and pursuit of more: more peace, more strength, more awareness, more balance. Jesus! I sound like a fucking fortune cookie!

During class, as we stretch our muscles and minds, I wonder what Cole values and what I represent to him. Am I still "Enna, with the theater and the long hair?" Or am I "Enna, the love of my life?"

Mal has a lunch meeting after class, and so, after tidying up the studio, I bundle up and walk to Prospect Park. It's frigid, but still the dedicated joggers puff past me. I forgot my gloves, so I walk with fingertips clamped under my armpits. Since Cole sent the cell phone, our communication has mainly been via text. It is tentative. I think we are both aware of our former miscommunications. I read and reread my messages before I send them, paranoid I might still be misinterpreted. They are becoming more frequent though, more chatty.

Mum and Dad have called a couple of times, "just to check their chickadee is still alive," but largely when I hear the cell phone ping or feel that little jiggle in my back pocket, I know it will be a message from Cole. I'm excited to hear from him again. There is less to fear from this potential word bomb.

A friend had told me once, "Texting should be like fencing. Short, cute and funny. Never get into the dull, humdrum, how-is-your-day shit." So, really, never be real? I'm not sure I'm very good at cute and funny, and I know I am certainly never short. I'm British. Of course, I use fifteen words when I could use three; I am verbose by heritage.

Another jogger runs past me in the same direction. She is heavy-set, and I hear her breathing before I see her. She plods along, punching her fists into air so cold, it's almost solid.

I hear her groan or roar and then shout at herself. "Just one foot in front of the other. Keep just one foot in front of the other!" And she keeps jogging on, disappearing from my view as she jogs around the long sweep on the east side of the park.

I'm not going to burst into a Bambi gazelle leap around the park—it is much too cold to expend any energy on that level—but I gasp her mantra and add it to my new collection:

Breathe through the uncomfortability!

Five breaths. You can do anything for five breaths!

Let go of what doesn't serve you!

Keep just one foot in front of the other!

The cell phone pings as if on cue, and I wrestle it from my pocket, my fingers so numb to its hold that I almost drop it.

This touchscreen iPhone is much more difficult to operate with no feeling in your fingertips. I punch in my code like a determined drunk, and the screen lights up.

Cole Krupski. The Polish Italian mishmash of coal-mining heritage that I had once thought would join family history with mine.

I touch the first line and the bubble of blue appears enlarged on the screen.

Hey Enna! Listen, something has come up at work.
I know it's totally my turn to travel to you,
but let's reschedule. Okay? I need a vacation!

The excitement of having a message from him and the crash of reading its contents for a millisecond makes me want to fling the phone into the trees, but I stop myself. Instead, I hold the phone tightly in front of me, overpowering my inner tantrum, and I walk as if grasping a set of water diviners.

My fingers tap out discouraged vowels and consonants:

But I haven't seen you for two weeks!

I read it out loud to the park. Who cares if people think I am crazy?

"But I haven't *seen* you for two weeks!" Needy.

"But I haven't seen you for *two* weeks!" Demanding!

"BUT I HAVEN'T SEEN YOU FOR TWO WEEKS!" Psycho.

Text interpretation is an exercise that seems to call upon all the multi-expression drama exercises we used to play at college: how many times can you say the same sentences imparting different meanings?

I delete my message. I'm always such an impulsive responder. I need to breathe. The river of tarmac my legs have been meandering along brings me back to the entrance of the park. The high and grand entrance leads out onto the plaza with an arched monument. It reminds me of the Arc de Triomphe in Paris and surprises me that bohemian, pacifist Brooklyn should have anything as military and patriotic. Brooklyn, in general, at least the part of this enormous borough I have seen, seems proud of its anti-false finery feeling. It's boho. It's punk. It's hippie. It's conscious, political, liberal. It's art. It's vintage. It's food trucks and flea markets. It's poetry readings and local IPAs and indoor bocce ball. The streets are lined with brownstones, side-by-side at attention, which contradict the laid-back, casual feel. I suppose everything, everywhere, is contradictory. Everyone can have many meanings, feelings and intentions.

I follow the path out of the park to the enormous stone arch, trying to make out the statue on top of the arch. It's a woman in her chariot. What's the history? What's her story? Tara would know. She looks victorious, in her dark firm lines against the blurred wintery daylight. On my walk around the neighborhood with Tara, I had never seen this before, and yet, I don't know how I could have missed it. Maybe I was too engrossed in conversation—I was probably talking about myself—to notice before. It wouldn't be the first time I've been too consumed by other things that I have not noticed what's going on under my nose.

I walk toward the monument now. I see the descent into the subway across the street—Grand Army Plaza. It's fairly deserted, not like other subways with stops along Seventh Avenue that seem to suck bodies down the stairwells like a vacuum and spit them back up at desired destinations.

The cars flow up to the monument and from there ricochet off in different directions, a car *Space Invaders* game. I lean against the granite under the arch, staring up at the masonry intricately carved into the ceiling. The uniform images look like rows of flowers, or maybe they are stars or medals; whichever, they must have taken such time and love and gentleness to complete. Is that what Cole and I need? Time, love and gentleness, and why does that sound like an awful nineties song?

I touch the screen and bring it to life again. I am disappointed. I can be real and tell him that. I tap out my response.

Sorry to hear that. Do you have vacation time soon?

Innocuous enough, I decide. After all, when we were dating, he seemed to make his time according to his schedule, so why not ask about vacation? He's entitled to a weekend off every now and then, isn't he?

He pings straight back.

Yeah, I can pick and choose, but if there is something big going on at work, I like to set an example and be here.

And there, under the arch of victory, commemorating soldiers and sailors, those lost in battle and those lost at sea, it strikes me, hooks me, gaffs me and brings me up: I know what Cole and I need! We need time alone together, just us, to see if this is still what we want, if we are who we want. We need to be lost at sea.

Chapter 14

I charge up the stairs, thumping down on every creaky floorboard. I fling open the door and bulldoze into the apartment. I have one sleeve out of Tara's winter coat as I stand in front of the fridge and shake myself free of the other sleeve. There it is, magnetized to the door, the "At Sea" itinerary. I let the coat slip from me, pooling like a puddle on the floor, and make my way to the computer.

The screen lights up its usual electric blue home page, and with a few clicks, the booking page is before me: Seven-night cruise to Bermuda from…and various prices dependent on cabin size. Can I do this? Should I do this?

I have to prove I am serious, right? Well, what could be more serious? And don't I want to get to spend some time without work pressures to find out if this is still worth salvaging? Yes.

But what if he's busy? What if he doesn't want to spend seven nights in a cabin with me? We haven't had sex since that first appalling car ride.

I must stop thinking about that.

Then there's the money. It's a lot of money, especially when one has no real income to speak of. What Mallory pays me covers food, and the rest I pay directly into Tara's account toward her rent. I categorically should not be spending the best part of two thousand dollars on a trip for two. Do I even have two thousand dollars in my account?

Absolutely not. I can't justify an expense like that. I shouldn't justify it.

I lie back on the bed with a thud, seeing the ship sail away on the high seas of the ceiling. It could have been so romantic, his big arms wrapped around me as we stood on the deck, watching the dolphins ride the ship's wake and whales fluke and dive for cover. We could have lain out on deck, still a bit chilly, but with a cocktail in hand and towels swathed over our shoulders. We could have bundled up. We could have watched Tara's show, then enjoyed four-course dinners, copious drinks, and tumbled into bed, all limbs and laughs and long, passionate kisses.

I can see him on top of me, the coarse hair on his chest, the trail narrowing down toward his belly button, below, narrowing further into a line of dark brown, forming an arrow south.

I bolt upright. "But…"

I pull the laptop toward me again and click the computer keys to navigate to my British account. Of course, I put everything into the theater, and Will had stolen every single penny.

Two thousand dollars, though. That's really nothing in British sterling, is it? Maybe fifteen hundred pounds? Nothing! I could easily pay that back when I return. Easily. Can I, should I put a cost on the man who could be the love of my life? He didn't put a cost on mine. I think every living, breathing romantic would do it, to take that chance to make that huge leap of faith.

And really, with all the rewards systems these days, who doesn't have a credit card? No one. It's the savvy thing to do. Everyone does. It is the normal way to live life, right? It's living in the present. It's yogic!

So I fill in the online credit card application with the only person in the whole world whose personal details I know like the back of my hand besides my own: Leo, my brother's.

Chapter 15

I have not just committed terrible online fraud. It's borrowing. It's different. Sharing is caring and all that. Isn't that one of the purposes of having a sibling, so they can be there in times of need?

"Leo, I need you now!" I announce to the ceiling. Announcing vocally, packed with powerful yogi intention, makes me less twitchy. I'll pay it back before he even notices. Leo's cool. He's all about living for the moment and following your heart. He would absolutely agree with me. Absolutely. Unequivocally. Without a shadow of a doubt.

I think.

Yes, I'm sure. He would say, "Life's too short, Enna! Carpe diem and whatnot!" Well, that's Latin. I don't think Leo would ever quote Latin, but something self-possessed and positive.

Besides, what more noble cause could there be?

None.

Well, maybe donating a kidney, or funding schools in Africa, but after that, buying a trip to prove my commitment and test out my love seems pretty bloody noble. How else are Cole and I ever supposed to come to a conclusion? We can't go on with this crazy so-near-and-yet-so-far rubbish. We need to be together to spend time in the same room, or claustrophobic cabin.

The temporary number and credit limit "Leo" is easily granted pops up on the screen. I write it down—they'll send the corresponding plastic in ten to fourteen working days, which is jolly kind of them—and I purchase the tickets. It's like ripping off a plaster, a bandage; the quicker the transaction, the better. My fingers drill over the keys like a concert pianist. I don't look at them, just the screen, watching the number as it grows on the screen. The credit card is interest-free for six months. Then, almighty financial hell breaks loose, and I'd *have* to sell a kidney. But six months? I can pay it back by then, without question. There! Ta da!

The booking confirmation and various forms churn out of the printer. The screen becomes a little too daunting to witness, so I rush to the kitchen and grab a box of kale chips. The bottle of organic wine to celebrate lassos my attention. Well, all right then. Just the one. Just to toast my purchase with.

This is how we roll in Park Slope.

Cross-legged on the bed, with my little mattress picnic, I plan the logistics with military precision, a pad, and a pencil.

Things to do! (Not necessarily in this order):

~Surprise Cole with said travel documents without really revealing where and how we are going (and praying to every god, saint and lucky charm he is free to come).

~Get a glimpse of Cole's passport so I can complete his on-board check-in. Do I have this info in fiancé visa file? Check into this.

~Earn extra money with any cash job that is legal and does not involve clothing removal and/or sex.

~Purchase a nice bikini.

Between mouthfuls, I rip off the top sheet of notepaper and frame it with fridge magnets.

In my eternally romantic brain, I like the idea of completely surprising him. Sending him no details, but just… "Be at this address at this date and time." It's so Cary Grant. *"Meet me at the Brooklyn Bridge"* or *"Be at the Waterloo Bridge before a bus hits me,"* or something like that. Of course, I will have to tell him he needs his passport. That's a shame. And he might feel odd wearing suits in Bermuda, so maybe I'll give him teaser details.

Going somewhere hot.
Please bring your passport.
You can lose the suit.
Don't ask questions.
Just be mute.

According to the site, Bermuda is not exactly tropical and will still be in spring, not summer temperatures. The high will be sixty-eight degrees for that week. Bah. More reason to cuddle up, I suppose.

Going somewhere warm,
Where there will be lots of gourm—
—met offerings to eat.
You make me all at sea.
I hope you'll come with me.

It's amusing, writing little ditties to send. I scribble down different rhymes in my notepad, some flowing, some stilted and awkward. I read them to the ceiling, to the wine, to the dehydrated kale. Truth be told, it sounds like I rap more than recite. Oh Will, look how you changed my perception, conception, shit, my introspection! I can't send Cole a rhyme. Rhymes and riddles were Will's thing. I will just have to take a less fun approach.

The accidental thought hooks and reels me in, dragging me through the watery visions since, moments in freeze frame, all the way back to him. Although I have schooled myself in this month of devastation and disappointment to not think of him, to stay buoyed up above the surface, the current of thought pulls me down. He is there on the bed, whispering Shakespearean rap into my ear, making me giggle with his words and gasp with the patterns his fingertips circle over my skin.

Was it all pretend?

I close my eyes, and it's almost as if I can feel his hands cup my face, like his fingers, those cunning digits that signed my signature and released all the theater funds over to him, had left an impression on my flesh, like dough, or putty. Was there a part of me he hadn't grabbed, kissed, squeezed, smacked? With eyes still locked tight, the vision of myself under a forensic lamp, I see the stain of him illuminated on my skin. The showers, the sweat, the tears have not washed him off me.

What would he be doing now? Would he be thinking of me?

Stop it, Enna! Don't waste your time!

I can see him, as if he stood, leaning in the door frame, holding a pint and lifting it toward me, as if to "cheers," smiling with that smug, self-satisfied grin.

How could I have let him in?

Stop it! Don't let him steal into your thoughts.

I close my eyes, but he's still there. I roll to the side of the bed and feel for the radio alarm clock. Perhaps music will drown out other, non-planning thoughts. The twangy intro to Pink Floyd's "Wish You Were Here" resounds through the mini speaker. It plays for a full verse and chorus before I chuckle at the irony. Will would not be wishing me here…there…wherever in the world he is.

Wherever in the world *is* he?

Enna, it's not your problem.

Well, actually, it *is* my problem.

Yes, okay technically, but leave it to the police.

Ha! Because they have done an amazing job of tracking him down so far!

Enna! You're losing focus. Move on, let go, proceed.

I shift off the bed and take the one stride to the window. A change of scene.

Plan, Enna.

I have been in the Slope for over four weeks now. The ship sails in six. I must look into extending that visa. Maybe I can get a student visa and say I am training with Mallory…or something. I'll look into it. For now, priority one is getting Cole to save the date! I stride back to the bed and spread all the document printouts out. I bundle up two envelopes, a big one and a smaller one. On the smaller, I write:

Only to be opened at the place you get to after you drive your car to this address: Port Terminal Blvd, Bayonne, NJ.

I cover the address up with a piece of cut out, colored paper and attach it with a bit of sticky tape. I write on the paper:

Only reveal at the beginning of your journey. Start heading toward NYC on the 580. Give yourself two and a half hours.

Of course, the blurb takes up too much room, so there are asterisks and arrows leading to squished writing, then more asterisks and arrows.

It looks like an ADD child has had a sudden spurt of genius and covered the paper with flow charts. Cole will never have the patience or the eyesight to interpret the scrawl.

I unseal it and try again, this time rewriting neatly.

Cole, I am taking you somewhere secret.
Somewhere fun!
I'll be waiting for you, hoping you'll come.
Please follow the directions below
and no peeking in the envelope!

Maybe it rhymes a bit. But not much. Short, clear points. That's what every man needs. Right?

I lick the envelope—which is just revolting because it's one of those pre-gummed ones—and hack like a cat with a fur ball. Signed and sealed and addressed, I take it to the post office and complete my busywork in fraud and travel agency all before the afternoon yoga class. Heart open, chest open. I breathe in and out. This is going to work. It has to.

Tara Skypes and is surprised and delighted.

My parentals e-mail and are surprised and delighted. They assume this means things are going really well. Who am I to disillusion them? All will be well. My parents are just premature, positive, predictive people.

Of course, I breeze over the actual purchasing of the tickets and focus on the fact that it's Bermuda, and a real deal too.

The one person who is not seemingly surprised or delighted is Mallory. "I just think you're jumping the gun."

"Erm…we've traveled to lots of places. It's not like this is a first date."

"That's not really what I mean." She sips her coffee stirrer straw and closes the lid of her laptop. "I mean, you really haven't had all that much time together."

"Exactly."

"Life is all about choices. Let me ask you this: does he make you happy?"

"Yes!" I reply without pause.

Mallory leans in and tilts her head questioningly.

"Well…he used to. Now, honestly, it's still hard. I feel there's an anchor weighing us down, but I think time together will help. It's the right thing to do."

"Okay, grasshopper. Your life, your choices. Just beware of your own idiotic compassion."

She tosses her coffee in the rubbish bin and passes where I stand open-mouthed, making her way to the blue yoga room.

I take her place behind the desk, ready to welcome and check in the evening session.

Did she just call me an idiot?

It's there. It's on the tip of my tongue. "What's idiotic compassion?" I want to call out before anyone arrives. But I don't. I bite my tongue. I can Google it when I get back tonight.

I know Mallory was not calling me an idiot. Was she? She's not the sort of person who would suffer idiots.

Why am I so miffed?

Because someone thinking of me having below par intelligence is so important? Yes! Yes, the good opinion of others is important. Being intelligent and making intelligent decisions is important.

Why?

Because.

Ego.

Ego is not important, Enna.

Who cares what anyone else thinks, as long as I know; to thine own self be true and all that. Oh, if noble, yogic thinking were only that easy. How do I learn to recondition my thinking? How do I un-care?

A few now-familiar faces slip through the door: a professional lady—Diane, I believe—talking in hushed tones into her cell phone, giving final instructions to someone down the line before she can switch off for the day; Leah, rushing in for an hour of "escape time" from her role of mum to her two delightful little boys; Katie, who doesn't usually do the evening classes—she's on one of the dating websites and seems to have a constant stream of dates.

As these three shuck their shoes and boots, coats and gloves, as they sign their names and exchange a few words, as they pass me and file into the studio, it hits me again, the draw of the studio. It's not the warm, mellow, buttery light that shines through the window like a lighthouse for lost women, the peaceful sanctuary within these walls—yes, all of that is important—but it seems more that we collective souls congregate here to be ourselves, not a professional, or a mum, or a serial dater, with all the baggage and head space that takes up. But it's where we can let go of those enforced roles and just be, without judgment. Maybe Mal is right. Maybe I am happiest here because I have permission to be myself. And, yes, this has been like heart rehab for me, healing and learning and growing, but I wonder if it is for these other women too. What are their stories?

It's five past the hour. I lock the front door and tiptoe to the back of the class for the last time today. It's a slow flow with restorative postures. Not the kind of class to have when the shit swirl is tornado-ing one's brain. The lengthy hip-opening *asanas* just give me far too long to think, to forget my breathing, to fidget and shift. My forehead rests on my blue mat. It's just resting, sweat-beaded skin to rubber, yet it feels like my third eye, my *chakra* of intuition and insight, wants to headbutt the floor.

Does my intuition agree? Do I really want to spend a week with someone who seems so unlike the man I thought I loved?

I can get it back. I can find him. I just need time away with him. We'll get back to the place of trust and love. We just have to try. That's not Ego wanting to win; that's my heart longing to be loved.

Longing, such an onomatopoeic word in a way, so full of desire, so much fuller than *want*. My heart just longs to be loved.

Mallory pads softly around the class in between the maze of mats. "Where are your minds going, ladies? They are probably telling you to flee, to get out of this uncomfortability, but you are strong. You are going to breathe through it."

There! I could flee from Cole. I could run back to England as I did before, for the theater—maybe that was Ego—but now I am staying and fighting for him. Idiotic or not. And maybe Mallory is right. Maybe it hasn't been a great relationship lately, but it was, and I can't let that go without a fight.

Mallory cues a gentle flow, and we rest back down into pigeon. I have liked pigeon in the past. I have rather enjoyed this version of the splits with the leading leg tucked under, *a la* nesting bird, but today, five breaths seem like fifty. In a coffin. Crawling with fire ants and many-legged creatures. I cannot keep still or my thoughts in check.

Maybe I did jump the gun with the tickets.

"Enna?"

Why is it that when a man does something bold it's romantic, but when a woman does it it's desperate?

"Enna?"

Huh? Me? I look up from my prone position. One thing here is not like the others! Mallory, Diane, Leah and Katie are now back, standing at the top of their mats.

"Oops!"

I shake out my left leg, spring back into downward dog, and bunny hop to the front of my mat.

"Nice of you to join us," she says with a smile. She knows she's caught me over-thinking.

I don't spend much time chit-chatting or extending the niceties after class. I feel a strange, unusual calm, and I just want to be quiet and have my thoughts to myself. Diane and Katie decide to have some wine and the *fromage du jour* at Brookvin, the trendy little bar with the trendy little tapas offerings. I nod and smile and tell them I have a bit of a headache, which is not an out-and-out lie. I did fall out of an arm-balance today and knocked my head into the wall and floor. It's not like a migraine, of course, but I don't think wine and cheese and a loud, claustrophobic bar will help matters.

Mallory doesn't look up from her computer as I say goodbye and tell her I'll see her at five thirty in the morning. I walk through the now-familiar streets, zig-zagging across to stay in the well-lit pools of street light and stopping at the deli for some necessaries. It's a single-girl kind of night, where a tub of roasted pine nut hummus and multigrain chips will make a perfectly suitable meal.

I rush up the stairs but with considerably less energy and enthusiasm than at lunchtime. I click on the computer and listen for its telltale whir into action as I busy myself in the kitchen, arranging a carpet picnic on a tray.

Clearly, hummus is the popcorn of the yoga world. As I read page after page of Buddhist thinking and psychology logic, drinking in the words and trying to filter the meaning, I crunch down on mouthful after mouthful of creamy, grainy hummus. How can I try to be so mindful on one thing and mindless of another at the same time? I replace the lid on the half-eaten pot and push the tray away; this reading takes more concentration than hummus-multitasking allows. Have I been an enabler, not a helper? Have I bitten my tongue and gone along with things because I didn't want to fuss and lose the good opinion of others?

No. I am doing this because I do want to help us! I just want to find what was there before, to shine a light on the waters and see if it reflects blue. I have to give us a chance so I know, so I am not just giving up and throwing it away again. And maybe that's Ego thinking, and maybe that it's because I hate to lose. And after Will, losing Cole as well would be a real zinger. But I have to find out. It's not idiotic to find out. It's the bright people who go searching for answers, right?

Or are the most content the people who stay at home, never knowing anything different? And why am I now thinking of masked ax-murderers at the door and the intelligence level of the girls who go searching for answers?

The italicized Buddhist quotes float upward as I scroll down further. It is the straight, bold Arial font of one blog that holds my attention and my breath:

Ah! The world is just full of compassionate idiots!

I type from experience. I used to be one. I thought I was helping people, but my intention in doing so was to help myself, to self-medicate, to indulge in "thought masturbation." You see, a compassionate idiot is one who does things, says things to help, not to necessarily be beneficial, but for the sheer self-gratification. Compassionate idiots do things to feel better about themselves, rather like an addict would. It's a sanctimonious high. Go on, admit it. You're a compassionate idiot! It gets you off!

I scroll to the top. The blog is entitled "Yoga Cabaret." I can't escape all things theatrical, it seems.

Chapter 16

"Hey, I got a package today."

I gasp and sit bolt upright. I shouldn't be surprised. I did post the thing two days ago. I wasn't sleep-mailing. Of course he received it. Yet, I am suddenly riddled with anxiety about it.

"Surprise," I say lamely into the small piece of plastic that transports my voice to his ear.

"What's this all about, pickle?"

Pickle! *Pickle!* Oh, how two silly syllables that don't really mean anything mean so much right now.

"It's a surprise, and I am trusting you not to peek, okay? All you need to know is that I am taking you somewhere, and you should secure a week off work and leave your suits at home."

"I bet that's what they said to Jimmy Hoffa."

"What?"

"Oh nothing, pickle."

I want to talk to him, this happy, normal version of Cole, but I am now on pins about giving too much away. Instead, I yap on about yoga and—huzzah—my new, fortuitous money-spinner.

"Well, you see, Diane, one of my yoginis, has this business. It's in P.R. or something. Anyway, she loves my British accent and wants me to record her voice greeting! Cash in hand, of course. Well, that got Mallory—she's my yoga guru—asking if I would record hers and maybe record a little clip, doing a virtual tour of the studio for the website. Isn't that great? She's not really into all that in-front-of-the-camera stuff, and so I told her, 'I'm your girl!'" I barely pause for breath.

"Just be careful. You don't want to get deported. I don't want you to get deported."

My jaw goes slack, and my tongue lies inert in my mouth like a mussel. I don't know what to say, but instead my eyes water, an upsurge from out of nowhere, and a tear escapes and flees like a fugitive down my cheek.

Maybe Hemingway was right. To earn someone's trust, you just have to trust in them. Maybe Cole just needed evidence that I was committed, that I wanted to be here, that I would work like a student with dedication and devotion, that I could survive without the theater, without Will, that I was content with me but still wanted to make room for him. Maybe he thought, like Mallory, that I was some kind of addict, dependent on the theater high as much as Mal thought me dependent on the dicktard high. But I don't *need* the theater. I don't need a large paycheck. I don't need a dicktard to treat me like a disposable tissue, or any other person to provide for me. I complete me. Just sharing completeness with Cole would make it more complete. Completer!

"So, you think you can get those dates off?"

"Yeah, I think I can. Shouldn't be a problem."

It's like a weight has been lifted. The anxiety of the last month ascends like the curtain rising. We are okay. We are going to be okay.

The recording goes well, so well, in fact, that a few of the other yoginis recommend me to their friends, and voila! More freelance projects! Holy social networking, Batman. Have accent? Will take a cash job mercilessly milking my mother tongue!

I book a wedding video to promote a new location in the Carol Gardens section of Brooklyn. I have never done anything quite like this. It rather reminds me of some perfume commercial with much running, looking over one's shoulder, trying to not fucking trip up, as I look deliriously happy.

giggle giggle

The commercial is shot with a handheld and a steady camera following me around as I romp around the ornate brownstone, giggling, holding my "groom's" hand—though only his hand and quite delicious arm are in shot—out through the stained glass French doors into the brilliant, clear, and fucking freezing sunshine of the patio, where I giggle some more. Then, it's back across the oriental rugs, eyes sweeping over the stiff Victorian sepia portraits, past the highly polished wooden banisters, up the stairs, to the marshmallow cloud of the bridal suite bed, giggling some more and making snow angels in the duck down comforter.

I say, "I love you!" to the metal tiled ceiling, and the commercial for Eden House is a wrap. The shoot takes only half a day but earns me a whopping thousand dollars. Never have I appreciated my accent more. Heck, why not? It's legal. Well, sort of.

I could send the money to Leo as the first part payment of the slightly unexpected credit card bill he will receive in the next billing cycle. The card and bills will be sent to our Ashtead home address, of course. Forgiveness is much easier than permission, right? So, I'll just apologize. A lot. I just needed the money for the tickets. He can cut up the card, and by the time I get home to England, I can pay him in person, probably before the first bill is ever delivered. Maybe I can even intercept it in the mail. Maybe he'll never actually have to know?

I could pay him now, but really, why risk it?

Besides, I am pretty sure from what Tara says, Bermuda can be pretty pricey. What good is going there to surprise Cole and finding I can't actually afford to treat him to anything whilst there? No scuba, no glass-bottomed boat ride, no dolphin swims, no shopping in Hamilton or bike renting, none of those fun things that Cole has always put his hand in his pocket for, for me. Nothing was too much when we went away. Those exclusive nights in New York, with theater tickets and restaurants and VIP penthouses—I never paid one cent. This was my idea, my surprise. I have to make it all from me. It's *my* commitment.

Another freelance job comes up for Saturday—modeling fascinators for an artist I meet in The Tea Lounge. After twenty minutes of chitchat about my accent—she hears me ordering a café au lait—we exchange names. Hers is "Brandee. With two Es."

"Enna. With two Ns."

Brandee travels extensively but works her business from her apartment and sells her pieces on Etsy. Since standing and sipping in the walkway seems a blockheaded place to be, we decide to sit on the low green velour sofa. She dips her quarters of apple into peanut butter as she compliments my cheekbones and tells me — now biting down and spraying spurts of apple juice on my face — that she will pay me a hundred dollars and the free fascinator of my choice for a shoot. One hundred dollars is hardly very much, but every penny helps! That could be five minutes with a dolphin or something!

The only day her photographer is available is Saturday — "It's just his side thing" — and since Cole has tickets to an Eagles game with a buddy on Sunday, I remain in the city for another weekend, working and planning. Working and planning.

It's rather strange, these monastic, regimented weeks of focus toward this event, this reunion that I know will be a crescendo of energy, bodies clashing into each other like heat-seeking missiles. Every text from him, every call, every sunrise and sunset is another step toward togetherness. I feel this amazing sense of expectancy, like a mother about to give birth, not exhausted and scared of what is to come, but energized and exhilarated by it, the latent possibilities.

He will love the surprise. He will gather me in his arms and sweep me off the deck and whisper his hot breath into my hair. He will kiss me furiously, deliriously, the wind whipping my hair in his face, catching on his stubble, but neither of us will stop to tuck it back behind my ears. And our kisses will be open and hopeful and tender and passionate. It will be simple and unlock all the complexities two souls have held back. I can picture this union so clearly that it drives me like an engine, roaring from my core.

With the wedding commercial, the fascinator shoot, Mallory's virtual tour, and various voice mail greetings, I have amassed an extra fifteen hundred dollars. It's not masses, but it does mean I don't have to dip into other funds.

I spend time thoroughly reading the US Immigration website and am delighted to find that there is indeed a B-2 tourist visa extension, form I-539, that I can download for $49.95. With a new acceptance and patience that I know I never entertained when form-filing the first time, I work through every page methodically and gratefully. It all seems quite easy without the frantic pressure I felt last time.

In the following weeks that pass, I receive the notification of action from the USCIS, a tracking number, and the advisory that my extension is under review and could take a maximum of two hundred and forty days! Well, two hundred and forty days! That's eight months. Perfect!

The universe is unfolding just as it should.

The weeks pass pregnant with hope. I *chaturanga* through the days, read through the nights. I am asked to record two more voice mails. I chomp kale like a cow and have never felt so good. The cruise is so close I can smell the coconut sunscreen.

I walk to my final day at the studio, the mornings so much lighter now than when I started. I can breathe without panicking, without looking at the time or worrying about the "to do" list. I'll get to it. I'll pack. I'll clean, but now I want to notice every little detail of Park Slope and savor it. The sounds of the morning, the smell as I pass the coffee shop, the "Hey!" from Frank the barista as I pass the open door. It's amazing how nearly three months can pass so quickly and how this little neighborhood can feel like a home. Not *my* home, but a home, a safe haven. I think of Park Slope as a technicolored jigsaw of people each belonging to a place. I follow the stone steps leading to the yoga studio and slide my key into the lock, pushing the door gently through its old oak harbor.

The lights are off and, for the first time, I have arrived at the studio before Mallory. I switch a few lights on but think better of it and light the candles instead. As I flow from the studio to the reception, I pass the mirror on the wall by the coat rack and lockers, and I stop, caught by this odd reflection. She's no stranger to me, of course, but it's still surprising not to see the woman in the skirt and pearls and clippy-cloppy heels, always late, always frantic, but instead this bare-footed, wide-toed, Spandex-clad, simplified version. How odd the transition from theater, a black box of pretense, to this studio of light and color, being real and true.

As the yoginis filter in, as Mallory leads the practice, I hold my *chaturangas* longer. I breathe deeper. I bend further. I balance firmer. I have found my intention, and only time and space hold us apart.

It's a bittersweet moment when finally, I close the door of the studio at the end of the day. There have been no bells or whistles, no goodbye cake or hoopla, and that's okay. What did I expect? A fanfare and a goodbye party? I'm the illegal worker who has been here for a heartbeat and will return next week, with a tan and with, hopefully, a fiancé.

Mallory switches off the lights in the back studio and floats through to the front. "So…this is where our paths divide for a time and your journey continues elsewhere."

"Yes. Look, Mal, thanks so much—"

"Thank you. We have enjoyed sharing your love and light. Be kind to yourself, Enna. Remember, it's a practice, not a perfect. In yoga, as in life, we all fall down. The trick is to get up again and again and again."

"I'll only be gone for seven days. I'll be back before you know it."

"Here." She hands me a little brown paper bag.

"What's this?"

"It's 'valor.'" She says this with a huge beam across her face, like I should know what *that* is.

"Oh. That's nice." I don't know what it is.

"Here." She grasps the little bottle from the bag and unscrews it, wafting it underneath my nose. Frankly, it smells of some hundred-year-old musty perfume. She tips a drop of the liquid on her fingertip and presses it to my left temple, then my right, then my third eye.

"Are you…anointing me like…Jesus?"

"No! Good God, I'm Jewish!" She chuckles. "But, I am anointing you like Enna, the special spirit you are. This is to empower you! To allow you to access the strength and courage and self-esteem that you already have inside you. Harness your power. Don't let anybody take that away from you. You understand?"

"Got it." I raise my arms like branches in tree pose, and she nudges me in the ribs to knock me off balance.

"Now, travel safely and go boldly where no yogi from Jaya Studio has gone before."

"Is that *Star Trek*? Mallory, did you just quote *Star Trek*?"

"Life is full of surprises. Now, don't forget your mat or your oil. Here's your last pay for the week. Don't spend it all at once."

"I feel like a wise man loaded with gold, frankincense and…mat."

She rolls her eyes and chuckles. "Go pack, young grasshopper."

"Okay, I'm going!" I juggle the oil, the cash and mat as I pull the door open and feel the fresh breeze on my face. "*Namaste*, Mallory."

She nods, twinkles, and I stride out into my future.

Chapter 17

Thank goodness I have been through this with Tara already: the packing; the transportation options; number of day outfits, beach wear and required evening dress. I say goodbye to the landlady and give her my return itinerary.

From the confines of the peculiarly smelling cab, I text Cole. The yogic control has firmly been elbowed out of the way by teenage excitement.

> *Just a few more hours until I see your face!*
> *Are you ready for a surprise?*

Within a minute, he responds.

> **Ready as I'll ever be. You're not going to tie me up**
> **and force me to marry you, are you?**

Cheeky sod.

> *You'll be lucky!*

> **On the road. Shouldn't text.**

I pocket my phone. In an hour and a half, I will be in his arms. In an hour and forty minutes, we will be in the cabin. In an hour and fifty, we will be erasing every dark memory of the last months as our bodies collide together and remember why they fit together so perfectly.

The taxi sails along the asphalt. The traffic is, for once, non-existent this Sunday, and I really couldn't have planned this better!

Why, thank you, Enna!

No. Thank *you.*

You are a veritable genius of surprise trip planning.

Donald Trump should hire you.

Why, Enna, that is very kind of you to say.

I owe it all to you!

I enjoy all sorts of smug Geminian conversations with myself as we pass through the Brooklyn borough on the less-than-scenic Gowanus Expressway, tolls, bridge, and hello, Staten Island, and finally, after thirty-six minutes, good day, New Jersey!

The taxi plops me out at the side of the Cape Liberty Harbor where I had deposited Tara nearly ten weeks ago, and I wheel my case, myself, and my papers through to the building every arrow and sign points to. It's a large warehouse, full of bodies snaking in a concertina. "No cell phone" signs are mounted on every available pole and wall. I glance at the screen just to check before switching it off.

One new text:

Pickle, I

The text ends. I look around for anyone official and hastily text from the innards of my purse.

Yessssss? What's up? Are you here yet?

I look across the simmering, bobbing sea of eager cruisers. Cole is always so easy to find in a crowd, always standing head and shoulders over everyone else. Unless he is sitting, of course. He's not here yet.

I'm wearing blue, I add, so he can easily find me.

I process my purse and laptop through the x-ray and walk through the machine that goes ping. I wait in this paralyzed conga line very impatiently, my head swiveling constantly for a glimpse of those hazel eyes and that strong, square jaw. He'll probably be wearing a baseball cap. He likes the incognito aspect of them. Never is he seen on the golf course without one.

Cole Krupski, never should he be seen in life without an Enna Petersen.

He'll probably wear one of his polo shirts that are his weekend uniform, maybe some khakis. He was always effortlessly well-coordinated.

Minutes seem hours as I stand sentry for him, catching snatches of head or hair through the crowd—more people are arriving by the minute—and gasping for a millisecond before I realize that the head or hair is not his. By the time I process to the front of the queue, the building is sardine-tin-esque. I can no longer see the newly arriving faces. Okay, so I won't see his immediate surprise as he walks in, but heck, he'll figure it out in the parking lot anyway.

"Passport, tickets, etcetera." A hand is extended to me over the counter.

"Oh, er…sorry." I hate this. I am the person who has been told for the last three turns of the line that I need my paperwork handy, and here it is, still tucked away. Sigh.

"You're traveling on your own?" she asks, chin down, brow and frown up.

"No, with Cole Krupski. We are checking in separately."

She seems satisfied, gives me a plastic room key card and a wad of papers.

"This is your key for stateroom nine hundred twelve. Your bags will be delivered to your stateroom around sailing."

"Great. Good. And, when does embarkation—boarding, this bit, you know—when does this stop?"

"Think of it just like flying on a plane. Safety checks need to be done, so we need everyone on board by three p.m. That's when we close the gates."

"Three p.m. Got it. Thank you." I take a last look, bobbing up and down to scan the crowd, and then, alone, I board the vast ship.

Twelve fifty-six, the digital clock on the wall behind the check-in desks declares. We've got time. It'll be fine. We've got time.

I find my way to deck nine and walk along the corridor to a chorus of cheery "hellos" from ladies and gentlemen in gray uniforms, bustling with towels, vacuum cleaners, consulting clipboards, but all looking very efficient. I find my stateroom and slip in. Technically, I should wait for Cole to ruin the crisp, white, untouched version of the stateroom, but I can't help it. I toss my purse, lay down the laptop bag, and dive into the white. There I lie, listening for the footfalls that belong to him.

I'm up and down like a mental Chihuahua. Each time I think it's him, each time the sounds of hefty shoes slow by my door, I am thrown into a frenzy of seductive readiness: hair tossed, lips licked, breath held. All lead to…nothing. No Cole to slide his card into the slot and thrust the heavy door open. After some while, I resign from the seductive welcome and decide to freshen up in the miniscule bathroom, re-do the essentials.

Ten minutes of preening ensue and a thorough investigation of all the mini bottles of shampoo, conditioner and body lotion. I take a whiff and apply a little daub of cream to my arms and thighs.

I check the time again. One twenty-nine. He is still not here. I open the cupboards, not looking for Cole or Narnia, just getting familiar with these new environs and distracting myself form clock-watching.

Oh! Fluffy robes!

The room is fairly standard, not the vast luxurious suite Cole used to book for us, but there's a balcony and large king-sized bed. What more will we need? Nothing! I venture onto the balcony, opening the slider door. *Woo. Windy.* I survey the Manhattan skyline and the Statue of Liberty for as long as I can stand in the breeze before retreating back within the cabin. I sit back on the edge of the bed and reach for my phone.

No texts. No missed calls. I look at his last text to me.

Pickle, I

Pickle, I'm running late?

I'm caught in traffic?

I'm on my way?

I'm stopping to buy you flowers?

I'll be there soon?

I scratch a note on the cruise line notepaper and prop it up on the pillow.

Surprise, darling! We're cruising! I have just gone to investigate and get us a cocktail, maybe not in that order. I'll be back soon!

There! Now I can find Tara and a drink, and get this cruise started.

Of course, the ship is a-bustle with cruisers having the similar idea, drinking and walking and pausing right in front of me. I weave through the throngs, ever-looking for that large head and shoulders, that contagious smile. The narrow corridors that house the staterooms are quickly dispatched. There's nothing to see or do, but either end of the ship on the tenth and eleventh decks are pools, the courts, the sun—wind—loungers, the nightclub, the restaurants and attendant menus. I race around the top decks, looking at the cars parked in the harbor lot, hoping I can see his black Suburban, but I can't. A car that is so conspicuous in its inconspicuousness!

He's probably in the room right now. He's going to walk in, and I'm not even going to be there! My legs whisk faster. My heart beats louder.

The drink! I promised a drink. I stop at the nearest bar on deck ten, give my cabin card, and order a rum runner cocktail. Re-pocketing the card, I take a slurp and steady myself. Holy mouth sanitizer, it tastes ghastly. But it does the trick to calm me down a smidge.

It's okay. It's going to be okay. Stop panicking. Breathe in. Breathe out. He's coming. He said he was on his way.

I take a breath at the door. How is it that important moments with this man seem to hinge around the opening of a door? I insert my card into the slot, watch it go green, and enter the cabin. I open the door, peering in to see his black trousers and body bent over.

"Cole!"

The body and head turn toward me. "Oh, so sorry, miss."

My stomach plunges from mouth to my shoes.

"I was just straightening the bed," he explains in an unplaceable accent.

"Please, don't worry." I draw a thin smile across my face, standing at the door as he exits the room.

2:17 p.m.

I check the phone. No texts. If he's been held up, why hasn't he called? Why hasn't he texted? He must be in line to board, surely. That's why he hasn't texted. It said on the signs at embarkation, "No cell phones." He's just being good. He's in line right now.

"Tickets…? Passport…? And here is your room key, Mr. Krupski!"

I close my eyes and listen to the footfalls.

Pickle, I…

Pickle, I…

Pickle, I'm…not coming.

There's a knock at the door and I lurch for it, opening it excitedly.

"Your bag, miss."

"Oh. Thanks," I muster without enthusiasm.

So many ups and downs. Where's the balance?

Enna, you are creating your own drama. You are choosing to be distressed here. You needn't be. Relax. There is a perfectly good reason for Cole to be held up. Perfectly.

I suck on the vile, tangerine orange colored cocktail, that clearly has nothing tangerine or orange, or in fact any real fruit in it at all.

I screw up the pillow note with a tight fist and throw it somewhere toward the trash. The loudspeaker relays some recorded message, and I close my eyes, waiting for him. He'll come to the room first, won't he?

I watch the minutes change on the red digital interface. I confirm them with the text-empty screen on my mobile phone.

I try calling. It goes immediately to his voice mail.

"Hi. Cole, are you here? Are you coming? I don't know if I emphasized it before, but you really need to be here before three p.m. That's really important, okay? So, if you have stopped along the way to have lunch or something, please hurry. Oh and—"

An automated voice interrupts. "To send your message press one, to erase and rerecord press two…"

AGH! I hate these. Why don't they make voice mails longer? I continue recording and try not to sound as anxious as I feel.

"Oh, I'm back. It cut me off. Anyway, hope you get this message. Please hurry. Oh, and I have…" I'm going to say I have a rum runner waiting for him, but the automated voice jumps in again, and after a little scream, I just press one.

We will laugh about this later tonight. We will laugh. And laugh. And laugh.

I sniff back the cresting tears. I can't cry now.

Take control. It will all work out.

I bury my head in the plumped and pristine white pillow and breathe heavily through the thread count, the pillow stuffing. I hear my breath slow and darkness hide the clock.

My heavy puffed eyelids and ears prick to hear another loudspeaker message cut through the drowsy fog of sleep.

Sleep? How could I fall asleep?

It is the captain, Leonardo, advising us to ascend to the upper deck to see the Statue of Liberty as we sail from Bayonne. I see from the passing skyline out of our balcony window that we are moving, and the great Cole-shaped space beside me is empty. I grasp the cell phone and awaken the screen. No messages.

I spring from the bed as if it is covered in ants, reach for my key, and leave the cabin, the door swinging to a heavy thud behind me. Where can he be? Why am I searching again? I searched for Will, unreliable, traitorous Will. I never thought I would be searching for Cole who stands out, who is reliable. Who *was* reliable.

I run through corridor after corridor like a horror movie heroine being chased.

Where is he? Where is he? Where is he?

Music fills my head, as if Rachmaninoff is playing some ghastly minor version of the concerto I had so loved, the grand sweeping climax of strings and woodwinds and piano that seems to only increase my speed and desperation.

I get to deck ten, the gym, the pool. I scan the bodies, the woman with non-x-ray eyes, trying to conjure some type of superhuman senses.

He will be there. He must be there.

I dart across the deck, tapping practically every man—and one woman—over six foot two on the arm. On deck eleven, facing the wind, freezing but too frantic to care, I look down to the open deck below, the massing people taking pictures of the Statue of Liberty, sucking up frozen drinks and swathing their shoulders in clean towels for extra warmth.

Recalling Cole's new penchant for a drink in hand, I make my way to each bar before returning to the room to check that…he is still not there.

The steward in the corridor—who seems to just pop out of the room whenever I walk by—tells me that no gentleman has been here yet, nor any gentleman's bag. An alarm sounds, and the voice on the loudspeaker informs—no, commands—all passengers report to their muster station. If Cole were here, he'd make a joke about "mustard station." Maybe that is where he will be. Maybe he got lost?

I file into the large auditorium/mustard station and swivel my head like the girl in *The Exorcist* sans projectile vomit. The actor in that film… what was his name? Jason Miller. Cole had told me about him. He came from Scranton. He drank like a fish in Scranton. Just like Cole.

Oh my God!

He's not here.

He didn't come.

He didn't love me enough!

He chickened out and just went back to Scranton!

Drowning on these depths of possibility, I hardly see any other faces. I am only looking to recognize his, so in the auditorium, as we are meeting the cruise director, and as we are told what to do in case of emergency—the waffle I hear as if underwater and expect to be the spiel about "women and children to the life rafts"—all the activity of thousands of people contained in one floating hotel, is peripheral, like the radio in the background, the TV flickering. I am bubbled in despair, cocooned in self-pity, diving in the dark depths of disappointment. I am, in fact, completely unaware that the face—the beige oval with long lashed eyes, one nose, one mouth moving mechanically pulled across to reveal white teeth, creating the short two-syllable word, En-na—floats up the aisle, repeating the strange familiar word over and over, closer and closer.

"En-na!"

"Enna!"

"ENNA!" She shakes my knee.

"Ugh!" It's not a scream, more a rush of air and jolt of recognition. "Oh!" The itemized list of features finally merge together and create the person in front of me. I propel myself from the velvet seat into her arms.

"Hey! Hey! *Mon petit! Arrête!* Stop! What's wrong."

"He's—" I sniff back the snot "—not—" gasp for breath "—here."

"Darling, I can't understand you. You sound like an asthmatic guinea pig."

"He didn't come." I then proceed to wail embarrassingly, but I can't help myself; it just comes out.

There are murmurs from the passengers sitting around me, shifting and disapproving glances.

The director makes a comment from the stage, and the audience laughs. Tara must be aware of the hubbub, as she continues to hold me tight and whispers in my ear, "Let me take you outside."

Like a lemming, I follow Tara as she leads me to deck four outside the auditorium. The whir of the casino machines hums through the next archway.

She holds my shoulders, bracing my limp limbs. "Come on, buck up. It's okay. It's going to be okay."

I breathe in and try to possess myself, to stand up straight and find some shred of my yogic self. I am not dead or in any physical pain. Check.

"So, Cole didn't come?"

"He said he was coming," I mouth between sobs. "He said he was en route. He should have arrived hours ago." I gasp for breath. Why is it so hard to cry and make myself understood at the same time? "But I waited—" breathe "—and I have searched—" heave "—and I am pretty sure, unless he has shrunk or undergone radical plastic surgery, he's not on board. He didn't come!"

"Okay. Calm down. Take a breath. He could be here. It's a big ship. Let's check the passenger listings. That will tell us definitely. No one can get on or off without passing security and being photographed."

I don't have the energy to argue, but I know. He didn't make it. I don't understand why he would change his mind or string me along, but he's done so much I don't comprehend; why be surprised now?

I blindly follow Tara through lots of passageways that I am pretty sure I am not supposed to be in. The carpet style has changed, and it looks generally less polished. We are somewhere on the lower decks, maybe two or one, with no natural light, when Tara turns into a little room and talks to a white-uniformed official. I hear her, but it's a muffled, submerged sound. Literally and figuratively.

I can't believe it. This mantra repeats, resounds, echoing like some terrible Halloween recording.

I can't believe it. Why would he do this? Lead me on? To punish me?

I can't—

"Enna." Tara's arm is around me again, shepherding me out of this submarine cabin. "Let's go and get some tea, huh?"

I turn to look at her. "Oh, I think I'll be needing something a *lot* stronger, don't you?"

"*Bien sûr,* absolutely."

And so, I follow her again, back up flights of stairs, passing hordes of people but not seeing a thing, into a little lounge off the main walkway. It's oppressive with its dark wood and studded leather, but it seems the perfect place to shut the door on my dreams and drink myself into oblivion.

Tara doesn't even ask, doesn't hand me a cocktail menu; she just orders. I am not a fan of martinis, but liking it doesn't really seem to be important right now. The first sip makes the sinews of my neck stand to attention. It's like medicine, acrid, corrosive chemicals.

Tara disappointingly drinks water.

"You're not joining?"

"I have the opening show tonight or else I would, but it's hard enough to keep my balance on stage when the ship is rolling. I don't want to add a martini to the mix."

I nod and sip again.

I haven't asked. I don't need to, but as if waiting for the perfect time, which of course never arrives, she places her water on the table between us and says, "He wasn't there. On the listing. I'm so sorry, Enna."

I sip. No, really it's a long gulp.

"I hope he's okay. I mean, sure, I didn't really know or sing allelujahs for the guy, but I do hope nothing happened."

Her words, her lips, the movement of her tongue between her teeth—they form a kind of aural poison.

"You…you mean…you think something could have happened? You mean, aside from him just not getting on board? You think something happened to stop him? Like what?"

"Stop! You will drive yourself crazy. Enna, he's not here. There is nothing you can do. It is now beyond your control. So, now you have three choices."

I sob. I slurp. I spill some vile martini. I sob again.

"Are you going to listen, or are you going to keep on sobbing like a demented lamb?"

"But, Tara, you don't understand. He said he was coming," I bleat on, taking the napkin already soggy with a martini ring, and I blow my nose loudly to punctuate the end of the sentence.

"Jesus! The way I see it, Enna, is this, you have choices: either you can spend the next seven days moping and being miserable, blaming, flogging and flagellating, masochistically torturing yourself with all the many things you said and did, and what he said and did, and how you should have reacted differently so he would be here with you now, and you can sigh and lament and drive everyone who has real problems and concerns fucking bat-*merde* crazy—which, quite frankly, achieves what? Fuck. All. It won't change anything but fulfill your inexhaustible quota for melancholy and drama; or, you can rethink, realign, focus on you, celebrate instead of commiserate and actually enjoy yourself."

It's like an aural slap.

"I do not have an 'inexhaustible quota for melancholy or drama,' thank you very much."

"No, I said inexhaustible quota for melancholy *and* drama."

My chest heaves, puffs and prepares for a fight, but it quickly deflates with Mallory's calming voice whirring through my head: "*You know, the thing of it is, you don't always have to be right. Let go of the need to be right all the time.*" I slump back into the leather and gag on another sip of martini.

"Choice three?"

"I don't have a choice three. I was vamping."

"Ah."

We sit in silence. I twirl the stem of the martini glass.

"We are sailing on the Atlantic Ocean. We are so blessed! We're alive; don't lose sight of that, Enna. Cole didn't hop aboard. Maybe that's a blessing. Maybe this is the slipped rope that releases you from your former self-imposed obligation to this man who, *excusé moi*, did not seem to treat you as well as you remembered. Don't jump ship and swim back to shore, searching for solid ground."

I take the last sip, the briny olive juice rasping at my tongue and summoning forth my gullet. Quite without notice, my jaw yawns wide. "I'm going to—" A surging tidal wave of puke surges into my mouth, and in a panic, I charge for the bar, no bin in sight. I bolt through the door to the deck and decorate the planks before the feet of a couple linked arm-in-arm. It's like I am making some sacrifice at their feet.

Oh, ye happy couple, I make my intestine semi-digested sacrifice to you.

He wears Sperry deck shoes—how appropriate. Now they are spewy deck shoes. She wears some rather impractical heels with a cork platform, perhaps four inches—woof! Another surge, and the puddle spreads, the feet now dancing around it accompanied by little shrieks. Tara's flat palm is there behind me now, patting my back, the soothing "coo" of the familiar British tones, quietly uttered but louder in my inner ear.

I taste the olive and alcohol again, my throat open, unleashing these ghastly gasps of breath as if someone has punched all the air, semi-digested breakfast bagel, rum runner, dirty martini, hopes, disappointment, bile, up and out. Gag, yawn, heave! Gag, yawn, heave!

The shoes have disappeared. Tara's red Crocs remain to the side of me until she kneels mid-deck too, and now we are knee-to-knee. Apparently she is not concerned that spew could at any moment sail across the inch or two of deck and soak her Spandex capris. She rubs my back as the tears brim. My mouth tastes rancid, and I stare at the contents of my stomach.

"Don't ever be an international spy," she says, rubbing my arm and helping me up to my feet.

"Why?"

"Because you are too good at spilling your guts."

"Nice one."

"Seriously, if this was a diversionary tactic to make me feel sorry for you, it was a goody. Come on, sit over here. I'll get someone to clean this up."

She disappears for seconds or minutes; I have lost concept of time and perception of where anything is. I sit hunched over in a fetal position, and I just want to get to bed.

The red Crocs arrive back.

"How are you doing, *mon petit* puke-face? *Le visage de vom?*"

I don't speak, my mouth so full of revolting taste, so instead I extend my middle finger and aim it at her.

"Touché." She levers herself under my arm and pries me from my seat. She takes my arm and limps me in the direction of the staterooms. "You'll feel better after a nap. Sleep, restore, rejuvenate. Then, eat something—"

I clamp my hands to my mouth. Even the suggestion makes me dry heave.

"And come to the show. Don't stay in your room and mope. Life is too short, and one hundred and one other clichés."

It sounds so easy coming from someone else's lips.

She tucks me up and draws the curtains.

I imagine him being there when I wake. He is Cole. He can make things happen—maybe not today; maybe something kept him away—he could find a way to helicopter in. He'd fucking row if he had to.

And I am surprised to wake, what only feels like two minutes later, alone, in the dark. I look immediately to the undented side of the white comforter to my right, and the disappointment swells again. What did I expect? That he would be there, standing above me, waiting as I return to consciousness as I did in the hospital?

Too late, Enna. You realized too late.

Why couldn't I have woken then and had the sense to throw my arms around him and be delighted he was there? Why couldn't I have recognized that face then? I trace the ramifications of my non-waking, the non-Disney ending of *Snow White* or *Sleeping Beauty* according to Enna Petersen. You snooze, you lose. You sleep too long, and Prince Charming just meets someone else. It doesn't make for a happy ending, but that's oxymoronic anyway, right? Endings are never happy. Endings are final. Endings are death. Chew on that, Walt Disney.

I imagine him now, on the sofa. Did he skulk back home to watch the Eagles game? Is he sitting there, an arm slung around Patricia, the easy, convenient choice? Could he really give up and give in so easily? After all the trouble, the visa form-filling, the expense, would he just throw his hands up and walk away?

Out of habit, I check the inert cell phone again. I am a lab rat who just likes to confirm the electric fencing still shocks. I run my fingers over the screen, finally landing on "settings." I switch to airplane mode. There! I accept it.

You can't message me even if you wanted to, you great shit!

I launch my pillow into the mirrored wall facing the bed. Though I really want to lob the phone with all my might, the pillow seems a less messy option. It hits the glass and flops to the floor. It doesn't even bounce. No bounce back-ability. I look at the woman in the reflection, so different from the purposeful yogini in the mirror yesterday. It was not supposed to be this way. This was the mirror I was supposed to see his bare triangular back in as he ripped off my clothes and kissed my neck, my shoulders, my breasts and as I watched my nails dragging at his skin and clinging to him as if to life. This was where we would make up for the forceful car fuck, the dry-ramming, where he'd take his time, his tongue over every inch, his weight pressing against me, and everything would just dissolve.

I look out beyond my little floating cabin. The sky through the balcony glass door is a royal blue now. It must be late.

Tara!

I must get to Tara's show. I am a terrible unfiancée, but I refuse to be a terrible friend too. I toss the comforter aside and get to my feet. My stomach refuses to let me stand up straight, and I hunch like a little octogenarian.

I shake out my hair, hope it doesn't smell of spew, spray lots of perfume, and slip on my wedge heels. I have to support Tara. The show must go on.

Chapter 18

I slip in at the back of the balcony, whispering excuse me's as I squeeze past knees. Of course, the only available seat is the one furthest from the aisle. At least this ducking movement means I don't have to stand up straight. My stomach feels so tight, like I've had liposuction and too much flesh has been moved to straighten. Maybe this is true heartbreak, not felt in the heart at all, but the guts. I've been drawn and quartered and stitched back up again.

Tara's on. Concentrate.

She appears on a rock—probably just polystyrene—elevated through the stage. She looks beautiful in her long red wig, her iridescent scales, her shell bra, the fishnet body stocking. She laments on her rock, flipping her tail, singing of love lost and never finding her sailor.

The microphone taped or glued under her cheek bone—I can't see from this distance—gives great sound quality, and her voice is as lovely as I remember. There is no trace of British accent; it's all very general American. The dance portion is limited for her, wearing a fishtail and all, but during the chorus, the dancers in various brightly colored costumes—a jellyfish, an octopus, a clown fish, coral and sequined seaweed—pirouette on from the wings and prance balletically, throwing in some gasp-worthy lifts through a very competently synchronized, contemporary routine. They whisk away whilst Tara has some dialogue with some other mermaids, a blonde and brunette. I'm not really listening to the words, but the costumes, the sparkles, the adrenaline, and for the first time since leaving Ashtead three months ago, I feel the pangs of the profession. My feet itch to be up there, to feel the lights on my skin, like a thespian's vitamin D. I want to see the faces, the glints of spectacles, of smiles, not the back of balding pates and bouffant blue rinses. I want the stomach rumble of waiting in the wings, the anticipation of my entrance, the millisecond of fear that I have forgotten my lines, the rush and relief of remembrance.

My stomach churns noisily. How long has it been since I have eaten? Too long. I glance at the wrist to my right. The gentleman's watch numerals conveniently glow, and I see it is nine fifteen, both dinner seatings missed, but the deck ten buffet should be open. Not how I imagined Cole and I would spend the first dinner.

Concentrate!

The musical passes as I expected in rip-off Disney fashion, and in a nice nod to female empowerment, after the sailor/prince type chappy rescues the mermaid from spending a soul-destroying existence singing for the underwater Mafioso of sharks in their submarine nightclub, she rescues him right back.

And they sing together, hoorah and huzzah. They are in love, and I want to rip my head off and use it to vomit in.

I don't. It's lovely; it's just…he was not for me. Clearly.

Tara's tail slips off, her scales shucked like lobster meat from its shell, and in sequined hot pants and a trail of diaphanous silk, she performs the fishnets off the last number, belting those alto notes and kicking her leg over his shoulder with astonishing accuracy and flexibility. He bends her back and, with one hand in support, she kicks her legs over and back flips, the sequins flashing, like a Catherine Wheel I remember from British fireworks displays, whipping around, and she lands and slips into the splits.

Shit, where the hell did she learn that? We did not do that at National Youth Theater! We did squats!

Impressive.

Her lead male is tall — unusual for musical theater — and the typical blue-eyed, blond-haired hero. He croons with his hand extended imploringly in practically every number, like some throwback to

Spandau Ballet or some other romantic and stylistically-challenged eighties band.

There is applause, nothing thunderous. The cast smiles and jumps off the stage to line the aisle and greet the audience. I suppose it's a nice touch to be "of the people" and warm us up for the next week of shows.

I slip from the balcony through the massing crowd waiting to press palms with the company. Tara shines her way toward me, every inch of her face and limbs dusted in glitter.

She smiles beatifically and hugs me, hard. My post-puke, octogenarian walking corpse does not like to be hugged so hard.

"You made it!"

"I wouldn't have missed it." I whimper, asphyxiating on her hairspray.

She draws away from me, still with my hands in hers. "Come on, let's get out of here."

She nuzzles through the crowd, smiling and accepting compliments, and I follow, irrelevant and unspoken to. It's such a strange feeling to be in a performance space and not have people asking me about sound, lights, box office, board members.

We weave around backstage. "Come on, I'll get some clothes on that don't require me to travel around the ship with a defibrillator, and I'll take you on tour."

Oooh. It's different, of course, but it is so nice to be backstage where it's homey, full of smells and sights that make me want to nestle in a corner, burrow in some stray tutu and sleep. I pick up the hairspray and just nudge a little out, just to see if it smells the same. I run my hand over the wigs and hot rollers. I sit in the bright fluorescence of the many-bulbed makeup mirrors, so tempted to grab the stick of thick stage makeup and smear it over my lids and under my eyes. A little brightener, a little yellow, and ta da! No one would suspect the woman in the mirror had been crying, retching her guts up.

I inspect every bottle, realign the products like soldiers, stab the loose bobby pins into the netting doughnut. I eye the railing sagging with the weight of costumes, the unbelievable collection of shoes lined up at each dancer's station.

"Dear God, you could open a shoe emporium."

"No joke. Thankfully, I am not a dancer. They have about ten pairs of shoes for that show: ballet shoes, blocks to go en pointe, tap shoes, modern jazz slippers, Irish dancing shoes, and a backup pair of each. It's crazy. How they dress so quickly between numbers and manage to change their shoes is nothing short of miraculous. I think every night, 'What will I improvise when they don't make it on in time,' but they haven't failed me yet!"

She peels off her Minnie Mouse fake eyelashes, unpins her wig, and replaces both on the polystyrene model head, lashes over eyes, wig over head. Without any ceremony, she whips off her hot pants and shimmies off the fishnet body stocking.

Other cast members call in the corridor, and a female dancer runs in. "Great job tonight, Tara!"

"Thanks, Liz," she replies, unperturbed by her own nakedness. My expression must say it all, because Tara laughs and says to me, "Don't look so bloody shocked. We really don't have time to be prudish with all the quick changes. We just whip it off, whip it on, and move."

Whip it off, whip it on, and move. Maybe this is how I learn to forget how wretched I feel. Whip it off.

The loudspeaker comes on, interrupting my thoughts or ideas on repost.

"Sorry, I'm…just a little shell-shocked. Probably not helped by my nutritional choices of breakfast bagel, rum runner, and martini."

"Understood. Staff bar or nightclub or…"

"Can we just walk slowly, maybe up to deck ten? I need a piece of bread or something."

She smirks. "Hmph! You are too adorable! Here you are at sea, on a cruise line where the waitstaff's mission to serve you is like they are competing in the *Hunger Games*, the battle to get to you first, and you…want a piece of bread. At least have some smoked salmon with it or something."

The mere mention makes my stomach lurch into my lungs. "Just something bland. Delicate, you know. I promise I will dine like a complete glutton every other night. How is that? Deal?"

"Deal."

"By the way, you looked and sounded great out there. I'm proud of you."

We circle the buffet, a myriad of colorful cuisines: the steaming soup station with poppy seed rolls, flour-dusted ciabatta, and some nutty, seed-topped offering; the salad station with stray leaves and beans around the metal self-serve tubs—oh, quinoa and chickpeas and thick magenta discs of beetroot; the portly chef in his whites shovels a just-baked pie from the oven to join the staggering collection of round pies with various toppings — mushroom with globs of white goat cheese is his latest — the waft of pizza fumes filling my lungs; the pasta bar with milky Alfredo, chunky marinara, verdant pesto and the ivory quills and bows, ribbons and laces of pasta; the next chef wields an impressive knife, slicing through a joint of beef, oozing red juices on the carving board, a ladle for horseradish dousing in the other hand; the mini desserts with their little puffs of fresh cream piped from a bag in perfect swirls decorating the dense vanilla cheesecake, the glassy-topped crème brûlée, the raspberry tart, the apple pie, the *mille feuille* with its layers of pastry and custard, the icing marbled beautifully.

How much food must they serve in a week? How many cows are butchered? How many eggs, pounds of cheese, gallons of milk, pineapples cut into chunks? The hordes captive on this ship swarm around the food.

I am hungry — I think I am — and yet nothing, nothing appeals.

"So, what are you going to have?"

And rather, more because I am embarrassed by my indecision and getting in the way of diners who seem intent on getting to whatever food station I stand in front of, I grab a poppy seed roll, and Tara takes a slice of pizza. We sit at the window, staring into the darkness outside. The wash of waves, fringed in white, illuminated by moonlight, fans out behind us.

There we sit in silence, the *thump-thump* from the nightclub above rumbling the ceiling tiles. Were there even any young people to enjoy the nightclub? Was it empty or full of geriatrics grooving with their fruity cocktails?

It was not supposed to be like this.

The first night of my romantic cruise for two. Here I sit, nibbling mouthfuls of bread, collecting poppy seeds in my teeth and staring blindly into the wash. They really should have the dining deck at the front of the ship so one can look toward the future instead of ruminating on what's behind.

"I'm not going to go on about it, Tara. I don't want to be miserable and pathetic, but this really hurts."

"I know." She wraps her arm around my shoulder. "And I didn't mean all those things I said earlier, pre-the-great-deck-puke. I know you are not a drama queen. I was just trying to make you focus. And, you know, really and truly, things could be worse."

"I know. It's not like anyone died, but it rather feels like someone did."

"You're mourning your relationship. That's normal, Enna."

"I'll be better tomorrow. Promise."

She turns to me. "Want me to come and spend the night so you don't have to be alone? Like the good old days?"

I reach for her hand and hug it in both of mine.

"I think being alone is what I need for the night."

"Understood."

Someone calling in the corridor wakes me up from a dream somewhere during the dark o'clock hours. I try to grasp the trailing wisps of the rapidly fading dream but forget it almost instantly. The red numbers on the alarm clock read 1:32 a.m.

I rotisserie chicken myself on my half of the bed, around and around, unable to get back to a comfortable unconsciousness. How funny that I keep to this half, leaving his so pristine, untouched. As if by keeping it unruffled, smooth and neat, he will be more likely to appear.

Enna, Cole is not Jesus, nor the angel Gabriel, nor David Bowie. He is not going to appear in a vision of gold blinding light or a drunken dream. He is human and flawed.

I stare at the red numbers glowing by the bedside, trying to catch the exact moment of change. I count seconds, whispering them to the untouched, plumped pillow, and still, the digit change surprises me.

This is maddening. I can't sleep. I don't want to imagine Cole anymore, where he is, what he is doing, what possible explanation there could be. Because there is none. I throw the comforter off.

Whip it off, whip it on, and move!

I fling the wardrobe door open, the dry-cleaned emerald wraparound dress taunting me from the wire hanger, but this isn't a wrap dress kind of feeling. I seize a pair of yoga pants and a fuchsia yoga top and slip them on, nudging my toes into some ballet flats. I grab the cabin card and run up the flight of stairs to the gym, realizing on the top step that I am no longer hunched like a granny. My stomach is tight but all right.

The gym is a ghost town. One white-uniformed gym attendant swings his feet off the reception desk as I enter. "The gym is closed, ma'am."

"I don't want the gym equipment. I just need the space. Would you mind?"

He looks the other way as I shuck my shoes and face the mirror.

Breathe.

I cycle through a couple of sun salutations to warm up. Then, feeling the heat, I come to do what I had intended. Placing my forearms down on the ground, I kick my legs above me into a handstand. My legs flail, not making it over my hips. This is all psychological. I am frightened of going too far and falling down. I kick up again, without momentum, but use my legs like a lever.

Kick up.

Fall down.

Kick up.

Wobble.

Fall down.

I can almost feel the acid in my shoulders; it burns.

"Work through the uncomfortability. You are strong. You can do it." I hear Mallory from the mirror.

With a grunt, my hips move this time. The shift is subtle and sudden, drawing my lower belly in. My hips seem to float over my shoulders, pike, then up above me, straight! Vertical! I hover for a few seconds.

"I'm doing it!" I tell Mallory in the mirror.

My back arches, and my legs drop over my head in a scorpion pose before I fall to my back, an inelegant sprawl, breathless and elated. After a minute of repose, I throw the towel up, get to my feet and tell the mirror, *"Pincha Mayarasana,* bitch!"

It's a small victory in the face of ultimate defeat, but I am strangely elated by this yogic accomplishment. I jog down to the fourth deck, sweaty and with adrenaline pumping. There is no way I will sleep now. The casino machines are still whirring, dinging and chanting, *"Wheel of Fortune."* I pass the ill-fated martini-puke bar, the coffee bar, the gelato and patisserie display, amazed to see so few cruisers still up. The walkway leads into a red and purple carpeted lounge, dark but for the spotlight on the piano singer in the corner of the room crooning softly into the microphone. It's something that sounds faintly Bublé/Connick Jr., a bluesy lullaby.

I pull up a barstool, hand the bartender my cruise key card, and ask for a Pinot Noir.

Oh God, It's "Moon River." Fucking bloody "Moon River."

He pours a satisfyingly large glassful. It's late. I look like shit. I guess he thinks I need it. I swirl the goblet in my hand, watching for the tears that run tracks down the inside of the glass. What do the wine enthusiasts call them? Legs? Not that I really know what to look for, but Cole used to do that. His little habit when he would order a bottle of wine for us, and the waiter would bring it to his side to approve of the label and take a first sip: he would swirl the glass and sniff it. I take a sniff, a sip, and I feel the flavors run over my tongue like velvet, comforting and warm. As I sit and try not to give in to the tortuous thoughts pounding at the door of my brain, I look around the dim lounge, the low slung chairs in red velour, the banquettes at the side. There's a couple in the corner, holding hands and tapping feet.

Am I the only person in the world to hate "Moon River"? Thank God, it flows to its end, and the couple in the corner applauds limply.

The pianist nods in their direction and thanks them. I clap one-handed with my glass, unable now to put the thing down. It's good to hold something, steadying somewhat.

It was him. It wasn't just me.

Sip.

We're both to blame.

Sip.

Oh God, now it's Elton Fucking John.

Slurp.

We both had a right to feel bitter, but we both took considerable transatlantic steps to mend things. I cannot take responsibility for his actions.

Glug.

So, if he decided not to come, if he failed to make that effort after saying he could and would, then it is about him and not about me.

I drain the glass and steady it back on the bar.

"Same again, miss?"

"Yes, please." I turn back to him, the dark face with the bright white smile.

His name badge—which all crew members seem to wear—boasts his name and country. Cedric from Cameroon.

He tops me up again.

"Thank you, Cedric from Cameroon."

His beam broadens, if that is possible. "'S my pleasure, miss."

I turn back to Elton John. If he plays "Circle of Life" or "Don't Let the Sun Go Down on Me" at any time, I may bash the glass over the bar and slit my wrists.

It's not about me.

Glug.

He clearly has issues.

Glug.

I mean, the night at the Radisson—*glug*—in the time I had rolled my cases up his street, along North Washington Avenue and hailed a cab at the corner of Greenridge Street—*glug*—hailed a cab in the fuck-me freezing weather, driven all through the Hill Section and scenic route to Jefferson Avenue—*twirl glass stem*—and eventually to the grand façade of the Radisson…by the time I had paid the cabbie with what little American currency I had, rolled myself in, navigated around the furniture, and ordered a hot tea, he had arrived and already smelled of bourbon.

Glug.

Glug.

He's been irascible, unreasonable, late, unreliable, ungentlemanly, unaccommodating, completely contradictory…

Glug.

No. He doesn't have a problem like that. Cole is extremely controlled, self-disciplined, put together. Or he was.

The Skype! I recall the Skype, the drink in hand, the decanters in the background. Since when did Cole have alcohol in his office?

Glug.

The staccato chords of "Benny and the Jets" feel like two mallets clubbing my chest, my brain, my liver. I drain the second glass of Pinot.

Is Cole an alcoholic?

It seems too outlandish, too unbelievable. He is the clean-cut, all-American Cole. The man who, I had imagined, would be helping to coach Little League, football, the dad who'd be in charge of the BBQ grill at the Fourth of July cook-out as the kids played in the pool or wrestled in the grass.

And yet, what was an alcoholic exactly? Shit, according to the government recommendation, don't I drink too much? Yes, I jolly well do. But I don't have a problem. I could stop at any moment, couldn't I? I just choose not to.

I look back to the bar. Cedric has refilled the empty glass.

It certainly would explain a lot, wouldn't it? The lateness, the mood swings, the alcohol in the office.

I remember watching a play at the Edinburgh Festival about one of the *Monty Python* men, Graham Chapman, who hid glasses of gin around the set, everyone believing them water.

Is that how Cole got through the day? Did he have to hide drinks?

Did I cause this? When I left? Was that when he started this social/anti-social behavior? Surely it wasn't in his history before. Oh, we imbibed, but it was always with friends. Maybe a beer in the sunshine, maybe a whiskey after a grueling day at the office, but never the need, the itch, the un-ignorable compulsion, the addiction, the inability to get through the day without the clink of the ice cubes, the metal cap as it twists off the glass bottle, the long unmeasured measure as it flows over the crackling cubes and into the tumbler.

I hold the globe of burgundy liquid in my hand, simultaneously repelled yet compelled to drink it. I sip and feel the velvet richness on my tongue. It floods into my cheeks and runs over my taste buds again, down my throat, warming and leaving a trail that begs to be followed with another sip, and another.

Shit, I'm method drinking.

But I don't have to get drunk to see what his motivation was. It was because of me. It was my fault. He drank because of me.

The infamous chords crash down, and I steady the glass on the bar top and get to my feet. It's pretty ironic, really, as the things that aren't steady are the two I'm standing on. I catch myself on the bar and ground my feet to the floor—not easy when on a rolling ship and three glasses of wine deep—and applaud the pianist, who bids us few standing soldiers goodnight and closes the lid on the ivories.

I take the petite glass jar full of rice crackers, wasabi peas—I'll pick those out—and nuts and pour a little handful into my palm.

With peas extracted and left in a neat line on the bar, in three pinches I fill my mouth and munch on the salty goodies.

"Do you like the peas, Cedric? They're a bit spicy for me."

"Erm, no, madam."

"Ah. Shame."

A rice cracker fizzes and dissolves to nothing on my tongue.

"Cedric?"

"Yes, madam?"

"Cedric, are there rules about playing the piano?"

"It's not encouraged, madam."

"Ah. S'not encouraged. Ah. I see. But you won't tell anyone on me, will you?"

"Depends if you sound any good, madam." Cedric smiles his bright white smile and winks.

I take the stubborn cell phone out of my pocket and lay it on the bar. I check its dull face again, and even muddled in Pinot Noir as my brain is, I recall I wouldn't receive messages now anyway. I am quite, quite drunk. And, damn it, I should be! I was supposed to be here with the love of my life. Instead, I am drunk, by myself, the bartender and some lovey-dovey — oh, shoot me — couple.

With a stumble, I launch toward the piano.

S'like a bike. You don't forget how to play.

I used to be good, well, passable. I played those audition pieces until my fingers were nubs.

I sit at the piano stool without falling off, or back, and anchor my fingers to the ivories.

The chord has drama. Nothing else follows as my memory blanks, but it is a *very* good chord. I look up, and from the darkness of bar, Cedric smiles again.

"Go on then. Show me what you can do."

I don't really think about notes or chords, or the fact I haven't played in years. My fingers, warm with wine, find the keys, stretch, and press.

And there they are, quite without thought or attention, and then, after one chord strike, my mouth opens, and out tumbles the words to Eponine's "On My Own" from *Les Miserables.* The song is completely perfect for someone deserted, with such an ideal of their love who doesn't give a fuck. The fingering comes back, as do the words and emotions which I, for once, do not have to look for motivation to conjure. It's all there: music from my marrow, tripping off my lips with saliva, rolling down my cheeks in grief.

There is masochistic joy; it's almost therapeutic, and I sweep my hair back and crash into the climax. As my fingers slow, I drop my head, focusing on the keys, which my fingers miraculously seem to find, but my eyes are having real trouble differentiating.

Quietly, as I end the ballad, I fold the lid and wipe the tears from my cheeks.

In the background, somewhere from the bar direction, a lone pair of hands claps air between them. I close my eyes, breathe, and look up.

The couple on the banquette have left. Clearly, I was a big success. Yet the lone clapping continues.

I peer into the darkness of the bar and expect the smile of Cedric to shine some light on his clapping hands, but it's not Cedric. There is another person present—shiny shoes, trousers, white shirt, sports coat...

My stomach launches into my mouth. "Cole?"

The figure gets up from the stool and walks toward me. With the light shining in my face, all I can see is his dark shadow, large shoulders coming closer, until...

"Hey! Either the lounge singer has gotten much prettier, or I am drunker than I thought."

He is not Cole.

Of course he is not Cole! Enna, get it through your thick head: Cole is not here and will not be here. He is a drunk, and he does not care.

My disappointment in Cole and in my own stupidity seems to absorb my answer, and I remain painfully embarrassed and rudely mute.

"Well, this is my first drink of the night, so I don't think it's the latter." His American twang kicks in, though from which state I am too addled to tell. It takes a moment for my brain to translate that he means "latter" not "ladder."

"Oh. Well, I've had plenty. But I know I am not the lounge singer. I'm Enna."

"Yes, I know."

"You know I'm not the singer, or you know my name?"

"Both, actually. I'm Tim."

"Huh?" I look into the light more closely at this stranger, and the wooden, stable piano stool beneath me just vanishes. "Oh, fuck."

I hit the carpet with a bump, and now I just hear his laughter, so rich and round and annoying. There's a flurry of hands, "sorrys," and "excuse mes" in a split second, and he pulls me to my feet. The red carpet retreats.

"And now I can say I know you by beautiful face, melodic voice, and acrobatics from a piano stool!"

"Excuse me?"

"I'm Tara's…well, I suppose you could say we work together."

My hand is still in his, but he re-clasps and gives it a proper shake of acknowledgement.

He's Tara's what?

Perhaps it's the seeming familiarity he has, his casual way, that makes me a little suspicious, or perhaps it's the alcohol that makes me paranoid, but I am reluctant to move. He urges me to follow him and I root myself firm despite my previous wobble.

"Come on, let's sit over there." He takes my arm as well as my hand, and with me unable to shuck him off, he double-handedly steers me to the banquette nearest the bar.

Cedric appears through the swing door, and it's a comfort to see his broad smile.

"Cedric, I'll take two waters please."

"Sure thing."

Tim has two heads. He might be handsome. His heads seem to be nicely proportioned ones, just with the wrong number of features, which is a smidgen alarming. In duplicate, I am not overly sure which of the four eyes I should focus on. I fix my eyes on his mouth instead. There are only two of those, and they overlap, so if I go for the center, surely I'll be focusing in the right direction.

"Tara's an angel. She's been excited for your visit. It's been a good distraction for her."

"She is an angel," I repeat. Something we can agree on at least. "When I arrived in America, we hadn't seen each other for years, and she just took me in, no questions…found me a job…though shhh! I'm not supposed to tell anyone about that!"

"Your secret is safe!"

"Sssshe lent me her clothes. She helped me…Did I tell you she took me in? We hadn't seen each other for…years! Took me in!"

"Yes, you said."

"She's like an underwire bra. Supportive and uplifting!"

I am shitfaced.

He laughs. "I like you!"

Cedric places the two glasses, jingling with perfect cubes of ice, between us.

"You met Tara at drama school?"

"Yes. That's right. She went to Broadway afterward, and I ran a theater into the ground, but other than career success, we're both pretty similar."

"You have a fabulous voice."

"ARE YOU FLIRTING WITH ME?"

I am definitely ssshitfaced. www.shitfaced.com/ennapetersen.

I don't know where it came from.

Where did it come from?

Maybe I have Tourette's.

He laughs again. Why is he laughing? Why is that so annoying?

"I mean…what I meant was…"

"No. Not flirting. Complimenting. I know a good voice when I hear one."

"Phooey!" I say, managing to spray more than I say, dusting his lapel with a little pinot saliva.

"Well, I am the entertainment director of the ship. I hope I'm able to pick out a good voice. Otherwise, you are in for a really long week on board."

Shizzle.

"You're the entertainman-er. Ah. I'm really verrrrr professional, you know."

"I'm sure. You're on vacation. Holiday."

"Well, I was supposed to be, Tom."

"Tim."

"Exactly. But I wasn't supposed to be here on my own. I was supposed to be—"

"I gathered from the song."

"But he didn't come! Cole was supposed to join me. I sent him a ticket, but—" *hic* "—he didn't come! Never appeared. We sailed and he didn't! I was so sure he would come, Tom—"

"Tim."

"Tim! Yes, and it's just so ironic—though not in a mildly amusing Alanis Morrisette way—that I had to choose between my fiancé and my theater, and I lost them both. I lost them! And I thought I could win him back, but what's the point? He's some alcoholic who couldn't give a damn, and I'm a washed up director, actress, yoga-imposter and…what the fuck am I going to do?"

He chuckles. Chuckles? He seems to find my heartache endlessly entertaining.

"You are not washed up…maybe a little lit up right now, but you'll feel better in the morning. After a bucket full of coffee. Enna, this business is hard. Life is hard, but it's just like horse riding: when you're thrown off, you get back on."

My eyes flicker. What is he saying? He wants me to go show jumping with horses or something? His two mouths move in duplicate. It's quite mesmerizing, the shape of his top lip that curves from rosy pink to tan skin pixilated with brown stubble.

"But I can't go show jumping. I haven't ridden for years."

The mouths move slower, the noise deeper and less distinct, a record being slowed, and with my head held up by my palm, my elbow slides across the table, and the lights go out.

Chapter 19

Oh. My. Head. How can blinking be an effort? And yet, it is. I have to try several times before successfully parting partnering lids.

Where the fuck am I?

The shoes peeking from the open cupboard door appear to be mine. The view from the balcony, the furniture, the mirror lurking there to frighten me, all suggest that I am, in fact, *dans ma chambre.* My cabin. *Thank God.*

I lift myself from the pillow, and it's then that I feel them — the evil team of midget Irish dancers doing *Riverdance* on my brain.

Oh. And the remembrances of yesterday rush to mind and amplify the pounding. I roll to the right, to the bedside bottle of water, and see the sky and the ocean in the distance. What a perfect view it would have been for the two of us to wake up to.

Would have been.

My unattainable expectations dance before me as I huddle, a little lone kidney bean-shaped woman in a large, overly empty bed. The soporific sway of the water beneath, the motion of the ocean is comforting in its constant, reassuring presence.

I am not drowning. Not drowning. Not drowning.

I grab hold of the white linen, ruffling the precisely-tucked sheets on *his* side, clinging on as if this rectangle of fabric and wood and metal springs is some precious raft. This king-sized disappointment, where my hopes curl up in the fetal position and cry themselves dry.

I can't believe he didn't show.

How could he not show?

It was supposed to be so perfect.

The perfect reunion to show him how much he meant to me, to prove that I was committed. And yet he was the one who didn't care in the end. It was He, the capitalized version, my Him, my rock, my Cole. Not mine at all. Oh, and all that money! What a waste. What a bloody waste!

A fresh fall of tears run their regular course. I am almost surprised they have not, by this stage, eroded my freckled skin, carving grooves from cheek to chin. But I am still whole. A disillusioned Alice in Wonderland, crossed with Dorian Gray.

The ship rocks and rolls. The noises from the corridor of deck nine punctuate my thoughts—a slam here, a door handle grind there.

"Hello! And how are you today, Mr. and Mrs. Calloway?" sing-songs the ever-attendant deck nine manager.

I pull the sheets higher, over me, cocooning as I used to in my sleeping bag when I was young, and my mind falls to the place it can't help but plummet to; it's drawn there magnetically, kinetically, chemically: where is he and what is he doing now?

Is he having breakfast with her? Is he alone? Is he already at work, having a drink to take the edge off? Is he thinking about me at all?

A flash of reality bolts me upward, away from yellow gingham kitchen scenes of Cole being content without me.

Tom! Tim! How did I get back here?

I examine the fully clothed, puffy-eyed, bed-headed vision of unkemptness in the mirror. Surely a temptress of the night!

But really, he's Tara's friend. I would remember if he touched or kissed me.

My shoes are neatly lined up, my zipper and buttons still firmly zipped and buttoned. Thank God. That would have added a new great low to my pit of pathetic self-pity:

BRAZEN BROAD ABOARD!—Yes, it's bon voyage to decorum as recently failed theater director boards the good ship *HMS Inhibition* and says tallyho to sobriety and her underwear!

The knock at the door interrupts the news headings echoing through my brain, and I will my wobbly legs to move.

The cabin manager is there, all smiles, with a tray and folding table.

I must look puzzled. He continues to smile and gestures — rather like he's shaking imaginary laundry or something. I stand back and let him enter and fuss about.

As he uncovers the metal lid, revealing a plate of toast, scrambled eggs and crispy bacon, I try to interrupt him, to say he has the wrong room, but my tongue summons a syllable and just stops. "Per…per… per…per."

By the time he lays out the napkin, the cutlery, and leaves for the door, no "haps" has followed.

The Irish dance troupe has vacated my head and instead kicks their little cloggy dance shoes into my stomach. I am starving. My head and hunger are clearly in league against my mouth and override any complaint. It does look very nice, the bacon just that right kind of crisp, the eggs that right kind of scramble solid. So I limp feebly to the table, sit on the edge of the bed, and watch the ocean chop and swoosh as I survey the feast and the stiff white card propped between the *cafetière* and the tall glass of orange juice. It's obviously not a menu, and the handwritten cursive confirms that at a glance.

At first, I imagine it is handwritten from Cole. He used to do such things — leave me notes, send me gifts. I fold the card together in my hand, so I can't read or see the writing, keeping alive for just one second more the hope that it could be — it could be — from him. I pour myself a cup of coffee, the weight of the card sinking fast into my lap. I allow myself one long, restorative sip. The strong, thick brown liquid draws me to attention, opens my eyes wider, shunts blood to my capillaries, and my fingers twitch at the feel of the card smooth against their rough whorls.

It won't be from Cole.

Breathe.

It'll probably be a sweet, thoughtful gesture from Tara.

I slide my hand between two thick leaves and spread the card flat on my lap.

My eye connects with the opening and the closing, sweeping past the middle.

Dear Erna,
Cheerio and pip-pip!
Tim.

I collapse back on the bed, the embarrassing visions of myself taunting me as they replay and rewind, replay and rewind, always with the same graceless, classless, drunken slur and unremembered ending. It takes a forkful of eggs, a rasher of bacon, and another three glugs of coffee before I feel at all able to even peer at the wide loops of blue ink on the card.

Oh God, Tara's boss, the entertainment director! I verbally vomited on the entertainment director! If actually chunk-blowing vomiting at a couple's feet wasn't bad enough, then I hurl drama at Tom.

Tim!

Damn it!

I need to do yoga. Food, then shower, then yoga. Maybe then I can face reading it.

But after another rasher of bacon, I fold, pick the card off the floor from where it has unceremoniously been flicked, and I read.

Dear Erna,

I hope you are feeling better this morning. I thought this breakfast might help. I always need a good hearty breakfast after a liver workout. ☺

I'm rehearsing in the auditorium at 12pm. I'd be so glad if you'd join me. Do wear flat-soled shoes if you have them.

Cheerio and pip-pip,
Tim.

Oh God. I can't not go, can I? I've been summoned for public ridicule.

Breathe.

I hear Mallory's voice resound in my brain. It cuts through the whirring hive of "what ifs" and embarrassment, and mines to the core, the reality, the *satya*. I am the one standing in my way. I am creating obstacles for myself. It's simple. I should be gracious and go.

Let go of what doesn't serve you.

Life is all about choices. You choose to be happy.

You can be the victim or the victor.

The Malloryisms repeat and resound.

I have been choosing drama. I have been making this whole shituation about me, and it's not really, is it? I am not responsible for Cole's choices. I cannot be responsible for Cole's choices, and the more I obsess about things I cannot control, the more I react to it, get wasted and self-destruct, the more unhappy and dissatisfied I will be. And it's a cycle, a loop of feedback; the more I play into the drama, the more drama the universe will dump at my feet.

So what now?

Can I let go of the need to be right, to win, to direct the show, to be so rigidly fixed on my version of how things are supposed to be? Maybe just focusing on me and being happy with myself like I was — almost by accident — in Park Slope, being consciously aware of my choices…maybe that — that — is what I should strive for?

I sigh out a long exhale. It seems a poetic way to release the thoughts, like a tangible knot of hot air blocking my throat is being expelled. And I feel some kind of satisfaction and relief and accomplishment in my self-diagnosis.

In my clothes from the previous night, with *Riverdance* now somewhere in the distance in the far right of my head, I open up the balcony sliding door for a fresh breath. The ship carves through the Atlantic deep below me at some pace, and the wind whips my hair like a raging Medusa. I open my eyes wide to the endless vision of blues and grays. Blue is truth, *satya*. Maybe now I can see into the truth of things as they really are. Maybe now I will find the voice to communicate what I want. Maybe.

I reach my hands high overhead and feel the delightful stretch of my arms, my spine, my neck, and then I fold like a rag doll, enjoying the rush of blood to my head and the engagement of muscles as my hamstrings extend. I dangle and it's then, apropos of nothing, that I recall something missing.

Where's my phone?

I snap to attention and back to vertical, eyeing the bedside from the deck. One alarm clock, the old glass with the dregs of rum runner cocktail from the day before, but a quick glance yields little else. I dash back into the cabin. I check my shoes. Maybe Tim placed it in my shoe? Nothing.

It shouldn't be this important. I can't get messages anyway, and yet...

In the stale clothes from the night before, I hustle as fast as my legs and body can go to the bar with the lounge singer. There are couples loitering, admiring the artwork, enjoying a coffee and the view of the vast, choppy waves.

"Hello, my name is Armando from the Philippines" stands up from behind the bar, pouring a carton of juice into a plastic container.

"Hi! Hello. I was here last night and I believe I left my cell phone here?"

"You want a drink?"

"Oh, no. I was just looking for my phone. I left it here. I think. A cell phone? Mobile?"

"I don't know. You ask ship services, lost and found, deck four."

"Okay. You're sure it's not here? I was at the bar very late. Oh, what's his name...Cyril...Cedric! Cedric from Cameroon was bartending."

"Sorry, ma'am. There is the cleaning crew that came through before I opened the bar this morning. There was nothing here. Try lost and found."

"Thanks anyway, Armando."

Between the bar and the center of deck four is ship services. I breathe and realize that this is not the calamity it might be elsewhere. I can't receive calls anyway, and does it mean in a week when I disembark that I am cut off from Cole? Well, maybe that is as it is meant to be. No temptation to leave questioning late-night texts.

The petite blonde, "Hello my name is Agata from Norway," sits behind the help desk, waving me across the marble-esque flooring. I explain this, my latest thoughtless move, and Agata nods sympathetically. She makes a few calls, a few clicks of the computer, but ultimately the initial search yields nothing. She promises to let me know if it's found. She is cheery and hopeful, but my gut cannot return her positive sentiments.

Chapter 20

"Darling!" Tim cries as I emerge through the unlit auditorium, freshly showered hair wet and beating against my back. The cast stops collectively and turns toward me. I had been trying to be discreet, but Tim is obviously welcoming the interruption.

He strides down stage right and guides me up the stairs that lead from the auditorium.

Tara gives me a small wave, and the circle of actors opens into a crescent around me.

"Guys, I want you to meet Enna. She is an actress and director and has the most delightful sound."

Fifteen pairs of eyes are on me. Assessing.

Remember, a graceful lady accepts compliments.

I smile back and mouth a thank you in Tim's general direction. I look into the eager faces, all so incredibly young and tanned. I feel proportionately old and pale. He asks the cast to introduce themselves and give a brief snippet of background. It's jolly nice of him and really welcoming. I must have given him quite the sorrowful story last night for him to give me such special treatment.

I try to catch Tara's eye, but she remains steadfastly fixed on each cast member until it is her turn. "Well, you know me. But I haven't told what fun I have been having with this cast and crew. It's really been such a great opportunity, and any performer would be lucky to be on stage with you guys." She wraps her bright red cardigan around her, and Tim, clearly enjoying all these testimonies of how great this ship's production is, grips her arm for reassurance.

"That's great, guys. Why don't we sing something for Enna? One from tonight's show."

Through some performer telepathy and series of nods, the cast launches into their version of "A Whole New World" from Disney's *Aladdin*.

Tara takes my hand and lays her sheet music on the piano in front of us. "Sing! Join in," she whispers in my ear.

I look at the open throats and impassioned faces around me. They are all going for it, having fun. Why not?

Tara squeezes my hand again and smiles at me. "Louder!" she mouths between verses.

I laugh and carry on, swept away by the infectious Disney melodic magic! It's like being back at National Youth Theater, standing around a piano, believing that talent would take me places, that I could go anywhere, be anyone.

One of the crew hands Tara a microphone, and the cast hushes as she starts the next verse on her own. She has such a mellifluous voice. She recaptures my hand but sings to the tall lead man she pirouetted, back flipped and generally canoodled with on stage yesterday. He takes a step forward into the circle and takes the microphone, singing the "Azaddin" part next. I didn't see it from the balcony yesterday, as I was blinded by Tara's sequins, but he's really very good.

I sway uncontrollably. This is delightful. Quite the tonic after yesterday's disappointments. And then, it's there. The black metal mesh over the top of the mic directed in my face.

Oh. Blimey.

They want me to sing. The piano plays on, regardless of the fact Princess Jasmine should be high on her magic carpet right about now.

Tara nods expectantly.

I swallow and open my throat and…floating somewhere on the Atlantic, somewhere between New Jersey and Bermuda, I find my voice—my sober, balanced voice—and some unexpected kind of happiness and truth.

Azaddin and I finish the rest of the duet, and as the final chords are struck, there is just silence. Tim exchanges looks with Tara, then Azaddin, then the cast.

Well, this is awkward.

I busy myself with finding the off switch on the microphone and setting it down on the piano top.

"Good job." The pianist nods, closing the lid.

"Yes, good job, everyone!" Tim choruses. "Okay, why don't you get back to your run-through and I'm going to take Enna here on a tour."

"Bye, Enna!" they sing-song in harmony.

Tim places his arm around me, ushering me through the stage right curtain. Pieces of set fly overhead, and larger pieces like the polystyrene rock of last night's mermaid musical sit inert in the wings, waiting for the lights and the velvet to lift.

We pass through the green room and dressing room, Tim enjoying his new role as tour guide, waxing lyrical about the shows he was in and the places he traveled to.

"I started as a company member in two thousand and one. The theater scene in New York is not what it had been because of 9/11. I got lucky, as I missed the auditions—they're held in Great Britain—but I met someone who knew someone, and bam! I got the role. Now I get to travel the world!"

As we circle all the way around and he chatters on, uninhibitedly, in the darkness of the wings—stage left now—I realize I haven't, in fact, spoken for twenty minutes. After we have relived the highs and highers of his fifth "tour," he pauses long enough for me to interject.

"That's really so fabulous, Tim. But, and forgive me if this sounds blunt, but why are you telling me all this?"

"Ah. Yeah. Sorry, I get a bit carried away. I guess I wanted to paint the vision of how we operate, how this all works. You see, Enna, this is a unique setup we have here."

He's rather like an American Hugh Grant, I realize, with his floppy hair that seems to have expressions all of its own and his enthusiastic roundabout explanations.

"When performers audition for the production company in England—yes, your mother country—they put the cast, set, costumes, everything together, and the ship buys in the productions for a set amount of time. We are on a seven-month run. After that, the set and costumes will go to another ship with another cast. We can apply to audition for another tour, perhaps with a different ship, perhaps the same; maybe with different cast members, maybe the same. But here's the thing: we get close like family. It's hard work, but it's also a great deal of fun. We sweat together, dance together, laugh, cry and get drunk together."

With his arm in front leading the way and his other hand in the small of my back, he leads me out into the auditorium, ignoring the performers on stage, and out past the seats to the deck. I turn to catch Tara's eye on stage, to wave goodbye, maybe mouth something inappropriate to put her off her lines, but as I turn she does too, and her glance is uncatchable. Like a foul ball, it goes in the opposite direction.

"So you've been blunt with me. Now I get to be blunt with you, but it's rather…what would you Brits say…delicate?" He pushes open the door to the outer deck, and we walk into the wall of wind.

"I'm listening," I say a little louder, my mind a mix of expectation and trepidation as to what he might be about to say.

"She wanted to tell you herself, but I felt it was best if I handled it."

"Who?"

"Tara."

"What? She hasn't told me anything. I've barely seen her but to throw up everywhere beside her. Long story. What's wrong?"

"Tara got a message yesterday, just before we left, that her mother has been taken to the hospital. She's not doing well."

"Oh, no." I stop walking.

Tim continues talking. "Obviously, Tara wants to go to her, but the contracts are strict. I mean, we perform come headache, stomach ache, sprains and pains. We practically have to bleed from our eyes not to go on. We have swing singer-dancers we could promote, but then we end up a singer-dancer short, and then…there is you. Tara says you were a great performer."

"Me?"

"And judging from last night's impromptu song and the number on stage just now, I think you would be a great replacement. You are the same shape, height, vocal range. You did say last night that this vacation wasn't going to be what you had anticipated. So how about it?"

"How about what? What exactly are you saying, Tom?"

"Tim."

"Damn!"

"I'm saying, would you be willing to learn Tara's parts and step in so she can fly back to Blighty and look after her mom? It means, of course, you'd be onboard for more than a week, but that might be a good thing? Right? I'd sort out all the logistics. You wouldn't have to worry about a thing."

Holy, giant cock-a-doodle doo.

"I would. For Tara, I absolutely would, but...but I can't stay! I mean, there's the apartment, the yoga studio. There's my extended visa—that's granted on the proviso that I don't work. Legally, I just don't think I can, Tim."

"I know. It sounds crazy, but Enna, hear me out! It's not a US work visa you need; you won't be working in the US. How do you think the British cast does it? It's a special type of visa. You can't work in the US, but we never have shows when we are in port. It's okay. I can pull strings. This is not my first rodeo. If you are willing, I am able!"

"But...Well, there's a lot to think about. A lot. I mean...aside from the fact I haven't actually performed for years, Tara's landlady expects me back. The yoga studio I help at expects me back..."

"Nothing's insurmountable. So, is there any reason why you wouldn't want to step back under the spotlight?"

The wind buffets my face. What am I thinking? Am I even contemplating this?

Enna, are you bonkers?

It's been literally years since I performed. Directing is different. Very, very different.

"But what about Cole?" I blurt out and spill to the breeze, to the seas.

"Ah! The real objection! Of course, this is a matter for you. Certainly if you want to charge back to Scranton and stand at his door—yes, you were very chatty as I took you to bed; don't worry, I was a complete gentleman—then be my guest, but I think we both know that ship has sailed. Pun intended."

I can feel the strain of my brow puckering. He stops me and turns me around, the wind rippling my long locks into his face.

"Think about it, Enna. You can learn the parts this week and sail with us for a few extra weeks as Tara does what she needs to do, and then she'll come back and relieve you. You'd be earning money and getting to travel."

"There's nothing to think about. If Tara needs me, I'm in."

Chapter 21

"You could have told me, you know."

"What? Welcome aboard, sorry Cole fucked you over, and, by the way, I think my mother is dying. Yes, I can see that would have been quite the delightful bon voyage!"

"You know what I mean."

We sit in the spa on deck ten, swathed in black capes, with two stylists fussing around us. The male stylist combs through my long hair, tutting at the wind-teased tangles and holding it at different lengths next to my face to find something that inspires us. The female stylist holds different swatches of hair to Tara's roots. We have decided we both need a change and a treat before the intensive rehearsals and performances begin.

"I have a wig for every show, Enna. You don't have to lop it all off on my account. Don't go crazy."

The stylist, "Hello, my name is Mario from Argentina," seems to second that emotion. "I have to ask you, you are not having babies or…what is this word…'ormonal?"

"Definitely not having babies. Do you usually ask your clients that, or is it just me?" I dare to ask, warily watching the scissors and razor lined up on the tray next to him.

"Oh, but sure. With troubles of the heart, ladies often want to change their hairs something drastical." He is so animated and horrified by the thought of "drastical" change, and I just want to hug him for his wide-eyed sincerity.

"It's okay, Mario. I need a change. I've held on to this same old, tired straight hair for so long. I want you to do something that will fit under Tara's wigs, something quick and easy that won't make me look like an alien."

"You've got it! I will do beautiful thing for your hairs."

Tara and I exchange glances and squeeze extended hands. Mario gestures for me to follow him to the sink, and "Hello, my name is Celeste from France" slaps some unbelievably blond paste onto Tara's head.

After an hour or so, I am washed, deep conditioned and combed through, and a halo of cut hair surrounds my chair. Not just little bits here and there, but hanks. Tens of inches of hanks.

It's fine. It looks longer when it's wet. Those skeins of hair lying sprawled over the floor are really much shorter than they seem. Anyway, if I don't like it, it will grow. It's replaceable.

For the first time in my life, that I can remember that is, there is no great weight, no scarf of heat around my neck, my shoulders, my back. I sit upright, touching the fine hairs on the back of my neck. My fingers expect to comb through inches, but instead they rake the air. It's official. I have done something "drastical."

"This is great for your eyes. You don't want to hide behind that hair. You have the beauty face to show to the world."

I'm not sure. Is that me? I feel brave and frightened silly at the same time. And I know it's only a haircut. I know in the light of recent parental health news, it is nothing. It also feels like something momentous, something indefinable. Some shift has taken place.

"Now, Mario, I do hope you are going to bag that hair up and send it to a charity like Locks of Love, right?"

Typical, thoughtful Tara!

"*Si!* Sure."

We peel off our capes and detach our stares from the mirror. My hand cannot stop bobbing up to the back of my neck, just to check. Is this what petting a squirrel would feel like?

We promenade the deck, ascending the steps to overlook the pool and, I admit, it is rather nice not having to extract hair from my lip gloss and eyelashes. There are no tendrils to whip in the wind.

Whip it off, whip it on, and move!

We find two vacant sun loungers and recline. It's still too cool to sunbathe, and I am covered from head to toe in yoga wear, but the sun is there, peeking out from between the clouds, brightening the afternoon. It feels good to close my eyes and absorb it all. What a crazy twenty-four hours.

"Do you have your phone?" I turn my cheek to Tara's lounger and squint in her direction.

"Of course. It'll get no signal here though. Why?"

"It appears I may have drunkenly misplaced my phone."

"No!"

"Yes. So I went to ship services and have reported it missing in action. Hopefully someone will turn it in."

"Shit."

"My sentiments exactly. But while I am phoneless here, pass me yours?"

"Sure, but…you won't get a signal."

"For photos, of course."

There on the breezy deck, as the sun passes through the clouds and we plough through the surface of the sea, we click a ridiculous amount of silly poses, pouts and open-mouthed laughter. We capture our renewed old friendship perfectly.

The lift doors open, and we alight on deck four and stand at the door of the auditorium, ready for our first rehearsal.

Here goes nothing. Or maybe everything!

Tara opens the large swing door that is always closed for rehearsals and quickly shuts it again, pausing before we go in. "I just want to say thank you. I know this journey so far has not been what you were hoping for, but isn't it weird the way the universe works? I needed you here and you were! Providence or divine intervention or something, but here you are."

My thoughts leap to Cole.

Did some divine or mystic intervention stop him from being here because I needed to look after my friend and not concentrate on him?

That's impossible. He is just an unreliable man I expected more from.

"Anyway, I want you to know I do appreciate this and my mum does too. I know she does." She pushes the great swing door open again, and we enter the auditorium, holding hands tightly.

I spend the next hour following Tara like her shadow, noting how she sets each costume change, watching like some strange voyeur as she applies her thick pancake makeup—the smell so achingly familiar to me—how she tapes her microphone and feeds it into a belt secured on her hip by her knickers, how she sings scales as she completes her sound check, her yoga-esque physical warm up. My head might explode with all the minutiae I try to log.

I'd read, oh somewhere on the Internet, that the average number of thoughts a day was fifty thousand. As I feel my brain spark with new nuggets of the order of things, cramming in this precise and practiced routine of Tara's, I bet I am logging at least a hundred thousand. No wonder she eats so much kale to keep her sharp and active.

Note to self: eat more kale.

I watch tonight's shows from the wings, script and score in hand, scribbling directions in the margins by the light of my little torch headset. I feel less of a spy, more a stage miner. The show is full of Disney-sounding songs that seem familiar and different, a slight change in key and lyrics, but ultimately the same melody. Lord, let's hope I don't revert to the popular known version and flout every copyright regulation under the sun.

It's fast and furious backstage, the dancers jeté-ing off into the wings, stripping as they go—here a nipple, there a nipple—appearing less than sixty seconds later with a new costume, wig and pair of dance shoes.

As the company sings the finale on stage after an hour of frenetic activity, I think I might be more exhausted than Tara. She smiles at the audience, unabashed in her Amazonian, Jane of the Jungle-type leopard print bikini top and loin cloth, batting her false eyelashes so hard she might take flight. Her *Zarzan*—even consonants must be sacrificed to save on royalty fees, it seems—with his orange glow of perma-spray tan, looks adoringly at her, and—oh, dear God—hoists her into his Day-Glo arms, grabs a rope, and swings her off into the wings.

I agreed to sing, but it seems a knowledge of ropes, silks, and aerial gymnastics is a bonus, and sadly, *Fifty Shades of Grey* is no help here.

"What was that?" I ask breathlessly as she enters the dressing room and peels off her spidery lashes.

"You didn't like the show?"

"No, the show's great. You are great. My faith in my upper body strength—even after the one hundred and eight daily *chaturangas*—is not so great! Tara, do I really look like the kind of person who has ever climbed a rope?"

"Don't stress. Honestly, you'll be surprised by what you can do when you have someone to show you how."

"Okay. Fine. If I shouldn't be worried, I won't be. I am just saying, when I swing out into the audience, slip, and land on some poor pensioner's replaced hip, I am not responsible!"

"Of course not."

"And Zarzan needs to know he might have to do more lifting than he is used to."

She is effortlessly beautiful and unflustered, and in minutes has peeled out of her Amazon leopard print and poured herself into aqua silk. It's simple, the lines just skating her curves, and yet it is completely divine, refined, and so Gatsby. "Do you like it? I borrowed it from Chelsea. She's the dancer with the brunette bob and the infectious smile."

"I love it! I can be found feeling utterly jealous at greenwithenvy-dot-com."

Herbie, or "Erbay" as he pronounces it, our little waiter from Honduras, welcomes us at the door and shows us to the central table. Tara, my role-to-be, is quite the beloved celebrity onboard I see. There are air-kisses and compliments as I get accustomed to the dim lighting, the wacky orange plastic furniture and black chandeliers.

"Oh! You are Tara's friend! Well, it is my pleasure to look after you tonight, laaaaaaddies!" Herbie flicks his wrists with delight. "Here are your two iPads. One of you has to be captain!" He giggles excitedly. "Is it you or you?"

I have no idea what he is asking, but Tara defers to me and tells him we'll have a bottle of the Veuve Clicquot. He almost skips to the glass-fronted wine cellar refrigerator and appears within seconds at my elbow, popping the cork with aplomb.

As instructed, I click on the screen and swipe through the choices.

"Life is all about choices!" we chorus, relishing our favorite Malloryism.

Each page gives another cuisine option. I see that staying aboard ship will allow the perk of getting to try all of these!

We select three cuisine choices and sip our champagne with giddy pleasure. Cole seems a million miles away. I catch myself laughing, and it strikes me as so odd that my brain is able to forget what has happened so very quickly, that the impulses to contract and expand the muscles around my mouth and form a smile could be so easily coaxed and created. Tara laughs too, yet thousands of miles away her mum lies in a hospital bed.

How can our bodies be so mutinous and be able to laugh and smile? It's almost insulting. For a second, maybe a minute, I let the melancholy of the shituation strike.

I could be enjoying moments like this at this bizarre little place with him, tasting all these mini-dishes and creating our own memories here, with the man I believed was the love of my life.

The world spins, and shit happens.

Herbie appears, all arms and flourishes, presenting the first round of little tapas dishes presented in a wooden box, almost like a doll's house, each open-faced room containing another Mediterranean specialty. I load the triangle of fresh pita bread with dollops of the eggplant and tomato, while Tara explains the apparent primary school level of athletic ability that is needed to "fly" on stage. I may be happier when I am fed, but I am not that gullible. Certainly, though with a surplus of delicious munchies to try — the hummus, the lamb chop, the chicken skewer, the tzatziki — my acrobatic neurosis is quelled for a while. A lady cannot argue *and* eat.

Over our second platter, the Italian selection — a collection of enormous meatballs stuffed with different surprise fillings — I listen as Tara tells me of childhood holidays and her mum's insistence on always packing sandwiches to the beach, which, with the Essex's wind from the Channel, would always be literally and figuratively *sand*wiches.

"Mum would say that dirt in anything was good for the immune system. A little grit in your cheese sandwich and that was extra minerals. Not just food either, but any gritty, shitty situation and she dubbed it as 'character-building!'"

"My mum would say things like that. Maybe it was the 'make do and mend' fallout after the war," I mumble through my mouthful.

"True. I wish you had met my mum," she adds wistfully.

And I truly wish I could remember; I rewind all those years, flashing through freeze frames of all those eager faces of parents looking stageward, but faces and names blend into a sepia reel of "past."

"She has always been my greatest cheerleader. When I came out to the US, during the lean times when I thought I would never book an audition, she told me that I could do it. She just had complete faith in me. She would send me these crazy care boxes, like I was some evacuee. Humph! Maybe you're right about that post-war mentality." She sips her champagne.

I stroke my hair and listen.

"Oh God! She would send random things that would make me smile. Nestle Lion bars! She would send chocolate bars, and a new lipstick, cuttings from her *Hello* magazines she thought I'd like, a hand-written letter. She had this emphatic belief that a new lipstick and chocolate would always make a woman feel good."

We chat nonstop through the Italian meatball selection and then through the Indian offerings and, finally defeated, Herbie pours the dregs of the bubbly, and we toast our evening together.

"You will come back soon, won't you? I mean, obviously take as long as you need, but you expect to come back, right?"

"Of course! I wouldn't, I couldn't, leave you with all four months I have left. Don't be silly. I'll message from England. Maybe we can even Skype, but I'll keep you updated."

"Okay."

"Don't look so doom and gloom! What happened to your yogic peace of mind? I am not going to desert you here and leave you prisoner. Promise."

Chapter 22

The next twenty-four hours rush past in a frenzy of sweat, hair pulling, and frequent curses of "What am I doing?" This "only a little dancing thing" is complete and utter bollocks. These are full-on dance routines and more than just a box-step. Tara and Tim—Tom!—Tim spend every moment they are not setting or warming up to run through routines with me, but I am not twenty-one anymore, and the swift kicks and ball-changes seem to take longer. I am forever a beat behind.

We record Tara singing so I can plug in and sing along and copy her sound and intonation.

I don't need to make it my own. I am just seat warming. This is just temporary.

As I help myself to another chunk of fresh pineapple—there seems to be an endless supply of pineapple—I watch the vacationers lying out for the snatches of sunshine, and I am so glad I am not sipping a piña colada, huddled in my towel, alone on the sun-lounger made for two. What was it Mallory said? It was a quote from someone, probably a dead philosopher oft reposted on Facebook.

"The universe is unfolding as it should."

Can it be that Cole was destined to be a drunkard, fated to let me down, so that I would be here for this? To help Tara?

It's a suspensory thought. I can't cut it off. It dangles unanswered as I lick the juice from my fingers, consult the wall clock, and leave the sprawling masses to get back to work.

I thought it would be different on a cruise ship, performing, but that same rush of adrenaline kicks in: the buzz of the challenge to claw into and cling on for the ride. Rehearsals clearly prove I have spent far too long on the other side of the curtain. I constantly correct myself and so desperately want to change the existing, and often pointless, blocking. Has no one ever asked, "What's my motivation here?" It seems to me that much of the blocking is from the school of "stand forward when you have a line." My pet peeve.

Enna, grit your teeth. What does it matter? Breathe. Flow. Be easy.

I watch the shows from the wings again, now getting quite acquainted with the crew whispering into their headsets and the charge stage left or right as the semi-naked dancers rush in and out like a tidal wave. It's fun to watch the interactions behind the scenes, the young dancers flirting with the only heterosexual male in the cast and fawning all over the homosexual ones.

After the two performances, we descend down the stairwell rather than up.

"Technically, you aren't allowed down here yet as you're still considered a guest, but you'll be crew in a matter of days so this is just more rehearsal."

She leads me down into the depths of the ship. The steps here are metal, not the heavily-patterned, fully-carpeted affair of upstairs, and there is no outside deck, so no natural light. It could be midnight or midday, and no one would know.

"While we're talking about where you can and can't go, you'll have to take my room when we port back at Cape Liberty. Another passenger will be booked in your stateroom. I hope you won't mind. It's not all that big or luxurious."

Oh. I had not thought of that, but I smile and shrug. Hardly worth adding to Tara's load and making a bloody fuss.

Enna, you are adaptable. You are evolving. Go with the flow. Be so flowy you make Niagara jealous.

As we peel off the staircase on deck one, I feel evermore that I am in a submarine, that I am sub-marine, underwater, yet I'm breathing.

Watch me breathe.

On the other side of this metal plating, and insulation, and wiring and all the stuff that must protect a hull from the elements, there could be sharks and whales and dolphin just feet away.

The crew lounge is dark and packed full of uniformed crew having a night cap. Faces from the restaurants, the bars, cabin staff, ship's crew, all in various outfits denoting their position. Most of the same color jackets stay together, even at sea. There are clearly vocational cliques. The table surrounded by the sequined, neckline-plunging, corset-cinching, hip-hugging, eyelash batting performers is easy to spot.

Is this post-performance drinkies or, in fact, an orgy?

There are rowdy waves beckoning us over, and the cast shifts and nestles in closer to make room for us. It's rather lovely to feel part of this little community. At the theater in Ashtead, there was never that feeling of being a team, except with Will.

I'm not thinking about that.

It was not your fault, Enna. He was as much of a team player as a mosquito. Anyone would have been sucked in. Sucked up. Fucked up...

We order drinks — there is a crew discount on drinks too! — and we join in the hubbub. I listen as the British accents banter back and forth over the bassy booming in the background. Usually someone is the brunt of a quick line of sarcasm that can only be quintessentially British. It's jocular; it's sophomoric, and it's fun.

I sit next to Chelsea, the petite, brunette dancer — she of the silk aqua dress Tara borrowed. Tonight, Chelsea sparkles in a metallic gray, slim-fitting cat suit, slit to the waist, with precariously-positioned yet perky, bra-less boobs. I suppose when aboard, the company of performers have no other uniform, so why not bedeck themselves in sequins, jumpsuits, and tit-tape? It defines who they are. That and the ability to turn every sentence I utter into the lyrics of a song. It's like some strange otherworld that is part *Glee*, part *Sex and the City*, set in a submarine that sparkles and shines so brightly; it's like the whole of Fairyland vomited glitter on these people. It's been two days of watching and listening and rubbing elbows with these glitterati, and if I hear "Let It Go" randomly belted out mid-sentence for no particular reason, I may run up to deck eleven and throw myself off the side.

Chelsea drinks a Stoli Orange and soda. "It's, like, nothing calorie-wise," she informs me, and as I look around the table, I see that most of the drinks are clear and probably burn more calories lifting the glass than consuming the drink.

It is my third night on board, and each has been doused in alcohol. It fits every occasion: commiseration, celebration, socialization. It's abundant. It's accessible. It's even low-calorie.

Is that how it started for Cole?

"What are you drinking, then?" the gilded Chelsea asks, animatedly moving her arms and jiggling.

Ah! Don't move. Mayday! Nipple on the breach. Repeat, nipple on the breach!

"Oh, wine." I cough, pulling the collar of my shirt closer. "I'm a wine-o. Oh, not a whiner, but definitely a wine-o."

"Never could get on with that, me. I'm just spirits." *Giggle, jiggle, jiggle.*

"That's very devout of you."

"Uh! I see what you did there! Devout, spirits, funny. You're a dark one, you are." The northern accent is so incredibly contagious to my ear, my throat, my mouth, my lips.

Must…control…accent overdrive. Must…signal that boobs are in peril.

I pull the sides of my shirt together again. Isn't every female trained to receive this wardrobe malfunction signal flare?

"Sooo, this is your first time on a ship?"

"Yes. You?"

"Oh, no. I've been on three cruises so far. I love it. I'll probably do this until I burn out at about thirty, and then I'd like to set up my own dance school back home."

I swallow my drink. Burnout age is rapidly approaching. On a cruise ship, I am almost retirement age. How very depressing.

What am I thinking? Second thought!

Thirty! What a great age to embark on new opportunities.

That's better.

"So, where next?"

"Well, truth be told, I really, really wanna get to the *Excelsior*."

"*The Excelsior?*"

"You've not 'eard of the *Excelsior?*"

Clearly, I am as in-the-know as a radish.

"Aw! Well it's only the newest ship in the fleet. It's bigger and better, and the auditorium seats tons more people. The new acts are just amazin'." Her eyes just light up with enthusiasm.

Mine light up with wardrobe concern. "Amazin'," I repeat.

"Yeah, some really wild, left-field ideas, and folks are really enjoyin' it 'pparently."

My interest is piqued. "Oh, aye," I say in brogue, automatically slipping into an accent from somewhere north of Leeds. "How are they left-field? What's so different about 'em?"

Enna! You are not Sean Bean. Stop speaking Northern!

"Oh, not the shows. Like, the company sends us in the same type of show, but they have other acts that take the stage on other nights. It's quite multicultural. They 'ave this Russian couple—I think they are Russian. Maybe they are Lithuanian or sommat. They have this silk dance routine like Cirque du Soleil on crack, and it is supposed to be amaze-balls!"

"Cirque on crack? That's catchy."

She places her vodka down and turns further toward me, double checking her frontage.

Yes, it's still there.

"Then they have this amaze-balls illusionist who flies into port on his own 'elicopter. I've never really been into magic tricks, but this bloke is mega. My friend Shelly—she's a dancer on *Excelsior*—says he makes his assistant disappear like that!" She claps her hands. "And he won't tell any of the cast how he does it. They have drinks together too, but he won't say a word.

"Shelly says the most popular on the ship though is this Irish bloke. He's a bit older, like you."

Charmed, I'm sure!

"And he has this weird show, like, with rapping. Well, not rapping as you think. That would never go down with the old folk, but it's like…fun poetry stuff. I don't know."

It's nothing. It's just a word. An entire music genre, and yet, I gasp.

"Oh, I know. I'm not really into that kind of music, except Jay-Z and Justin Timberlake; I could listen to anything with Justin Timberlake. But this bloke is, like, really intelligent and stuff, and he's supposed to be dead gorgeous."

I draw my chair back. I want to leave.

Enna, that's unreasonable! You are choosing to react to this.

"You all right? You look a bit peaky."

Tara leans over. "Oh God, you're not going to puke again are you, *mon petit* puker! *Merde!*" She turns to the other ruddy faces flushed with laughter and Stoli. "You should have seen her on the first day. A couple of sips of martini, and Holy Pukeville, right on the outside deck! Don't worry, *ma petite*, you'll get used to it! I had to wear one of the ear plasters for my whole first week."

I smile thinly and without teeth. What's a little poetic seasickness between friends? "I think I need some air. I feel…claustrophobic down here."

"You'll get used to it!"

"Feel better."

"We'll be in Bermuda by morning!"

I press the button for the lift and gnaw my cuticles as I watch the illuminated floor numbers above the door go up, not down. I turn toward the staircase. I must get up into the air, into the moonlight. I climb the first flight two stairs at a time, then break into a run and shorten my stride, dodging the older couples in their bugle-beaded jackets and pantsuits.

At deck ten, I have run and climbed the panic out of me. Panting for air, breathing is now more urgent than thinking, or remembering. I fill my lungs with Atlantic breezes, my new crop leaving no locks to buffer the breeze and cover my face. I can see everything around for miles. I can see another cruise ship in the distance, like a toy, lit with hundreds of little windows.

Could he be on a boat? Is that why the police haven't found him? Because he's not ever-so-English Will, but some charming Irishman, some Dylan, or Shane, or Patrick, using his cunning linguistics to have audiences, women, lone females traveling and dreaming of romance, vulnerable and unsuspecting, pliable, willing, and cash-ready. It makes perfect sense. What an ideal opportunity for a shark to make a quick killing.

It could be nothing.

I should let this go.

I'm choosing drama.

I'm choosing justice! I can't just let it go and *namaste!* If it is him, if there is any chance it could be him, I have to try. Then maybe I can repay all the favors and all the loans from Cole, from Leo, from Mum and Dad. Then I can cut this thing off, release it. Until then, there will always be this parasite of doubt, of disappointment, malingering, sucking incessantly at my soul.

The stars are out in their numbers tonight, too many to count, but I stare out at them and try anyway. I am the sole passenger left on the dark and chilly deck. It's another stage, another audience of silent witnesses. If the universe has a plan, if this is, indeed, as the cosmos conspires, then it's pretty twisted and unbelievably, yet delightfully, fitting that we should both be drawn to the ocean, off the coast of America.

It does fit though, doesn't it? We met in the embassy on course for the States. Theater was our livelihood…the dots connect. Where better to disappear than on a floating hotel, surrounded by strangers, sailing free and easy, with no fixed address?

The wind picks up and needles through the fibers of my clothes. I loop back to the covered Jacuzzi, the ice cream bar—still serving—and through to the escalators, stairs, spa, and gym. I peek through the window to the gym, the lights still bright but the machines deserted. With the expanse of bare flooring, I cannot help myself and push the glass door open. The same gym officer mans the desk, nods, smiles, and gives me the floor.

I roll out a mat, not facing the mirror but the vast black shimmering mass ahead, and there, while other passengers snore, gamble, eat or drink, I plank until my palms sweat and my biceps swell. But my mind is noisy tonight. I cannot focus and quiet the noise.

Oh God, it's him. I know it's him.

Chapter 23

The skies of Bermuda are decidedly gray and overcast as I look out of my balcony the next morning. The ocean is surprisingly dark and uninviting. I thought Bermuda was supposed to be all pink sand and crystal clear water. There's some kind of fort building high on the wharf, and the road seems to snake around passing parades of shops and arcades. Not that I will be doing much shopping today.

Tim—Tom—Tim has a brutal military schedule planned for me today, one-on-one coaching with the musical director. It's exciting to sing again. I say *exciting*, but what I really mean is terrifying with a little bit of head rush. I think I have become so used to singing under my breath in the wings of Ashtead or only when very, very drunk, that this chance now to find my voice again, to focus on something that makes my heart soar, is like some strange masochistic thrill.

Cole never really liked me to sing. There! Maybe I should focus on that: he's a drunk and didn't like me to sing. Of course we weren't a good match. What a good job he is not here.

I smear a coat of gloss on—gloss that my hair can no longer reach and stick to like fly paper—and take a final inventory before I leave. Three months of yoga and a new hairdo are quite the transformation. It's pleasing to see this stronger version of myself. I grab my room key card and head down to Tara's cabin.

"I know you've probably got a million and one things to do before your cab comes, but do you have a minute?"

She opens the door wider. "My room is yours! Well, half yours."

Oh. What? Wait. There is a twin bed. With a…person in it.

I whisper, alarmed, "There's a bed with a person in it. A sleeping person!"

"Oh, yes, didn't Tim tell you about that?" she says nonchalantly at normal volume.

"Erm…let me think." I hiss, "No!"

"Enna, it's just Lauren. The dancer with the really long legs. You know, she wears the octopus costume in the mermaid show. And you really don't have to whisper."

"It's rather small to share, isn't it?"

"It's just how it is. Look, maybe I can speak to Tim. Have him find you something else?"

I'm being a diva.

Enna, why are you reacting like this?

Because I'm surprised.

Hello? Life is full of surprises. You are being ridiculous.

"It's fine. Just a surprise. That's all. Look what fun we had when we shared your apartment, and we probably had even less room."

"Truth! So, what do you need? You've got all the scripts, scores, and daily schedules, right?"

"Oh, yes. That's all fine. My brain is boiling. It might explode, but I think it'll cool down soon. I didn't come about the show. I came about…"

I came to tell her about Will. Well, Irish Will. About my conversation with Chelsea and my gut-twisting feeling that this *Excelsior* performer is indeed the man who swindled me, but, looking at her face, the heap of packing on her bed, I know she has her own baggage to deal with.

"I just…came to say goodbye and thank you. I never thought I would get on stage again, but I suppose I really didn't realize how much I missed it. God, it feels good to be singing and dancing and reciting terribly cheesy lines, dressed in ridiculous outfits!"

We hug, and she hugs so hard the words I didn't say reabsorb into my throat. "Have a safe flight. Send my love to your mum, and don't worry one bit about me," I try to say encouragingly.

"I won't worry about *you*. It's everyone else I worry for," she replies to the side of my head. "Now, hop to it before you make me cry or something."

The first night moored at King's Wharf is an evening off for the cast, as a former Broadway star who used to stand in for Barbra Streisand takes the stage. It's a wonderful one-woman show, flowing from anecdote to song, anecdote to song. It's a nice change of pace from the many-costumed, and somewhat plastic productions of the musicals.

After a day of intense singing, hot tea, an impassioned edict from the musical director who bans me from any dairy product — *"No, Enna, cottage cheese is still a dairy product, even when consumed with fruit."* — the chance to sit back and appreciate a beautiful, unfettered voice without the kick line and headpieces is glorious.

The doubts that nibble at me as I sit alone in the dark remind me to keep looking forward. I choose to ignore them until I can do something about them.

"Don't worry about Bermuda. It'll still be here by the time you sail back here next week. Isn't it more important we get this polished?" Tim jollies me along, and it doesn't occur to me to mind. The good spirits — and bad ones from the below-deck staff bar — flow, and the cast doesn't seem to mind being brought in for a special first rehearsal with me. It's for the good of the show, the team, the community.

They are amazingly accommodating. When I forget the words to the song, Lauren covers the gap. When I lose my place, Michael — he of the perma-orange-glow — presses a guiding hand into my back or a whispered line into my ear. Chelsea shoots me a wink as a cue to speak. We get through it together, and it's not half bad. It's not as slick as Tara's performance, but by tonight, the lines will be quicker, the movement sharper, the notes less tentative.

As we hit the dressing rooms, change, and check our costumes for laundering, catches, rips, de-sequined areas in need of repair, Chelsea is, as luck would have it, my station mate, sharing the cubicle of space in front of our mirror.

I re-hang Tara's costumes. *My costumes.* "Thanks for the prompt, Chelsea."

"Oh, anytime, like! We've been doing these shows for ages now. Everyone knows everyone else's lines. You don't know what's comin', just you look at us. I'll put you right."

"Thanks, Chels." Now, how to seamlessly segue? "Chels, you mentioned your friend is on board that ship you want to join next."

"The *Excelsior*?"

"Aye. Er…I mean, yes. That's the one."

"Yeah, what of it?"

"Well, I was just struck by the coincidence of things, because I used to work with a brilliant rapper at the theater, and we…lost touch."

"Shame. I keep in touch with everyone on Facebook or Instagram. It's really the only way nowadays, ain't it?"

"Yes, but not everyone does Facebook, and as for Instagram, is that like tweeting?"

She is peeling off her false eyelash and stops, the unstuck half now drooping lamely. "You don't Instagram? Enna, you 'ave to Instagram. It's, like, amazin'!"

"Oh?"

"Oh, aye. Look." She repositions her lashes, grabs her phone from her purse, and snaps a shot of herself, grinning into the mirror. "There. Now, you add a filter, a couple of 'ashtags, and *voilà!*" Her fingers drill over the touch screen faster than a concert pianist.

"So. Okay, Chels, where does that go now? Who have you sent it to?"

"Err…the world. Anyone who clicks on those 'ashtags for dance, ship, cruise, and of course, to my Instagram followers."

"A Whole New World" starts playing over the speakers as the techies check the sound on stage.

"So, if you hashtagged *Excelsior,* for instance, pictures from the ship would come up?"

"Exactly! Amaze-balls, right? Anyhow, that's how I keep in contact with all my mates."

I must check to see if my phone has been found, turned in to ship services. It must be somewhere, and suddenly it is more important than ever.

"Chels, I know this sounds so silly, but do you think you could ask your friend on board the *Excelsior* if she knows the Irish rapper's name?"

"Sure!" As simple as that.

"And, Chels, does your friend do Instagramming?"

She giggles. "Instagrammin'! You're funny! She 'as Instagram, but she doesn't upload often. Why?"

"Well—" *No asky, no getty, Enna!* "—I'd love to see if that rapper is my friend. Do you think you can ask her to do an Instagram with him?"

"Sure." She giggles again. "Don't worry, Grandma. I'll teach you the ways of the twenty-first century!"

There's a sense of renewed excitement backstage, a buzz as we do our group warm-up and vocal exercises.

"You're going to bloody kill it, Enna!" Michael says to me in the wings as Tim introduces the show on stage. I look at his young face, the tan "Azaddin" I had sung with just a few days previously. How can that even be possible? Time seems to cheat me. In the darkness, Michael's big eyes shine so sincerely, so reassuringly. If only he wasn't neon orange, he might be very good looking for someone young.

I inhale deeply, chest, ribs, belly; exhale, belly, ribs, chest. And I dedicate the show, as I would a yoga practice, to Tara. I imagine her now, waiting out the long layover at JFK airport, nervously picking at the side of her nails as she does when anxious, and counting every minute until she can board and continue her journey back home to her mum.

I hit the first note a little off-kilter, but Michael joins in, and it becomes a marvelous duet. Of all the lines I was rehearsing, the opening lines were the ones I had repeated over and over, again and again, whispering them under my breath in the wings, and they are the ones I stumble on?

Breathe. Progress. Move on.

The dance numbers will win no prizes, but with my long hemline, no one can see my feet shuffle out of time and miss the few ball-changes and the lifts. I largely rely on Michael to whip me up into his orange arms and flip me where he will, skirt allowing.

The ballad—based on "A Whole New World," peppered with sharps—goes exceptionally well. My voice melds nicely with Michael's and has the audience swaying, which is, I learn, oddly off-putting when the ship is rolling in a different direction!

The audience applauds politely in that soft palmed way older generations clap, and they seem to leave most satisfied. I glug water in the wings, run my tongue over my teeth, and return to the auditorium to meet the audience. Then, we reset props and costumes, reapply lipstick, and the second show goes on. I barely have time to adjust my underwire before, holy déjà vu, here I am again. Round Two! It flows and seems more natural this performance, every step, note and line reinforcing where, when, what and how I do it again.

"Champagne!" Tim announces as he pops off a bottle in the dressing room. It's a lovely gesture, and I am never one to turn down a glass of bubbly, but it would be a jolly lot nicer if one had the chance to get dressed first and not be toasted as I stand here in my knickers with my dress halfway up, bundling my head, shoulders and chest into what can only be described as an awkward sandwich. "Here's to you, Enna! Cheers!"

Lauren, one of the dancers, comes to my aid and pulls the sleeves to help me out of the dress. There, in slightly washed-out turquoise thong and sports bra, I receive the cheers, the hullaballoo lassoing the boys from the other dressing room. And all in stages of semi-nakedness, we grab plastic cups and toast.

Oh my God. Bubbles.

We descend to the underbelly of the staff bar and wash the champagne down with vodka sodas — I too have converted. Dangling on a rope while clad in a leopard print bikini and loincloth, does not fill me with the deep joy of body confidence. The daily alcohol — I know my limits; it's just social — and the twenty-four-hour buffet, not to mention the specialty restaurants, mean things could get out of hand if one were not very disciplined.

Eat less, chaturanga *more.*

At least "dancing" ups the heart rate, and the cheese ban should lower the cholesterol, as well as the throaty singing voice.

The cast claims our usual table, the horseshoe shape of sections of highly patterned sofas around it. After many congratulations and much back-patting, Michael, even more orange in a crisp white shirt, suggests a game.

Perhaps this is for young pups, and I should retire. It is nearly eleven p.m., but he holds my hand and pulls my arm back down to be seated.

"Enna, this will help you get to know everyone here. It's called Two Truths and a Lie." I must look horrified because he immediately continues with further explanation. "You have to make three statements. Two have to be truths. One must be a lie, and we have to figure out which is the lie. You can make them quite outlandish or fairly normal, whichever you think we wouldn't catch. Go on. It'll be fun!"

I may not know about Instagram, but I can be fun!

It's a harmless enough game. Many of the lies are silly and easy to spot. The more savvy players make their lies as normal as their truths. It's curious that, here I sit, so many facets I could reveal about myself, and yet I have a complete block. Lines come easily when they have been written for you. Nothing I compose seems to be appropriate or funny, or at all worth telling. So when the attention is turned on me, I lose my way for a minute.

It's quite without forethought that I blurt out, "I was engaged to marry an American."

Aside from Tim, there is an audible gasp of surprise. Being twenty-one and dedicated to dancing, marriage is for older people, like those approaching their thirties. Those too old for cruise ship dance companies.

And that's where I stall. "I'm sorry. I'm not very good at this."

"Keep going!" says Michael, patting my hand and giving me a nod. The males in the company are all very touchy. If Michael weren't so young, it might occur to me to mind.

I don't know what kicks in—the champagne, the vodka, my innate desire to be liked and accepted by this younger set, or to get a conversation going about the *Excelsior*—but I take another sip, and it loosens my tongue.

"I love rap and totally want to see the show on the *Excelsior*! And I once went to a party in Cornwall with Prince William—oh, this was way before Kate—and we drank like fish and got completely loaded together!"

They form a little conclave: a huddle of excited whispers, a few sloppy drink spills, a shout of "bullshit!" thrown in for good measure.

I sink back into my seat, sucking feverishly at the straw, waiting for their verdict, trying for my best poker face.

It is Tim who elects himself chairman, though barracking comes from all sides and individuals want to get their opinions in. "Okay, the majority say...the lie is...number two. There is no way you are into rap!"

Jesus, am I that uncool?

"INCORRECT!" I whoop—clearly, there has been just enough drinkage. "I *do* like rap. We used to have a Shakespearian rap show at my theater. The lie was Prince William. I was there at the same pub in Cornwall, but we didn't drink together. Maybe history would have been really different if we had!"

There are a few cheers, and one of the flamboyant dancers, Gavin, gets another round in. It's simple when everyone drinks the same clear, low-calorie concoction. Michael, now practically lying down on his seat, propped up on his elbow, rubs his fingers up my arm to get my attention. "So, you were engaged, huh?"

"Briefly, yes."

"What happened?"

"Oh, that's a long and complicated story. I was hooked on saving my theater in England. He was in the States. It just didn't work."

"But you don't run the theater now, right?"

"No," I say with quiet nostalgia.

"And you don't have a fiancé."

"No, and thank you for the reminder," I tease him for his untactful reiteration of my recent history.

He is silent, looking up at me.

I imagine he is trying to piece the bits he knows of me together. It's a faintly awkward silence, too long for a new acquaintance, so I babble on. "I had thought we could rekindle things, but...well, we didn't. Don't you have a girlfriend? A tall, strong chap like you must be besieged with offers. Like Patrick Swayze in *Dirty Dancing*."

"Who?"

"*Dirty Dancing?* Patrick...? Oh, dear God, really? You dance. You should have seen *Dirty Dancing*. It's a classic. I can recite practically every line. How can you not have...Really? Really and truly, you haven't seen it?"

"No...I heard of it."

"Holy shit, Michael. It's like I'm talking with a preschooler. How old are you anyway?"

"I'm not that young! I'm older than you think. Why, how old are you?"

"Old enough to know better."

"Well, no. There's no girlfriend. We can't fraternize with the passengers. It's funny, I'm here on a ship surrounded by people, but honestly, Enna, it can get pretty lonely." He fixes me with his sincere blue eyes.

Is this a line?

"Drinkies!" Gavin exclaims with a twinkle as he puts a round down and skips back to the bar to reclaim the ones he couldn't carry.

Michael rubs my upper arm again, two fingers skating over my skin. I am still digesting the fact that anyone, let alone a man who has studied musical theater, can have lived and not seen *Dirty Dancing*.

"I really shouldn't drink anymore."

"And why not? We work hard. We drink hard."

The little fair hairs on my arms stand to attention. His touch feels too welcome to continue. "There are other ways to celebrate, you know." I reposition on the cushions, shifting just so slightly out of his reclined reach.

"Oh, yes?" he replies with a suggestive eyebrow lift.

"Jesus, you're incorrigible!" And I knock his elbow so he falls into the cushions.

He laughs, and righting himself, he grabs the cushion behind me.

Oh shit!

I sink low, close to him again. The yelp I make draws the attention of the others who had been fully focused on Gavin doing his Graham Norton impression.

"Whoopsies!" I say, before I realize how uncool that must sound.

They turn back to Gavin.

"Stop flirting with me!" I hiss into Michael's ear.

"I'm not flirting. I'm just talking. We're adults. Can't we have a conversation?"

"I am far too old for you, young whippersnapper. You couldn't even carry the amount of baggage I have."

"I could try." He looks up at me again.

Enna, you must not. You cannot. It is absolutely not allowed to flirt with, let alone touch, kiss, or in any way get naked with this boy. Absolutely not.

Of course, we have kissed on stage. And we have already seen each other in our undies back stage...

It's no excuse. You are approaching thirty and should know better. You have a failed business and an ex-fiancé, and you are heartbroken. Isn't this what happened last time? You allowed someone to just swoop in and make you feel special, validated. You don't need it, Enna.

He blows on my neck. "You are really beautiful, you know."

But that does feel really good.

For a split second, I imagine it. Running through the deck corridors to slash my card in the door, fling it open, be thrown down on the king-sized bed that is unnecessarily re-made three times a day, and to have this tan, rippled, young buck hold me down and fuck the memory of Cole out of me.

Wouldn't that be living in the moment? Wouldn't it be comforting to feel wanted by someone, touched by those fingers, to feel the weight of someone between my thighs? Would that be moving forward and *namaste*?

"Don't you feel lonely, Enna?" he whispers. His hot breath just beneath my earlobe sends ripples that course through to my fingertips.

It would be so easy.

I smile and blush and turn away, and I see Cole holding me like he used to, that bear wrap-around, protect-you-from-the-world kind of hug. I can smell his Hermès aftershave. I can imagine his fingers around my ribcage, my waist, pulling my hips closer, driving into me. And although Cole has made his feelings very clear, although I could say, "What the hell! Seize the dick and the day!" and dive into bed with the grandchild of the great orange George Hamilton here, I just…can't, and I won't.

"You're very sweet, young buck, but I must go to bed. Alone."

His mouth opens, but no words come out.

I take another sip and wave goodbye to the cast and return to my stateroom. Only two more nights before I have to leave my stateroom to be submerged below deck in Tara's shared room. Goodness only knows when I will get a completely alone moment, without the high pitched chatter and laughter and song lyrics drumming my thoughts into hiding again.

Chapter 24

I don't remember my dream, but as I feel it trailing away from me, I am desperate to remember and hold on to it, but the sound—a knock? Is someone knocking?—snatches it away as soon as I open my eyes.

The knocks are quiet but repetitive and with a little rhythm. *What the fuck?* I turn over to the clock: 2:50 a.m. I pull the covers over my head, but the knocks continue with a little flourish every now and then. Paranoia starts to kick in as I imagine escalating scenarios, the life and death situation I could be ignoring.

Finally, I whip back the cover, shrug myself into the soft, white waffle robe, and squint into the bright light of the corridor as I open the door a fraction.

"Hello!"

"Michael! It is nearly three a.m." This is clearly not a life or death scenario.

"I thought you could use some company." He sways as he leans on the doorjamb.

Is this it now? Do I just attract a bunch of drunks? Is there something, some pheromone I am exuding that works like catnip for drunken idiots? Are my pores releasing some stealthy lure I can't smell, like gin? They smell it on the air and seek me out?

Okay, Enna, two. Two men.

"Michael, go away."

He pushes the door open, casting more light on the cabin. "See, look at all that room. Go on, play nice and share. I only have a little cabin below deck."

"No."

He takes a step forward and presses up against me. Judging by the pressure from his groin nailing into my abdomen, he is drunk, but there's no dysfunction here!

"Michael, no! This is not funny or charming." My body rebels against my brain and doesn't move away. I am rather intrigued as to what his plan might be next.

"I think you'd like it. We'd be good together."

"I'm almost ten years older than you!"

"And?"

"And that is a lot older. You need someone your age. There are plenty of pretty dancers on the ship."

"Yes, but they are not you."

"Goodnight, Michael." I push his chest lightly to maneuver him out of the doorway, but he holds my hand instead. "I so appreciate it. You're lovely for my ego, but it is not going to happen. Good. Night."

A whole day at sea before we port at Cape Liberty means another whole day of rehearsal for the last show. Thank God it's an easy one, a night of cabaret, singing our favorite show tunes with accompanying anecdote. Tim wants me to sing "On My Own" from *Les Misérables*, the "Legally Blonde" duet from the show of the same name, and "Defying Gravity" from *Wicked*.

"I think you do tragic very well," he says encouragingly.

Oh, that's just…peachy.

My scheduled hour with the pianist reacquaints me with the subtleties, the harmonies, the pacing. It's frightening to sing such revered songs in public to an auditorium of glinting spectacles and high-pitched hearing aids, but nothing more than I have already accomplished. The military routine, the dedication to the team effort is…fun.

I am having *fun*.

Amazing to think it, but sans responsibility of running my own theater, being involved, performing again, feeling strong and working hard has made my heart pump. It's like being on a holiday camp. The adrenaline flows as fast and frequently as the Stoli O and soda.

The *Legally Blonde* song—singing about a woman who runs back home, thinking she's lost everything, not knowing that there was a loyal and loving man by her side the whole time—strikes a chord, literally and figuratively.

Well, that was before he became an alcoholic with a personality disorder.

Michael strides up the aisle, no trace of morning head fog or embarrassment, just dazzling in his white shirt, dangerously unbuttoned and revealing his toned, tanned chest. My voice cracks. Jesus! It's like I'm some old cougar pervert.

Surely I'm not old enough to be a cougar. Maybe I'm just a puma, or a slightly less aggressive leopard of some kind?

Stop looking, Enna. Stop looking and sending him mixed signals.

He unfurls his sheet music, nods a "good morning" at the pianist, Harry, and as the introduction plays again, he holds his music to his lips and gives me a sideways sultry "Hello, you."

I think I must flush crimson. It's so audaciously familiar!

I am going to have to put a stop to this. After rehearsal, I will reiterate the many and perma-tanned reasons for not seeing him, and I will give him a damn good...telling off!

I fix my eyes on the notes and words and don't dare respond. I am a professional. I am singing about loss and feeling used, wasted, not about casual sex.

Michael switches it on and sings to me as Emmett. He actually turns to face me as I steadfastly watch Harry with laser beam focus. I probably burn holes through him, I stare so hard.

Michael sings about love, pleading, beseeching. I am an unresponsive lemon. I sing my lines with feeling, but really, we are around a piano. We haven't even blocked this. Surely I don't have to interact. We're just going through the notes, right?

Harry stops playing. "Enna, erm, sorry, let's try it again from the top, and this time remember that Emmett is not completely invisible. He's been your ally, your friend. You can look at him as you sing."

"Oh. Yes. Sorry. I thought we were just practicing."

"We are never 'just practicing,' darling girl. Life is a stage, and we are always on it. So, again! This time I want to see the connection between you."

Michael raises his eyebrows.

I could hit him.

So I sing as Elle, heart worn and foolish and so deep in my pit of despair that I cannot see him throwing a rope to get me out.

He holds my shoulders and sings. I have to break away to keep to my lines, but it works. Elle is fighting against it. She has to run away.

The shrink at the hospital, after my little accidental overdose, said I was a runner. *"Enna, you run from your problems."* But I faced them. I went to Cole. I stood on his doorstep. I wonder if he was nicely drunk then.

I don't run any more. I chaturanga *into my problems.*

"That's much better. Much better!" Harry encourages. "What a delightful couple you are!"

"See!" Michael whispers from behind his sheet music.

I am not playing this game.

There is a certain frisson in the air on show night. It's amazing that in less than a week, I have gone from being irreconcilably rejected and sick with sadness, to euphoric on the high seas, singing my heart out. The cast says they had chills, goose bumps, and Chelsea tells me, as I stick my false eyelashes back on the polystyrene head and peel my wig off, that she had "a full-on, hard cry" when Michael and I sang the *Legally Blonde* song. Michael was there, of course, but I imagined Cole, and it was a beautifully tortured performance. When will Cole stop haunting my days? When will I be able to let go of the thoughts of him as well as the person?

"Anyhow, you did brilliantly! Let's go and celebrate!"

I'll have one drink, just to be sociable, but vow to leave right afterward. I repeat it like a mantra. "Thank you! But I'm not staying. I'm just having this one little drinky, and then it's off to bed. I have the mermaid dialogue to learn tonight."

"That one's a piece of cake, and don't worry. Michael will be there to whisper in yer ear!" She looks up at me and winks conspiratorially.

"There's nothing going on!"

"Oh, aye! It don't matter. Anyway, I got news for you."

My face relaxes, and my smile contracts.

"I heard from my friend on the *Excelsior*. That rapper you asked about has been quite the naughty boy!"

"What do you mean?" I can hear my heart racing in my ear. It's like I'm underwater. I *am* underwater.

"You should see your face! Quite white, you are!"

"What did your friend say?"

"Well, between you and me, I think she probably has her knickers in a twist because she probably liked him too, but she said Liam is quite the ladies' man and is having a thing with the principal singer on the *Excelsior*."

I need a drink. My heart feels like it is bouncing against my ribcage and ricocheting around my chest like organ pinball.

Liam. Liam...? Will...Liam. Certainly not a stretch if one wanted to use one's documents but be known by a different name.

But would he be that obvious? "Anything more? Is he rapping songs? Shakespeare? What does he do?"

"Oh, he takes suggestion from the audience. Like that improv game *Whose Line Is It Anyway?* Then, he makes up a rap on the spot. I know that's the way the company wants to go, more audience participation..." Chelsea chatters on, but I only see her lips move.

It has to be Will. It *has* to be. And as much as I know that it's completely ridiculous and that there are billions of people on the planet, I know.

"Can I see photos on your Instagramming thing?"

"It's just Instagram. I'm pretty sure she's posted photos about twice. But if you 'ashtag ExcelsiorRapper you might get some photos."

"Can I see? I mean, can I see on your phone? I don't have one."

"You don't 'ave a phone?"

I see my cool points vanish in one withering, uncomprehending look. "It's a long story. I did. I don't. It went missing, or got stolen — I'm beginning to think the latter — on my first night here."

"Bummer. Well, I'll look when we get into port at Cape Liberty. I'm on airplane mode until then. How's that?"

"You can't check now?" It's the singing, the stage, the night; it's made me ballsy brave.

"No way! I made my mistake trying to receive calls and messages before. It was very expensive. We'll be in port soon anyway. Just be patient. Keep yer knickers on!"

It's oddly comforting to hear such British expressions; I am not so on my own.

I return to my room. I am sure I will never sleep tonight, chasing Will and tossing and turning through various showdown scenarios.

The mermaid script lies abandoned on my bed, spread open, an obscene reminder in bright white of what I should be doing. I slip off my pumps and dive into the cloud of duvet.

My head is a projector of reels I had vaulted away: Images of Will, swathed in his gray scarf as I first met him in the embassy. Will, as he appeared at the theater after everyone had gone, and he sat with a mercurial look in his eye, swirling my wine in my glass and taking sips without asking—was he hatching his plan then, to help me then leave me and take all of the money? Will falling on me, surrounded by paint pots and rollers and not kissing me. Will kissing me in the office, the dressing room. Will layering me with falsehoods as he planned his theatricks. Did he plan it, or was he just an opportunist?

It must be him.

We sail into Cape Liberty in the early hours of Sunday morning. I wait until ten a.m. to knock on Chelsea's cabin door, only to find she has already gone ashore to buy some essentials.

Bugger.

I shall have to wait to check her Instagram.

Jesus! Why am I such a tech-tard?! Aren't I young enough to understand these things? Can't I just download it, or is it only for cell phones? I chastise myself for not being interested in computers, cell phones and apps. I prefer the edible kind of apps, not the downloadable kind.

In the interim, I fill my time disembarking and embarking—a tiresome procedure just to be given a new ID and swipe card for Tara's room. I check the ship's service one final time in the vain hope that a passenger or crew member, after walking around with my mobile phone all week, now realizes that it belongs to me. I find and speak to Cedric, the bartender at the piano bar, who recalls he saw the phone but thought I took it with me; and I promise Lauren dinner if she will let me use her iPad and catch up with my e-mails home. Maybe there are perks to having a cabin mate!

I navigate to settings and find the secured Wi-Fi, tap in the impossibly lengthy password and reconnect with the world. It feels almost illicit, like returning to a bad habit: a hasty cigarette, biting a fingernail, pouring an unnecessary glass before going out or after coming home. I tap in my password and am glad to be locked away in a cabin where no one can see me give in to the lure of communication. Life has been so much simpler and less harried without the constant badgering of social media and e-mail. It's been easier living in this floating bubble without knowing. I suppose I have become numb to curiosity. But now there it sits on Tara's tiny twin bed, this portal, this gateway, this Pandora's box…with three e-mails from Cole.

The name, his name, is hardly unexpected, yet it still gives me a jolt. I laugh out loud, filling the cabin with hollow guffaws, because I don't know how else to feel other than naïve for being surprised, and betrayed that my stomach turned and chest pounded. Why is my body so quick to commit mutiny against my better judgment?

I click on the first he sent.

To: Enna

From: Cole

Subject: Sorry!

Enna,

I am so, so sorry. I hope you know that I am more sorry than a person could ever possibly be. I can't imagine what you are thinking now, and I don't know how I will ever explain, but I want you to know that I tried. Please write back.
Cole.

Sorry? I laugh again. What kind of effort or explanation is that? What is he asking for? Forgiveness? I growl in frustration, angry that my eyes sting with liquid. I lie back on the bed and bury my head in the pillow, the safety and darkness where no one can see my face. I breathe long, deep breaths in an attempt to quiet the fireworks of thought exploding chaotically in my brain.

Don't be angry. So his explanation is anything but. He has displayed, yet again, a complete lack of effort and disinterest, but you're okay, Enna. This is a positive. What's the message in this? You learned that people do change, and better to learn this now than after five, ten, or fifteen years of marriage, during which he gives approximately zero fucks about you or making an effort and is content to spend his time with a whiskey in hand rather than his wife.

He has made an effort in the past.

It doesn't matter! It doesn't count for anything anymore. Accept and move on, Enna.

I inhale long and deep and let a loud exhaled sigh muffle into the pillow before casting it aside.

Listlessly, I click on the other awaiting e-mails.

> Pickle,
>
> I peeked at the ticket in the envelope. That was such a nice surprise. Did you still sail? I haven't heard from you so I am guessing you did. I hope you manage to have some fun. I'm so sorry again.
> C.

It's numbing. Every inadequate word that gives no account, no explanation, just moves me mentally further away.

I scroll to the last inbox message, sent today at 9:29 a.m.

> Enna.
>
> I think you come back today. I hope you call me. I have tried calling you, but I guess you don't get a signal or you have let the battery die, as you always seemed to do when you lived here. If ever a girl needed a charger in every purse she owned, it is you.
> I'm still sorry.
> C.

I click on reply and contemplate all the choice adjectives I could use, but where would that get me? I hear Mallory's voice echo within my thoughts, *"Let go of the things that do not serve you."*

I close my eyes and remember to breathe. This man makes me feel…what exactly? Sad, bereft. Like something has died, something we just can't get back. Replying to a ghost seems pointless. Railing and trying to force accountability on him seems completely futile.

I write to Mum and Dad instead, ignoring the three unanswered e-mails that sit like kryptonite in my inbox.

> To: Mum and Dad
> From: Enna
> Subject: BIG NEWS!!
> So guess what? I am the newest member of the cast aboard ship! I took over Tara's roles as principal singer, and life is beautiful! I am having a blast!

After a nap and a salad at the buffet, I track Chelsea and her phone down while we are still in port.

"All right, all right. Keep yer knickers on."

Erm, that's exactly what I intend to do. "Chelsea, did you check your Instagram?"

"If I go over my data plan, I'm charging, okay?"

"Sure!"

We scroll through a reel of selfies, but none of her *Excelsior* friend. Damn. Yet what was I thinking? That he would be there, posing for the world? Yet isn't that exactly what that cocky bastard would do?

I will check every week. Every time we port, I will stalk that hashtag like a sunflower!

Chapter 25

After the frenzy of two weeks of non-stop rehearsals: singing rehearsal, blocking rehearsal, dance rehearsal, setting costumes rehearsal, make-up practice, quick change practice, and repeat—finally, the non-stop *Groundhog Day* starts to peter out, and a new routine is set.

The company is all much younger than me, and the nightly drinking, card playing, and general hullabaloo gets as old as I feel. My guts twist and wind me as I watch them all suck the clear liquid that is slowly poisoning them and making them fools. I wonder when I will swirl a glass of Pinot Noir in my hand and not think of Cole, a snifter of brandy, a tumbler of whiskey. The smell of bourbon closes my throat like a hand gripping my trachea.

Activity is my alternative. It's my entertainment, my therapy, my new addiction. The gym attendants know me well enough to leave me unchallenged and let me sweat as I flow through each sun salutation facing the ocean. Whether at sunrise, with the sunlight making the water a sheet of blinding, shimmering silver, or at midnight, staring into the darkest of nights, I practice, looking out toward the ocean full of whales, dolphins, sharks, and shipwrecks. There's something incredibly romantic about the thought of those grand wooden carcasses, the five hundred or more ship skeletons waiting to be found in the depths fringing Bermuda.

Maybe that is why the sand is pink. It's the blood of sailors leeched into the sand. It's these ideas that entertain me as I keep to myself; as I run on the deck track, watching for whales to fluke; as I breathe the salty air that whispers into my ear words I can't distinguish but that comfort me; as I hit my mat, stomach muscles engaged, and hoist my legs high.

I avoid Michael as much as one can when being held four out of seven nights, twice a night, in his arms. He gravitates to my side, and I have to fight the current. He is tenacious and very insistent.

Port days are the ones I live for, to fasten my trainers and get lost for a few hours through the coves and hidden bays of St. George's, to take a sandwich from the buffet and a book from the ship's library and wedge myself between the rocks, away from the tourists and the ship's passengers who hail me aboard and insist on telling me of their family history originating from some British city.

I love the rainy days — Brits seem far more waterproof than the average tourist. It gets decidedly foggy, and the passengers stay aboard to play improv games and get drunk. I catch the bus — this bus pass is a godsend — and watch as even the tiny uniformed children with tightly fastened pigtails climb aboard and say hello with a politely mischievous look in their eyes.

I'm glad to leave King's Wharf behind, with its touristy tat, and head for the hills and winding roads that lead into Hamilton. It's often a "close your eyes and hold your breath" bus experience. We pass the lighthouse and the pink sand beaches, through the boutiquey harbor-front shops of Hamilton, where I alight to use the free thirty minute allotment of Wi-Fi at the library, sending out quick updates. Cole writes a few more lame *I'm sorry* e-mails, but I know I must protect my heart and not think about it. Eventually, I won't feel a thing.

I hop aboard the bus again, out toward the crystal caves and on to the far northeast of this small island, the historic area of St. George's. Forts stand sentinel on every bluff of the island, looking out to ward away unwanted marauders. I spend hours alone, running through the thick stone halls, into every turret and lookout, watching and waiting. *Waiting for what?*

The cannons cemented to the ground — though God knows what opportunist thief could succeed in stealing them — must have been so gloriously threatening at one time. The cool black metal must have once run hot, smoking with action, but now they sit as relics, ineffectual and used, facing the Atlantic and the wide Sargasso Sea. I feel the bumpy pits of the metal, imagining its own war wounds from the counter blast, and all the soldiers loading the cannonballs, lighting the fuses and aiming at incoming ships. It all seems so quaint in the light of bombs and bazookas and impolite warfare.

Below the cannons, the fort walls run down into a three-sided moat, so overgrown with vast-leafed vegetation it's as if it's overgrown by triffids. It could be creepy here where the moss grows, where the sunlight and the rain is blocked by these umbrella-leaves. I run through the moat, hello-ing, delighted to hear the echo as the walls narrow and filter into the underground tunnels. I run my hand swiftly against the stone. So many years of history. So many hands have touched these cool walls. So many feet have walked, have run, have panicked through these tunnels.

Maybe it's the feeling of being imprisoned, caged aboard a floating palace of endless vodka and fifty-cent beer, but land beneath my feet makes me move. My legs churn like pistons, and my feet impact and resound with a satisfying crunch on the gravel, the rocks, the fantastical pink and yellow sand. There is something liberating about having a purpose. It should be the other way around, I know. That a purpose, a mission, anchors and ties one down, but it doesn't. Having a focus, an intention, is freeing from all the other craziness — the sadness about Cole, for Tara, the anxiety of not knowing how long I will be doing this — all the many shades of bullshit that do not serve me are left in my dust.

It's the second morning docked at King's Wharf, after four weeks of Atlantic back and forth, that I read a new e-mail from Tara, and it is crushing. How helpless and ineffectual it feels to read the words from your friend that her mother is slipping away. I spend my whole session at the library, typing and deleting, retyping and deleting. No words can create a hug, which is what I truly want to send.

It doesn't occur to me until some hours later, as I escape the rain and sit in a little coffee shop on the harbor front, drinking a steaming coffee, that this sad news would, of course, affect when she would return and resume her role.

You are only seat warming. Do not get attached, Enna.

But when she returns, what then?

Then, Enna, you have choices of where and what and with whom you want to be in the world.

I block the tentative needling thoughts of returning to Scranton to ask for an explanation.

What good would that do?

Hmm…umm…

Exactly!

I have my two wheely suitcases and could return to England, or go via Puerto Rico and sit on the harbor, waiting for the trail of *Excelsior* passengers and crew to spill out onto the street. I could forget both and choose something new, maybe a yoga school in Thailand. The messy coil of ideas unravels as I trace each to its own conclusion.

Where is my life GPS? Why does the universe consistently throw decisions to test me?

Because, Enna, you have to learn to make a decision and stick to it. You want so many different things. You drive yourself crazy trying to chase them all, and you miss each one. You cannot chase two rabbits.

Then, I must go to Puerto Rico. I can afford it with my saved wages. I must face the negative memories. I must accept losing the theater, the money, my dream, and move on, and I can only do that if I have done what I can to catch Will.

It feels good to have this mission.

I have hours before I have to be back on board. I leave the coffee shop with a hearty hail from the barista, and I head for the bus stop and weave through the narrow roads northeast to St. George's again.

I run from the bus stop and do not stop until I meet Fort St. Catherine, marking the northern edge of the island with its British fortifications and artillery. I don't go in this time. I stand on the wall, with the rain on my upturned face, the wind buffeting my short hair and filling my lungs with fresh, briny air. I reach my hands for the sky, feeling the energy from the sea, the wind, the sun. The whoosh in my ears that whispers my name, the crash of the wave below that drowns it out. The few wandering tourists congregate at the Blackbeard's restaurant, waiting for the sunshine, but I'm British and, therefore, waterproof.

I stand with my right foot on my thigh in tree pose and hold my hands to the sky, focusing on the sound of my breath, the waves, the wind, the birds, the flag hoisted from the fort slapping the air.

"Enna."

"Enna."

"Enna."

The elements swirl around me, and I root down, being grateful, albeit confused, to have choices. How life changes! How odd that in just four months the course of my life has changed so dramatically, been so blown off-course, buffeted and blown and wrecked on the rocks, only to be rebuilt on a small island, fortified as never before, and almost free to sail again. The wind rushes into my face and my ears, holding me up, not blowing me over.

"Enna."

My name on the wind fills my ears again, louder this time, and all at once I feel this pressure, a weight on my shoulder, and I lose my footing, my balance. I wave my limbs frantically, trying to grab something, anything, but seize only handfuls of air as I slip from the wall.

Chapter 26

I lean toward the fort and land on the stone ramparts, watching breathless as a few rocks tumble to the water and bounce on the shallow, jagged rock pools below. It all happens so quickly. My eyes are bulging at my near-miss-with-the-allelujahs as I imagine my skull cracked and body turning the golden sand on this beach to the prettier Bermuda pink.

"Are you all right?" The words suck into my ears, a swirling vortex of sound, and I remember to look back, startled that I fell, that someone was there.

I get to my feet without looking, dazed I suppose, taking in the feet, the khaki trousers, the shirt, the face, now bent over me, wide-eyed with concern.

It's like I've been punched, shot or winded, and I can't breathe without hyperventilating.

Don't go to pieces! Breathe!

I right myself so my lungs can fill. My eyes flood, but I will not cry now, so I open them wide and suck them back in.

"What…what are you doing here?"

"Pickle."

Four months ago, I might have shot into his arms, like the wayward sheepdog called at the whistle, but now, I don't know what to do but spread my toes within my trainers and root down.

"Don't 'pickle' me, Cole."

"Would you just let me explain?"

I look into his face now. He's lost more weight. His cheeks seem slack and his jaw more stubbled than usual. I could swear there is a smattering more gray through his short brown hair. His hazel eyes fix me so sincerely.

The wind whips louder.

"There's nothing to explain," I shout to battle the wind.

"There's *everything* to explain!"

"I waited for you! You said you were coming."

He drops his head, lifts his hands to his face, and rakes his fingers through his hair.

"Can we go somewhere?"

"We are somewhere, Cole. We used to be something. But now we are just two people with some memories."

"You're just giving up?"

"Not just! Cole, I tried. I said I was sorry, that I'd made a mistake, but you never once let me forget it. I tried to bring us together, and you just kept cranking us apart. Well, I deserve more than that. I deserve someone who will treat me with respect, to love and honor me like you used to. I don't like this new inconsiderate, unreliable, drunk Cole. There, I said it!" The wind flaps the flag as though giving a ripple of applause.

He sits on the wall, his head in his hands again. "I know. I screwed up, sweetie. I screwed up really bad." He looks up and at me now. "I was coming. I had thrown some clothes in a bag and was on my way. I was looking forward to seeing you."

The knife twists.

Breathe.

"It was so stupid and so fast. I just looked down to re-read your instructions, double checking where I should go and when I could open the second envelope, and this car, pickle—Enna—it came out of nowhere. Blargh!" He stands again, pacing in front of me. "It was a mess. The car totally T-boned, caved in completely, and the other guy was shouting at me. The cops get there, and I don't know...We were fine. I was fine, but...I guess it was a Sunday morning, and they were...well, they asked me to blow, and it was point-oh-eight and..."

"Cole!"

He was drunk driving? His face looks forlorn, and I am caught between my chosen indifference, complete incredulity, and wanting to hold him.

"They took my keys, my phone, your envelopes. They cuffed me and took me downtown." He stands and starts to pace in front of me. "I told them I needed to go, there was somewhere important I needed to be, someone important I needed to see, but instead they fitted me with ankle chains. Ankle chains! Like I was some criminal. They took my mug shot—Jesus! A fucking mug shot, Enna!—then to another room where they videoed me, did this blood test, the whole nine yards!

"I told them I needed to make a call. I needed to be somewhere. They asked me where, and I had to reply that I didn't really know. They said they'd make a call for me. I had to give them three names to call. What was I going to do, Enna? Have the police call you and frighten the crap out of you? So instead, they called Donny. I stayed in the cell all afternoon, just watching the wall clock and knowing I'd blown it."

"Cole!" I launch myself as if I've burst and thump his chest with the side of my fists. "What were you doing drinking in the morning? What were you thinking? Why have you let this overtake your life?"

"Hey! Hey! Enna, I know, it's awful. Please don't cry." He clasps my wrists and stills my fists. "It wasn't intentional. It's been there for me, you know? It takes the edge off. It helps me sleep. I'd had a skinful that night. I thought I was fine, but the shot of courage before I left home to drive to you, that must have been enough on top of what was still left in my blood. I was about to stop for a coffee and a bagel."

And it's almost funny. But not quite.

His hold slips from my wrists to my hands, palm-to-palm.

"Why didn't you call the ship? Why didn't you let me know?"

"I tried. I called your cell phone. I left voice mails. Then I wrote you e-mails. Did I call the ship? No, but I only expected you to be cruising for a week, not to take over the show! I even called the number for your address in Park Slope. I spoke to a lady who said she'd expected you back, but Tara had been in touch, saying you wouldn't be returning for a while. I was going out of my mind. In the end, I called your mom and dad, and they said they had been very puzzled by your e-mails, but you were floating somewhere between New Jersey and Bermuda."

His fingers steeple with mine.

"I did try, baby. I didn't give up. I told myself if I had lost you, I'd spend my days trying to find you."

I feel my strong core weaken.

He's still a drunk, Enna. Words are pretty, but they don't change the ugly facts.

"You have to get help. You know that, don't you?"

"I know. I screwed up. Hey, you changed your hair," he adds, extending his fingers to lightly stroke the hair and cupping my chin with his hand.

It seems such a trivial thing after the gravity of his story that I can't suck in the tears any longer, and a deluge breaks through.

"Sweetie, I tried to get to you. Honestly, I tried." His arms are around me, those shoulders, those arms…

I shrug them off and pull away. *This is important!* "It's more than that, Cole. You have a problem. I'm not going to accept that your DUI was merely an accident. An accident is when something happens without intention. You drink with intention. You drink too much, knowing that you drink too much, and it's changed you, Cole. You aren't the man I fell in love with."

"I know. Pickle, hear me out. Please? This was a big wakeup call. I fucked up; I know I did. Believe me, my bank account knows I did. I understand, Enna. I think back to that night you visited, and we went to Von Luger's. And I cringe at my behavior. I cringe. I wish I could take it all back."

I don't say a word, but I do bend a little at the apology.

He takes a step closer and he whispers, much lower, his eyes locked on mine, "Enna, ask me when I last had a drink."

So many words ball up like candy floss in my throat, but I manage to repeat his question. "When did you last drink?"

"That day. Donny picked me up from the station, drove me home. I immediately grabbed a beer—it had been a shitty day—but I stopped myself, and I threw out all the bottles I had. I tried to call. I e-mailed. Short of swimming after you, I did everything I could to let you know."

"No."

"No, what?"

"It's not that easy, Cole. Just stopping for now doesn't cure you. You have to go to classes, to see someone. I've read about this. You can't do it on your own."

"So do it with me."

"Go to AA?" I ask incredulously.

"No. I mean, be there for me. Cheer me on. It'd be a fresh start for you and me. Come home with me."

"No." I stand up on the wall again. I should be wary—once bitten, twice shy—but I suppose I am drawn to the precariousness of the wall, and this less-than-ideal romantic shituation. "Can you come here, please?" He comes before me, and for once we are at eye-level. "Here's the deal." I can feel the tears welling up. "I love you. I have never stopped loving you, and I want to believe that you will give this up. I need you to prove to me that you are not dependent on booze, okay? I'm giving you a month. By then, I imagine Tara will be back on board, and I will be free to leave the ship. I can go to Puerto Rico and get my theater money back."

"You found—"

"Do you accept the terms of this deal? Yes or no?"

"A month?"

"Yes or no."

"Yes! Of course, yes!"

And there on the fort wall, with the blue waves so steady and purposeful, crashing into the stone, Cole's delicious lips find me, and they fit so perfectly. The rain falls more heavily, and our kisses just become deeper and hungrier. As we both stand, wet to the skin, he holds me closer and lifts me up. I wrap my legs around him, and he carries me into the armory shelter and pushes me against the closed door, blocking the way against intruders.

It's been months since our unfulfilling romp in the car, and this is completely different. It's slow and sensuous, and as the rain hammers down on the artillery roof, he breathes hot kisses into my neck and hammers into me, and I moan louder than the concerto of elements, opening my eyes, not to the whitewashed uneven walls of the shelter, but to see the tree tops and daylight of Montrose, those same hands, that same touch, the light graze of stubble, the intoxication of his

Hermès cologne. In this fort, in this foreign island that is neither Ashtead nor Scranton, I feel at home, because he is here with me.

Afterward, we relocate and rearrange misplaced and disheveled clothes. We leave the shelter for the tourists who want to admire other types of weaponry. The rain stops, and we run around St. George's. I take Cole to some of the spots and sights I have discovered so far. I haven't forgotten and forgiven, but his hand feels so perfect around mine, and the thought of that opposing car slamming into his as he searched through all the silly little envelopes I put together, the thought that, really, I am lucky to have him here and in one piece, makes me squeeze his paw a little tighter. Would Mallory approve? She would tell me life is all about choices. You can choose to be happy or not. I grip his hand, kiss his neck, and inhale his Hermès.

We take a bus to the Crystal Caves, and hand-in-hand, we descend into the earth to see the stalagmites and stalactites, centuries old, mighty, cold, creamy, dripping rocks that almost glow in the torch light. The water is deceptively deep, and the stalagmites which appear just under the surface are in fact over fifty feet below the water line, so the guide says. After the crash of the waves above, this more inland, underwater, crystal-clear lake is fantastical.

Cole has booked a room at the hotel near the pink Gibson Beach, so we return there, and, still a little damp, warm up with a shower, followed by more comfortable sex in an actual bed, followed by a very necessary second shower.

"With all this water, I will grow scales and become a mermaid."

"You are already my mermaid on the rocks."

"Just as long as that's all you're having on the rocks." I turn in his arms, so I can look him in the eyes and see his expression. "This isn't fixed, you know. I think it's important we enjoy this in the present moment, but just because we had sex—"

"Twice."

"Yes, thank you. Just because we had sex twice—"

"Good sex, twice."

"Yes, okay, just because we had good sex twice, doesn't mean it's all fixed."

"I'm not expecting it to be magically one, two, three, but a step in the right direction is good enough for me now."

"We leave port soon. I have to get back."

He peels back the covers. I slip out and tug on my still-damp clothes. After the warmth of his arms and his bed, it's torture.

"I'll get you to the wharf."

"That's kind, but there's no point. I can't get you aboard. You'd just be standing there, waving for two minutes, and then I'd disappear. I'll get a cab."

"Okay, but at least let me get it for you."

And so we part again. I don't cry. I'm not sad. It feels exactly as it is supposed to be.

Chapter 27

"Something's happened. You're all…distant and quiet. Well, scratch that; you're even more distant and quiet."

"Am I?" I ask Chelsea, always very near and loud.

"Is it Michael? I knew he'd be a bugger to you."

"No. Michael knows where I stand. It's actually…" And for a second, I want to tell her everything, the whole convoluted saga of Cole and me, but I recoil and clutch the thought to myself instead. "It's actually good news, I think, but I have to wait and see."

"You're not pregnant, are you?"

I almost choke.

Wouldn't that be a little unexpected shituation?

"No. No, I'd hope not."

What starts out as nerve-wracking but exciting quickly becomes rather dull. The routine of yoga classes in Park Slope brought me such peace and calm. The monotony of being at sea, answering the same questions to a fresh ship full of faces every week, returning to the same small island, knowing that Will is aboard the *Excelsior* and Cole is back in Pennsylvania waiting for me, just makes me itch to mutiny and swim to shore. But, I don't. I promised.

As I sit on the deck, feeling the sun warm my back and the sweet chunks of pineapple compress to juice and fibers against my palate, I remember the excitement of putting *The Shakespearean Rap* together with Will, how easily I fell under his spell, how my eager broken heart clung to him and believed every word he said.

We believe what we choose to believe, don't we?

Is my renewed belief in Cole, his promises and sobriety, the same? That earnest desire to be wanted? Am I flinging myself, masochistically hurling myself on him, like I did with Will? Like an addict? Am I loving him because I like the idea of love, rather than because I actually like him?

It's different!

How?

Both appeared to be one thing but turned out to be something else.

True. I had bought into both men like they were Disney stock on sale.

And what have I learned?

To be self-reliant, to be present, to be open-hearted. For all the hurt and sorrow, love them anyway.

I think about it. I bounce the idea around in my head. I know Mallory and the yoginis would advocate letting go: loving Cole and lifting him up from where he is, and loving Will, letting him swim away. Maybe I am not such a forgiving yogini after all. I want to see Will's face. I want his face to see mine. I want his cheeks to burn with shame, and I want him to apologize. Then maybe I can let go. Then maybe I can say, "Fuck you and *namaste*."

While the ship restocks and the fresh set of voyagers embarks, I take my five hours off the ship to find an Internet café, toothpaste, and some other necessities. A quick scan of the inbox, and my eye is drawn immediately to Tara's address.

Finally, the sad news we were waiting for. Her e-mail is brief—I don't blame her; who'd want to be chatting—but she focuses on the logistics and her return to the ship when we port at King's Wharf in three days. In three days, I will be free. It's liberating and terrifying.

My heart flies to Tara, and I send her all my love and telepathic hugs. Then, I e-mail Mum and let her know that I will be home soon.

I perform the socks off the next three days of shows, hitting my notes stronger, extending my limbs further, pointing my toes harder. I spend more time in the top deck gym, facing the water ahead: downward dog, plank, *chaturanga*, upward dog, downward dog, float forward, stand, swan dive, repeat. I cycle through this sun salutation again and again, the sweat beading on my forehead and trickling down my face where tears used to roll. I shake them off.

I tell the cast that Tara will be back as soon as we reach the island, and there's a bittersweet response to see a new friend go, but an old one return. Though I have hardly been partying with them every night, we have become close, and I will be sad to leave this little midnight marauding community below deck. Even Michael, who in spite of his persistence has become like a sweet, ever-energetic puppy, wanting to play and chew on parts of me, will be sadly missed.

The morning we dock at King's Wharf, I process through security, my bags are x-rayed, and I disembark for the last time.

Tara is there, waving dockside. *"Mon petit chien!"* We walk toward each other, drop our bags, and hug. "Thank you so much for doing this for me. It means so much."

"Tara, don't be ridiculous. It was good to get back under the lights. How are you doing?"

"Meh. Journey was fucking brutal, the layover so long I wanted to kill kittens, but I made it. And no animals or air stewards were hurt in the process."

"I'm really sorry, girl."

"Thanks. It was hard going, but I am glad to get back to some amount of normality. I was going batshit crazy just sitting in England drinking tea. Mum has lovely friends. Lovely. And by the time I left, they had cooked enough meals to pack three freezers. Poor Dad will have enough lasagna and shepherd's pie to survive a nuclear apocalypse."

And as Tara speaks and reminds me that her dad is alone, a few tears roll in sympathy.

"None of that! I've cried enough for both of us!" Tara chides me and gathers me in for another hug.

You should not be crying, Enna. Stop it!

"I don't know where it all comes from!"

"I think that all the time!" I rejoin, wiping my eyes. "It's like we are human geysers and snot factories! You'd think it'd all dry up, but it doesn't. Our bodies just churn it out like fucking loaves and fishes. Fish? Fishes."

"Oh, gross, Enna! I will miss you. I wish you'd stay on the cruise."

"I will miss you too, but I have some big fish to fry."

"You look totally bright-eyed and mischievous. Tell!"

"Okay, well I suppose it started at Fort St. Catherine. I was facing the ocean...No! It really started when Chelsea told me about the new ship, *Excelsior*..." And on a bench at the side of the wharf, I tell her how I found "Liam" and how Cole found me.

"Wow. Enna, that is amazing. I hope this Liam is the right guy, and I hope Cole keeps his promise. Alcoholism is a tough one to break. It's so social, so accessible."

"Cole has always had extraordinary will power."

"That's an unfortunate name of one's power, in your case."

"I guess so!" And we laugh on the bench, wringing out our time together before we must say goodbye.

"So seriously, while I go back to performing on the ship, where will you go next?"

"Cole got me a room by the airport, and I fly tomorrow, back to JFK, then my connector flies straight to Puerto Rico. After then, who knows?"

"What will you say to Will when you get to Puerto Rico?"

"I honestly don't know. And you mustn't say anything to Chelsea or the other cast members. I don't want Will to get any kind of head start."

"*Oui, bien sûr.*"

After Tara leaves, I navigate to the hotel and their business center, checking last minute e-mails and double checking flight itinerary. I tap out a quick e-mail to Cole, asking him to alert Detective Shugard in England that I am en route to apprehend Will, and perhaps they could liaise with the local police force. I click send and scan the inbox for other notable messages. I come to a halt.

> To: Enna
> From: Leo
> Subject: WTF
>
> En, I have a credit card bill here. I thought it was a mistake and called the company. Apparently no mistake. Some arsehole knew my information and fraudulently used it to get funds traced to...a cruise line. You've got some explaining to do.
> Leo.

Oh my God, oh my God, oh my God!

I forgot Leo. I forgot I was only meant to cruise for a week and then return to England and pay it off before he even noticed.

I scramble to type a reply. But, really, what is there to say?

> Leo,
>
> I am SOOOOOOOOO sorry. I just...I got caught up in my own goings on here and asked to stay on board ship so my friend could visit her dying mother. No excuses. It was a terrible thing to do, and I am so sorry. But I meant no harm, and I will pay you back with lots of interest. Promise.
>
> E

What is there to say other than sorry? Any explanation sounds so far-fetched. Is this how Cole felt? Caught out, saying sorry until his lips bled with it?

Leo doesn't respond immediately, of course. It's probably the middle of the night in England. He'll get it in the morning. He'll understand. I hope.

How could I have done something so...criminal? That's what it is, really, taking something without asking, and certainly there is more pre-meditation to it than Cole taking a habitual drink. I am a terribly flawed person.

I fly out of Bermuda airport the next morning, bound for JFK airport and then San Juan. I sit at the gate in JFK. It's the same non-deals on offer at the duty free, and frankly I'm not jazzed by the idea of airport shopping anymore, so I hunker down in the row of chairs and watch the plane stand frustratingly ready-to-go through the window. Of course, it's *not* ready. I am the only nutcase sitting at the gate to wait five hours. I try to meditate, to focus on the present and all the things I am grateful for, to breathe, to let go, to manifest my intention.

I imagine seeing Will and try to plan out what I'll say or do. He'll be surprised, of course. He's too arrogant to even consider I would catch up to him. I see his tiger eyes grow wider and then calm, palming off excuses and apologies. Well, none will be good enough.

"Now, I felt sure you'd be sampling every perfume under the sun."

I look up to catch the voice and see his reflection in the glass window, the baseball cap, the square jaw, the broad grin.

"Cole!" Oh my God! My stomach rolls three hundred and sixty degrees. "Cole!" I spring up from the chair and launch into his arms, forgetting any British reserve or memory of former hurts.

"I thought maybe you might be able to use some company and maybe some backup."

I cock my head. *Is he coming with me because he doesn't trust me with this man, or because he wants to support me?* I shake the thought away. It doesn't matter.

"That would be lovely. You're coming? You're coming with me to Puerto Rico?"

"I've never been to San Juan, and I was figuring you probably hadn't booked ahead and had nowhere to stay, so it occurred to me—" he pulls me tighter to him, such a natural conjoining "— that maybe you'd like me around?" We stare at eye level into each other, sharing the joy of surprises.

The flight is not full, and we are able to talk to the steward at the gate and change our seats to sit together, legs stretched out in the exit aisle. The endless sitting has, curiously, exhausted me, and as much as I try to keep my eyes open and tell him about Tara's return and my terrible criminal oversight, my words drift off as I doze in and out of consciousness on his shoulder.

The flight arrives at four a.m. in San Juan. Cole suggests we get a few hours' sleep and meet the ship tomorrow.

"Killjoy! You know, we'll probably miss him that way. He'll disembark and disappear before we can get him."

"He won't disembark until ten a.m. I've done my due diligence. We have time for sleep. Or a little something-something anyway."

I shoot him a stare. "You're incorrigible!"

And it's lovely to have him by my side again. It is as if this whole period of being without him, being with someone else, being alone, seeing his dark side— it has made me appreciate the real Cole, the one I flew three thousand miles for, so I could stand on his doorstep and tell him I loved him. Old feelings I had blocked, cauterized, just flow back, an upsurge of dammed emotions; it was a trickle at first, at Fort St. Catherine, but now, here, with this man who flew to Bermuda and then traveled to JFK to accompany me here, they gush through every vein, artery, and little arteriole. I feel love from my core to my fingertips. How could I ever live without this man? Flawed or not, I choose not to.

All the doubts, all the fears, evaporate as he wraps his arms around me again and whispers words into my hair. He sways from foot to foot, and I realize we are dancing, and he is singing. It's so quiet I can't hear him, so I hold my breath and hold on tight. Through the open balcony doors of our beachfront room, the white sheers billow into the darkness, and the waves calmly crash on the rocks below. As we sway in unison, looking out into the darkness, I finally feel a lightness, that all the weight of fear, obligation, expectation lead-lining my bones has just dissolved and melted away.

There we stand, swaying, watching the night, wrapped around each other, neither willing to let go.

This is how we started.

I think of that chance meeting in Florida, and how we curled around each other on the balcony, trying to hold back the morning. Of course, things are different now. My immediate instinct is to open the minibar door, but in his arms, I eye it dangerously and know that must be off limits now. We have each other instead. My conditions about Cole being sober for another month just float away. Time seems so unimportant. We've wasted so much already.

In the morning, we both feel punch drunk without sleep, but our bodies work anyway, and the adrenaline of finally facing Will gives an extra alertness my fatigued body magically conjures from somewhere.

Cole orders room service as I blow-dry my hair. It's a strange yet familiar symbiosis. When the tray arrives, he pours my coffee from the *cafetière* and adds a glug of milk, not cream, just as I like it. With hair looking much slicker than usual, I cuddle up behind him, inhaling him again, as he pours a cup for himself, the delicate handles looking so ridiculous between his fingers.

"Careful, I'm pouring."

"Practiced with a bottle, not a *cafetière*, eh?" I say thoughtlessly. *Why did I say that?*

He focuses on the plunger and the stray ground of coffee trickling down the spout.

"Sorry, that was a joke."

"It's okay, pickle. Better you laugh and say it than brood and think it."

"Ferment it."

"Yes, better you are upfront. That goes with everything. If we can start again and make this work, then I need you to be honest with me. No hiding your phone and being shady—"

"I was never—"

"Listen, it is what it is. It's done. But now we can have a clean slate, a fresh start, and I want to be the one you can talk to about everything. If you need to act, or work, or manage the theater, we will make it happen. It might take time. You might have to do some voluntary stuff in the interim, but that wouldn't be so bad, would it? You'd meet people, make your own friends."

His almost yogic acceptance, this let go and move on, stuns me for a moment, and my tongue takes a second to catch up to my brain.

"I'm not sure I want that anymore. Losing everything has rather made me…review the shituation." I circle to the other side of the little dining table. "I don't need the theater, per se. I think I need a sense of belonging, of having a role to play in Scranton. It worked in Brooklyn. I just can't sit and do nothing all day."

"You want to move to Brooklyn?" He almost soaks the toast with projectile coffee.

"No, crazy. I think…I think I want to do this." I open the patio doors wide, the ocean rolling up the sand to the rocks and sea wall, a rumpled sheet of froth and shimmer. I place my hands splayed wide on the stone floor of the patio balcony. I look at the space in between them, suck in my stomach, and transfer my weight to my palms, lifting my feet up and in, perfecting crow pose, five breaths without a wobble.

"You want to crouch like some strange marsupial?"

"No!" I jump back and up and wipe the dust off my hands. "I think I want to teach yoga."

"Can you do that?"

"I can try. I can train as I wait out the endless period of time before I can take on paid work. Then, who knows, maybe I'll open my own studio?" The words appear and surprise my ears. My mouth, once again, has not consulted my mind at all.

Where the fuck did that come from?

The thought ignites and fizzes up the touch paper trail in my brain. Could I? There couldn't be anything less like theater! It's the exact opposite, really, embracing oneself and searching for *satya* versus pretending to be someone else and perfecting artifice. But a guru does direct, coaching others along to the best version of themselves; that is not so foreign.

I could do this. I really could.

"Sweetie, I think that's a great idea." He takes a contemplative sip of coffee.

My right foot effortlessly uproots my leg into my groin, and here I am in tree pose. Serene yet energized. I'm feeling very inspired by this sudden burst of clarity.

"Of course," he adds, "you might want to look into getting a small business loan."

My tree wobbles and I lose my balance. "Ugh!" I reclaim my coffee. "Because that worked out so well for me the last time. Thanks for the reminder."

"It's business. You got into business with someone unreliable, someone you couldn't really trust; that's all. Don't take it personally. It will drive you crazy. You can get back on the horse. I know you can. And you can trust me." He sips his coffee and just looks so ungodly good. He glances down at the paper, and I wrap my arms around his neck.

Trust. Isn't that what love is? Finding someone you can trust will look out for you, unselfishly and without agenda?

We stand on the disembarkation ramp. I worry that the bright green outfit might flag to Will, *Hello! I'm hereeee!* But I see the majority of milling tourists and Puerto Ricans are brightly daubed in color, and he'd have to be a prophet to know that, at the bottom of the ramp, there will be a welcome committee. Waiting.

"You're bouncing like a jumping bean." Cole holds my hand and stills me.

"It's nerve-wracking. I don't know what I will say."

"Well, just let him get off the boat first. We don't want some jurisdiction debacle. Ah! Here they are!"

What? Who? Huh?

I whip my meerkat neck around and see a familiar face with a trio of unfamiliar faces. "Detective Shugard? What are you doing all the way over here?"

"Ms. Petersen." He nods gruffly. "We've been positioned over by the decking for an hour or so now. No sign yet. But, thanks to your tip off, our intelligence at Interpol has confirmed the suspect is aboard, and we have the international warrant for his arrest. He'll be extradited to the UK before the day is over."

How fast does my heart have to beat to have a legitimate heart attack?

The policemen resume their stand-off position, and I hover, my heart in my mouth. The many dark heads that parade from the bowels of the *Excelsior* have me on my tiptoes, eyes riveted to the top of the gangway with laser beam focus.

"You'll let me talk for a moment, won't you?"

"Sure, pickle. But if he touches you or runs, I will squash him like a cockroach."

"Very Buddhist."

A dark head appears at the top of the gangway. He's wearing a baseball cap, but I know it's him. It's the shape of him, the frame of him, the swagger. That is the man who filled the stage, not with space but charisma.

Lies!

That was the man who held me in his arms, looked me in the eyes and lied to me, who left me waiting for him while he cleaned out every last penny in the account. My stomach turns. My heart drums. I can hear it fill my ears, the syncopated pulse shifting, stressing, pounding my chest. My eyes threaten to fill with tears, but I fist my hands and cut my nails into my palms to halt them.

Enna, you cannot, must not cry.

And he gets closer. He's listening to his iPod and staring at the screen in his hand. My gut lurches again, and I squeeze my fists tighter. His face is still beautiful to me.

Why is he still beautiful to me? Look for the satya.

He is beautifully bad, a Dorian Gray with an easy smile and a damned soul. He lifts his eyes, as though he must feel mine bearing down on him, but his glance sweeps away to the girl in the short shorts and bikini top walking alongside him.

He descends the gangway and steps up on the promenade that leads around the seawall. I am aware of a shift as Cole grows taller, and two policemen cross the gangway to block it behind him. The other officer circles in front of him with Shugard.

"Now, sweetie," Cole prompts.

I swallow the mass of fear lodged in my throat. This is my cue, but I have no lines, just truths.

Come on, throat chakra, *open!*

"Will!"

He walks on.

"Will!"

He pauses, displacing an ear bud and looking vaguely over his right shoulder.

"Will!"

He turns back now, whipping his head to the left. And then he sees me. For a millisecond, maybe less, I swear the corners of his mouth turn up and his eyes sparkle to see me, before instantly hardening, his feet skittishly dodging to bolt. He doesn't. He eyes the area and stands still.

"Enna."

I take steps toward him, slowly, gingerly. "I searched for you. I worried something had happened to you. I didn't let myself believe that you would have left without a word, that you would have cleaned me out."

"Enna...I..."

"What? No silver-tongued explanation to lie your way out?"

"Enna, I have missed you."

"Good. I hope you have, because that might mean that maybe there is an ounce of decency in you and not everything that passed between us was bullshit. And, maybe if you missed me, there is something you can work on as you rehearse yourself into being a better person. There! There's my director's note for you."

He chuckles, breathing out of his nose. "You know, Enna, you always thought with your heart and never your head."

"You say that like it's a bad thing."

"Survival of the fittest, baby." He smirks again. "Well, this reunion has been delightful, but I should probably go."

Cole takes a step toward him, and Will looks at him for the first time, perhaps unaware I was protected.

"Oh, I see we brought the goon squad! How incredibly quaint."

"I want the money back, Will. Not for me, but you can't have the theater's money."

"Enna, you're either truly naïve or have been drinking heavily if you think that I have a penny of that." He turns and strides away.

"Will!"

There is a flurry of movement, like a flock of startled pigeons all flapping at once. And in the seconds that pass, as his legs thrust into a sprint, Shugard, the other detective, and Cole lunge toward him. I breathe. I think of my warrior two pose, the strength, the determination, and I stand in front of him again, feeling fierce, as he writhes in the hold of the officer.

"No, Will. It's not that easy. You have to face the music."

"What? And dance? This isn't some revenge play, Enna!" He jerks his wrists against the handcuffs fastened behind him. "Tell them it's a mistake. You can call them off. Come on, we can work this out."

"No. No, we can't."

"Oh, I get it. Enna gets her little revenge scene to play out."

"No. Really. I don't want revenge. That seems a wasted emotion. I don't need that. Maybe I did for a while. After your betrayal, I was rather angry, but you know, now, I just feel rather sorry for you. Here I am starting a new chapter of promise and love, while you, most likely, have some prison time, and I know the kind of love demonstrated in there. But that's such a waste, Will. You could have achieved so much with your talent if you hadn't been so greedy."

There's a pause as he looks up at Cole, daring him with a mocking stare. "So, you're back with him now? You didn't think so much of him when I was fucking you on the office floor."

Before I can formulate a Zen response, a fist flies from behind my ear and lands solidly against Will's jaw. I hear the crack and look back at the retracted arm.

"Sorry. He asked for it."

Will licks the blood on his lips that trickles down from his nose.

"You know, Will," I feel compelled to add. "It wasn't the money. I was never sad about that. I hope you had your reasons. But never saying goodbye, never leaving a note, leaving someone dangling without explanation is spineless. You are a coward."

He coughs, and the red splutters. A shower burst of blood rains on the tarmac.

"Jesus! Get off me," he yells to the detective restraining him.

The detectives jostle him. "Come on, Shakespeare," I hear Shugard growl.

I look to the pattern of droplets on the ground, too pretty to be human damage. The blood shines red in the sunlight. Red, the color of the root *chakra*, influencing survival and self-preservation. Of course, Will—Liam—can adapt and evolve and survive, and I wonder how he will wriggle his way out of this in court.

We turn and walk along the promenade with the ocean steadily lapping into the sea wall, without the pomp and clash of churning seas. In our silence, with just the lull of the water, I can hear Will struggle, shout and tussle, but I don't turn back. I'm not going in that direction.

The sun is high now. It's approaching noon, and the ocean takes on an almost greeny-turquoise hue. We stand and stare at the expanse, the water, strong and steady. I slip my hand into Cole's right paw, its hold loose and easy.

"Did you really sleep with him on your office floor?" he asks into the breeze.

The drum beats again.

I swallow, inhale, exhale.

"I have done some things I regret."

"You fucked him on your office floor." His words ring with disappointment.

"Please, Cole. Don't." I turn to him and bury my head in his shoulder, jamming myself into the nook that fits me, but he shakes me off. "Don't be like this now."

He stands firm, immovable.

"Please. It's not important. It's in the past. Can you honestly stand there and tell me you didn't sleep with Patricia?"

He turns at this, moving swiftly, and for one microsecond I think he means to hit me too, but his hand passes across me and wraps around my back to hold me gently in his arms.

"Yes, I can honestly stand here." He stares into my eyes. "I never slept with Tricia. When you knocked at the door, we were watching a movie. It was our third date. Friends set us up so I would stop thinking about you. And even then I couldn't stop. The house was just too full of memories of you. I had started to plan renovations so I could make it different. That was the long-term plan; whiskey was the short-term plan."

I look up into this handsome face, his hazel eyes so sorrowful but burning with such urgency too. *He was waiting for me?* I think my internal organs might implode with guilt and regret. Words evaporate. My mouth tries to move, but I have nothing.

"Do you think we can start from the beginning? Can I erase him from you? Wipe clear those months?"

I inhale. "No," I say softly, finally finding my voice. I reach for his face as I would the sun, feeling the warrior strength possess me. "No, we can't start from the beginning, but we can start from where we are. We can be more open, more honest. We can move forward. I gave you a month, but I take it back. I don't need a month to know that you believe in us and that you will keep sober."

A tear rolls down his cheek, and I wipe it away with my thumb.

"You said something on my doorstep about me being your hero," Cole recalls. "I think I replied something dumb, like they needed to be saved too. I was being an ass, but actually, it's true. I never thought it would be you who saved me, but you did."

He draws me in and up, and his mouth is on mine, strong and solid. We flow together, unstoppable, like water.

I gasp as he clutches me tightly, a stabbing pain in my heart, and he loosens his hold.

"Pickle?"

I bend over and trace my hand over my sternum.

Am I having a heart attack? I'm too young for a heart attack!

My fingers twitch as they move to the source, find it, and hold it close to my chest. I chuckle with relief. I'm not dying.

"Pickle, what is it? What's the matter? Should I call a…"

I draw the chain out over my top, and the ring plops over and bounces audaciously against my bony sternum. "The culprit!"

"That's because it's meant for a finger, not a neck."

"I'm not sure it fits a finger yet."

"Ah. Maybe someday?"

"Maybe someday. Baby steps. It's a practice, not a perfect, Cole."

He turns from the sea view in front, the police car pulling out from the curb, to the side, and he finds me, his hands so big and gentle as they cup my face. "I don't want to be without you another day. Life is short. Enna, come on, we've been here before. Let's just go for it. Let's dive in. Let's choose each other. You and me against the world. You can do anything. You can go anywhere. You could probably find a million men more handsome, or smart, or wealthy than me, but I promise you this: you will never find one who adores you as much, who would fight for you every day if you needed. Pickle," he whispers, letting go of me. "Please, give me the ring?"

My stomach whirrs.

"Please?"

I stand motionless, wordless, frightened as he lifts the chain from my neck.

"Pickle, don't marry me because you feel duty-bound. Do it because you want to be with me, wake up every day with me, have adventures with me, see the world with me, have amazing little British-American babies with me!"

"I…"

The wind blows in my face, and a dolphin's dorsal fin bobs in the briny water.

"Absolutely, I do."

He throws the chain into the sea, and it disappears before my eyes. Instead, the brilliant jewel appears rejoined with my finger. This time it doesn't feel foreign and weighty, but at home, sparkling as it does in the Puerto Rican sunlight. It shines greener than ever. Green, the color of the heart *chakra*. Emerald, the gem of healing and of hope.

Acknowledgments

On December 16th, 2011, Michaela scraped me from her living room carpet, enfolded me in her arms and took me to Jaya Yoga Studio in Clarks Summit. Like Enna, my first candle-lit yoga session was not a huge success. I wept and sniffed through the class and spent the entirety imagining I was laced into the emerald taffeta gown dressed for the ball, where I thought I was supposed to be.

In fact, being on my mat was exactly where I was supposed to be. It was a safe place to fall, to be open and vulnerable, and where I found my feet again, and, eventually, my heartbeat. It took some time, but I got the message eventually. And what a sanctuary Jaya Yoga Studio is. What a community you have built, Hilary Steinberg.

To Michaela, for insisting — against my will — that I should put down the hummus and bottle of wine and come with you; thank you. To my yoga teachers, I have learned so much from each and every one of you: Hilary, you help me see the truth, reaffirm my worth and remind me daily that life is truly "all about choices"; Maria, you empower me to be daring and always tell me your honest opinion; Cat, Gravedigger, you prove that it is cool to be kind, to be a yoga badass and give all your love away; Erin, thank you for being the calming voice who put up with my snotting through my first class. Thank you for never saying a word about my guppy-eyes and red, wet face, and for the squeeze you gave me that communicated all that was needed.

How lucky I feel to have found such a circle of positive, inspiring people, not just yogis in the studio, but gurus in life. Nora Boczar, you have guided me, cheered for me, empowered me, taught me so much about how to be a boss in killer heels! Your last text to me was "Go high!" So you! You always made me feel like I could accomplish anything I set my mind to do, what light and hope you brought to me and so many others who were lucky enough to call you friend. I will miss the mischievous sparkle in your warm chocolate eyes, your laugh, your unrelenting energy. Namaste.

To Katie McElhenny, yes the answer is always "go to yoga" and, if not, it is surely "let's get Thai." How you make me smile. You are beautiful and you don't even know it. I love you.

Don Lafferty, whether near and far, your guidance, support, and love has never steered me wrongly. You always have a place in my heart. Cheers to you, my friend.

My Omnific editors! Joannie and Colleen, I have so enjoyed working with you again. Joannie, I am so grateful for your sense of humor and patience, and I hope my late night emails never disturbed you! Thank you to Enn Bocci! I will never get tired of saying, "My Publicist, Ms. Bocci..."

Thank you to my dear friend, actress Tara Gadomski, who showed me the ropes in Park Slope and has always been such a supporter and provider of kale! Thanks to Candice Oden, who shared with me the nitty gritty of being a cast member onboard a cruise ship, and to the crew of the *Celebrity Summit*!

I have such gratitude to Paul and Josh of POSH at the Scranton Club, and to all the lovely people who supported our signing and reading event last year! What a cracker! Your support meant so much; looking up from the microphone to see the smiles, the flashes of teeth, of eyes, of Hemingwayish cocktails! It was an evening I will cherish and preserve on the microfiche of great memories stored within the whirls of my brain.

To the great friends who organized book groups to read *Theatricks*, The NEPA Lady Lit group: Sheli, Pidge, Terra, Heather, Elizabeth; Janet Blaum, Heather Fox, Nicole Dixon (xx) and Sandi Graham, a thousand thanks. You are ladies of integrity and kindness and you like to party too, so HUZZAH for more reading parties! (I will be available for forthcoming *Jazz Hands* shindigs, and an appearance is really very reasonable; i.e., a glass of wine!)

To Matt Damon: you are a very difficult equation I don't think I will ever work out, but thank you for being in my life.

My fabulous Lionhearts who make it possible for me to work from home and write. You inspire me to live and holdfast to those Mary Kay principles and priorities. I love you. I hope I make you proud to be a Lionheart! My Customer-Friends who let me be your consultant, I truly appreciate you and your custom, and I am proud to serve you.

To my Mum and Dad, having you in Scranton still surprises, delights and completely bemuses me. I'm a lucky girl to have you as my parents and friends. Sorry for being ratty, for distracted phone calls, for eating all your hummus and cheese. You've seen my best and my worst, and you hug me just the same.

And lastly, to Matt. It was a frozen day in January 2013 when you texted and invited me to cruise with you to Bermuda. Who could have written what followed? (Wait for it, give me time!) *Jazz Hands* would not have been written without you: your ability to find good vacation deals; the balls to ask me and fight for what you want; your eloquence, your brilliance, your humour—all had a hand in the writing of this novel. Thank you, too, for your patience and for always loving me even when I didn't deserve it; for having faith in me when I started to doubt; and for cheering me on at work, in life and in love. Thank you for helping me find my own *satya*: you.

About the Author

Eleanor Gwyn-Jones lives in Scranton, Pennsylvania, but originally hails from Surrey, England. Huzzah! She studied biology at Southampton University before taking to the stage as an actress, agent and administrator of a touring theatre company. She performed in theatres, studios, schools and festivals across the British Isles before moving to the States. It was whilst visa-dangling and unable to take on acting work that she started to write and decided she far preferred it to anything else in the world! In 2008, Eleanor started her own "at home" business to afford her more time to be with her "book babies." Now she spends her time writing by day and teaching ladies to look fabulous at night. She is a travel junkie — it's research, darling, research! — a gourmand, a yogi, a sometime blogger and she adores her family and friends beyond all measure.

If she weren't writing, she'd like to think you'd find her in Downton, The Paradise, or having a goblet of wine with Tyrion in King's Landing.

←———→New Adult Romance←———→

Three Daves by Nicki Elson
Streamline by Jennifer Lane
The Shades series: *Shades of Atlantis* & *Shades of Avalon* by Carol Oates
The Heart series: *Beside Your Heart, Disclosure of the Heart* & *Forever Your Heart*
by Mary Whitney
Romancing the Bookworm by Kate Evangelista
Flirting with Chaos by Kenya Wright
The Vice, Virtue & Video series: *Revealed, Captured, Desired* & *Devoted*
by Bianca Giovanni
Granton University series: *Loving Lies* by Linda Kage

←———→Paranormal Romance←———→

The Light series: *Seers of Light, Whisper of Light* & *Circle of Light* by Jennifer DeLucy
The Hanaford Park series: *Eve of Samhain* & *Pleasures Untold* by Lisa Sanchez
Immortal Awakening by KC Randall
The Seraphim series: *Crushed Seraphim* & *Bittersweet Seraphim* by Debra Anastasia
The Guardian's Wild Child by Feather Stone
Grave Refrain by Sarah M. Glover
The Divinity series: *Divinity* & *Entity* by Patricia Leever
The Blood Vine series: *Blood Vine, Blood Entangled* & *Blood Reunited* by Amber Belldene
Divine Temptation by Nicki Elson
The Dead Rapture series: *Love in the Time of the Dead* & *Love at the End of Days*
by Tera Shanley
The Hidden Races series: *Incandescent* (book 1) by M.V. Freeman

←———→Romantic Suspense←———→

Whirlwind by Robin DeJarnett
The CONduct series: *With Good Behavior, Bad Behavior* & *On Best Behavior*
by Jennifer Lane
Indivisible by Jessica McQuinn
Between the Lies by Alison Oburia
Blind Man's Bargain by Tracy Winegar

←———→Erotic Romance←———→

The Keyhole series: *Becoming sage* (book 1) by Kasi Alexander
The Keyhole series: *Saving sunni* (book 2) by Kasi & Reggie Alexander
The Winemaker's Dinner: *Appetizers* & *Entrée* by Dr. Ivan Rusilko & Everly Drummond
The Winemaker's Dinner: *Dessert* by Dr. Ivan Rusilko
Client N° 5 by Joy Fulcher

Historical Romance

Cat O' Nine Tails by Patricia Leever
Burning Embers by Hannah Fielding
Seven for a Secret by Rumer Haven

Anthologies

A Valentine Anthology including short stories by
Alice Clayton ("With a Double Oven"),
Jennifer DeLucy ("Magnus of Pfelt, Conquering Viking Lord"),
Nicki Elson ("I Don't Do Valentine's Day"),
Jessica McQuinn ("Better Than One Dead Rose and a Monkey Card"),
Victoria Michaels ("Home to Jackson"), and
Alison Oburia ("The Bridge")

Taking Liberties including an introduction by Tiffany Reisz and short stories by
Mina Vaughn ("John Hancock-Blocked"),
Linda Cunningham ("A Boston Marriage"),
Joy Fulcher ("Tea for Two"),
KC Holly ("The British Are Coming!"),
Kimberly Jensen & Scott Stark ("E. Pluribus Threesome"), and
Vivian Rider ("M'Lady's Secret Service")

Singles and Novellas

It's Only Kinky the First Time (A Keyhole series single) by Kasi Alexander
Learning the Ropes (A Keyhole series single) by Kasi & Reggie Alexander
The Winemaker's Dinner: RSVP by Dr. Ivan Rusilko
The Winemaker's Dinner: No Reservations by Everly Drummond
Big Guns by Jessica McQuinn
Concessions by Robin DeJarnett
Starstruck by Lisa Sanchez
New Flame by BJ Thornton
Shackled by Debra Anastasia
Swim Recruit by Jennifer Lane
Sway by Nicki Elson
Full Speed Ahead by Susan Kaye Quinn
The Second Sunrise by Hannah Downing
The Summer Prince by Carol Oates
Whatever it Takes by Sarah M. Glover
Clarity (A *Divinity* prequel single) by Patricia Leever
A Christmas Wish (A *Cocktails & Dreams* single) by Autumn Markus
Late Night with Andres by Debra Anastasia
Poughkeepsie (enhanced iPad app collector's edition) by Debra Anastasia

Poughkeepsie (audio book version) by Debra Anastasia
Blood Eternal (A Blood Vine series single, epilogue to series) by Amber Belldene
Carnaval de Amor (*The Winemaker's Dinner*, Spanish edition) by Dr. Ivan Rusilko & Everly Drummond

◄— ⸎ —►Sets◄— ⸎ —►

The Heart Series Box Set (*Beside Your Heart, Disclosure of the Heart* & *Forever Your Heart*) by Mary Whitney
The CONduct Series Box Set (*With Good Behavior, Bad Behavior* & *On Best Behavior*) by Jennifer Lane
The Light Series Box Set (*Seers of Light, Whisper of Light, Circle of Light* & *Glimpse of Light*) by Jennifer DeLucy
The Blood Vine Series Box Set (*Blood Vine, Blood Entangled, Blood Reunited* & *Blood Eternal*) by Amber Belldene

coming soon from
OMNIFIC PUBLISHING

The Legendary Saga: *Claiming Excalibur* (book 2) by LH Nicole
The Runaway series: *The Runaway Ex* (book 2) by Shani Struthers
The Forever series: *Forever Autumn* (book 1) by Christopher Scott Wagner
Something Wicked by Carol Oates
Going the Distance by Julianna Keyes